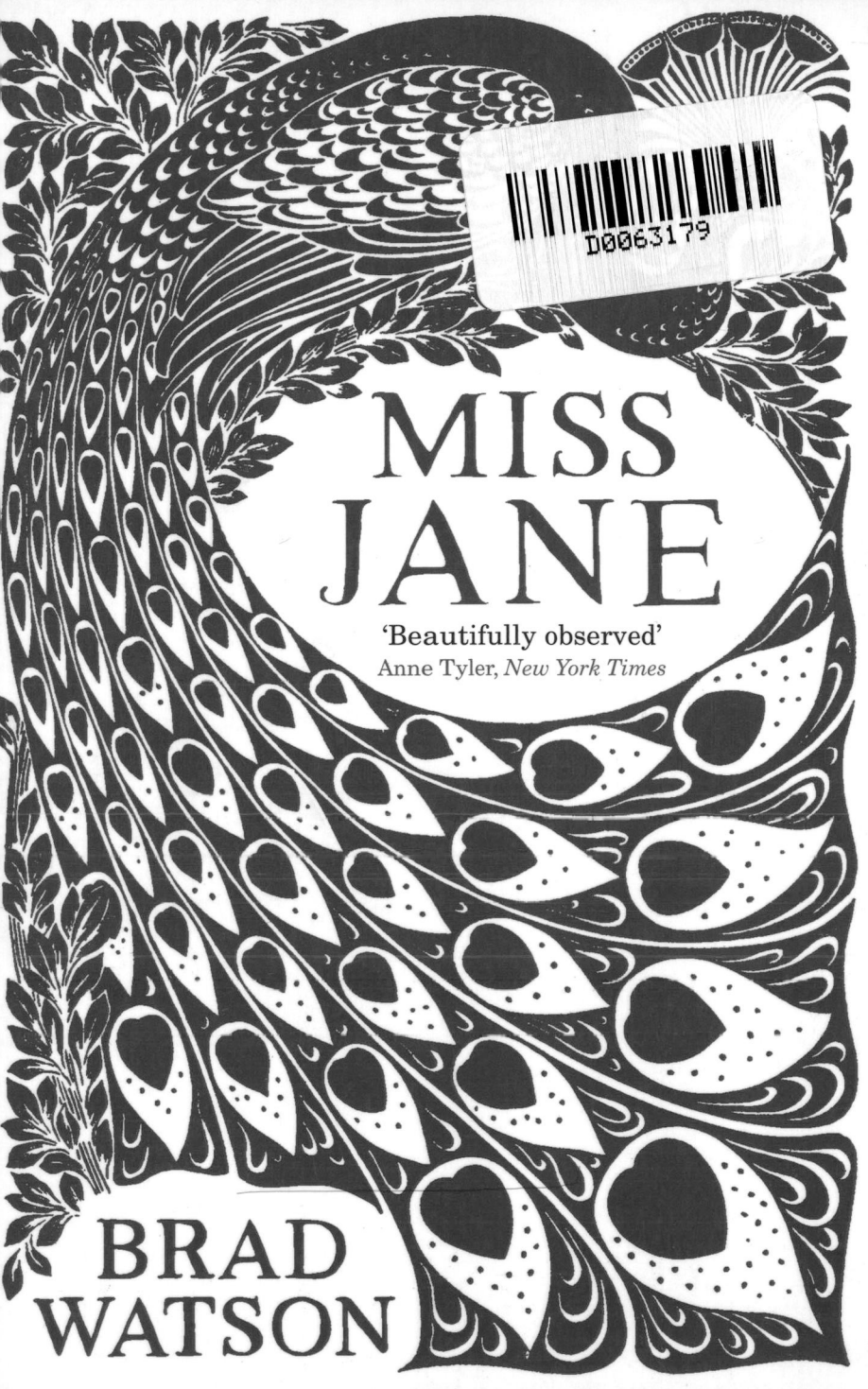

MISS JANE

'Beautifully observed'
Anne Tyler, *New York Times*

BRAD WATSON

'Miss Jane is courageous, resilient and enquiring; her parents are troubled souls, but loving . . . With the woods and fields of Jane's rural home seeming to cast a subtle enchantment on her life, hers is a history that is as unexpectedly beguiling as it is affecting.'

Daily Mail

'Watson's talent is singular, truly awesome; he reminds me of Raymond Carver and Flannery O'Connor in his bravery, his unflinching willingness to look at what might set others running.'

A. M. Homes

'Rich with profound meaning . . . Convincing, occasionally shocking and often overwhelming.'

Irish Times

'A quiet, often solitary lifetime enriched by the unfettered outdoors, the tough routine of farm life, and the ache of unconsummated love.'

Washington Post

'Exquisitely written . . . life in all of its unsentimental and symphonic complexity . . . *Miss Jane* is an artistic triumph, a novel that will linger inside you as long as your own memories do. Brad Watson's gifts are immense.'

Andre Dubus III

'*Miss Jane* is both winning and big-hearted in its embrace of and appreciation for what seems to be a disabling difference. One of its great pleasures is its young protagonist's flowering from loneliness to a new understanding of her place within creation.'

Jim Shepard

'*Miss Jane* is an especially timely novel for right now, when so much of our turmoil is dependent on how we view the Other, whether it be because of race, sexuality, religion, or where someone was born. It's also a novel that thrums with beauty, melancholy, and desire.' *Salon*

'I really admired Brad Watson's limpid novel *Miss Jane* about a woman born with an irreparable and humiliating physical anomaly who manages to fashion a rich and enigmatic life despite all odds.'

Tim Winton, 'Books of the Year', *Financial Review* (Australia)

'Here's a challenge for you this winter: find a book that's as beautiful as *Miss Jane*. Wait, don't bother. It's impossible . . . From almost the first page of this story of a hard-scrabble life, you'll find yourself basking in words that set difficulty awash in lushness . . . You'll just float on the sentences inside this book. Start *Miss Jane* and kiss your afternoon goodbye.' *LGBT Weekly*

'Watson tells this story with such tenderness, sensitivity and grace, at times I just wanted to weep . . . A beautiful novel . . . Watson says he based [the book] on the life of one of his great-aunts, and went through thirty drafts to get it right. He did.' *Seattle Times*

Miss Jane

ALSO BY BRAD WATSON

Miss Jane

BRAD WATSON

PICADOR

First published 2016 by W. W. Norton & Company, Inc.

First published in the UK in 2016 by Picador

First published in paperback 2016 by Picador

This edition first published 2017 by Picador
an imprint of Pan Macmillan
20 New Wharf Road, London N1 9RR
Associated companies throughout the world
www.panmacmillan.com

ISBN 978-1-5098-3433-4

Author's Note

Inspired in part by circumstances in the life of my maternal great-aunt,
Miss Jane is nonetheless a work of fiction: names, characters, places,
and incidents are the product of my imagination, or are used fictitiously.
Any resemblance to actual events, locales, or persons, living or dead,
is coincidental and unintentional.

Visit **www.picador.com** to read more about all our books
and to buy them. You will also find features, author interviews and
news of any author events, and you can sign up for e-newsletters
so that you're always first to hear about our new releases.

*This book is dedicated to the lost memory of my Great-Aunt
Mary Ellis "Jane" Clay,*

*to the beloved memory of my mother,
Bonnie Clay Watson Collins,*

*to her memories of my grandfather,
S. S. Clay,*

*and to my extraordinary in all ways wife,
Nell Hanley.
Thank you, love.*

In the wombs of the mothers, unborn embryos were growing, membranes and tissues folded and pleated themselves cleverly around each other, exploring without sorrow, without hesitation, the possibilities of topological space.

—LARS GUSTAFSSON, "GREATNESS STRIKES WHERE IT PLEASES"

She'd had, like anyone else, her love story.

—FLAUBERT, "A SIMPLE HEART"

CONTENTS

Miss Jane

You would not think someone so afflicted would or could be cheerful, not prone to melancholy or the miseries. Early on she acquired ways of dealing with her life, with life in general. And as she grew older it became evident that she feared almost nothing—perhaps only horses and something she couldn't quite name, a strange presence of danger not quite or not really a part of the world.

She didn't fear a fever of the kind that had taken brother William at the age of three, before she was born. To her mind such fate belonged to *that* child, not her.

She wasn't afraid of snakes, not even the poisonous kind, for she believed they wouldn't bite her if she simply left them alone. Mosquitoes, for some reason of their own, did not bite her, although she took no precautions against them.

She did not fear chickens, because she found them to be comically sage—in spite of what people said about stupid chickens. The same with pigs, although their frequent, abrupt, chaotic, or oddly orchestrated and deafening panic at first frightened her, until she saw the comical in that. The panic was sudden in its arrival and departure, both. Cows were so obviously a threat to no one, if you did not threaten a mother's calf. The bull was safely penned in his separate small pasture.

She didn't fear the coyotes that sang at night in the open fields, nor the panthers that sometimes screamed far off deep in the woods. She loved to kneel at the open window and listen to the coyotes sing and imagine what they were singing to each other, what their singing meant to them. She did not mind them tearing mice, rabbits, and squirrels to pieces, nor running down newborn fawns. Nor the panthers sometimes taking a newborn calf. Her odd fear of an unnamed beast, something we might call mythical, came from having thought she once heard one grumbling near the house at night, and she was terrified then.

She was not afraid of screeching owls in the night, nor of the possibility of coming upon wild hogs during her walks in the woods, nor packs of wild dogs that sometimes roamed the pastures and were to everyone more fearsome than the coyotes or panthers or bears, their having no fear of man. She was not afraid of rabid coons or foxes, of her father's guns, being a ten-gauge shotgun and a Winchester rifle. Nor of the hatchet used to decapitate the chickens, nor the long knives used to butcher the hogs, nor the smaller knives used to skin and butcher the occasional deer, nor the saws used for sawing their bones. Nor the large black kettle, used to boil water for washing soiled clothes and also for making soap in the yard, that she was told to *stay clear of* when she was small. Nor was she afraid of hell, although the preachers on the circuit warned of it, but she was not afraid of eternal fire or demons and the devil himself. She could not properly conjure them in her mind without a comical air. Jane, who rarely even went to town as a child, could not imagine going to hell, her imagination being neither successfully cross-country nor subterranean.

She was not afraid of cyclones in the darkest bile-green-and-black skies during storms that cracked off the limbs of oaks and the tops of pines and made the tin roof of the house and gallery pop and groan and bend upward at the edges. Nor of the hail that pocked the tin like buckshot raining down. Nor of lightning that split trees their length and left smoldering charred skeletons rooted to the wet, scorched earth. She was not afraid of God, with his sly and untrustworthy balance of love and wrath, who was yet curious enough to make himself vulnerable and walk among humans just like herself in the beautiful, harrowing embodiment of Jesus.

She feared horses because when they yanked their heads skyward and rolled their eyes she imagined they knew better than her what there was to fear in the air, in the inescapable physical world. She did not fear mules, which her father explained were smarter than horses and predictable, and later she liked it when she learned that they had no lineage. When she was small she feared standing bodies of water because for some reason she thought they were bottomless, but her father cured her of that by taking her fishing at their pond and coaxing her to wade in, cool off, feel the muddy earth safely there beneath the surface. Still, she would never learn to swim.

Her mother was more of an enigma than a threat, tending to lash out but seeming more angry at something inside herself than at others. Jane learned to weather the harsh and dark words, no more than a passing foul breeze in a world of variable winds of variable intensities but ephemeral and of no real consequence in a life.

She did not like the vexation of her incontinence, and wished she would outgrow it, but eventually accepted it as part of who she was, no matter how unsavory. She determined that she would live like any other girl as best she could, and when she could no longer do that, she would adjust her life to its terms accordingly. So she did not fear her own strangeness, even though her awareness of it grew and evolved as she got older.

In time her gaunt, dark-haired, blue-eyed beauty would be altered and sharpened by age, a visible sign of her difference, her independence, and a silent message to all that her presence in the world was impenetrable beyond a point of her own determination.

Purgatories

She was born into that time and place, in the farmland cut from the pine and broadleaf woods of east-central Mississippi, 1915, when there was no possibility of doing anything to alleviate her condition, no medical procedure to correct it. It was something to be accepted, grim-faced, as they accepted crop failure, debt, poverty, the frequent deaths of infants and small children from fevers and other maladies.

Her mother was thirty-nine and had not intended to have another child. Five years earlier she'd lost what she thought would be her last and youngest, a boy named William, who contracted a fever and died. The next year an unplanned child, her second girl, died stillborn. On William's stone were the words, How desolate our home / Bereft of him. The stone for the infant girl read simply, Chisolm Infant, with the identical dates of her birth and death engraved below.

For the first few months she was pregnant with the girl who would become Jane, she pretended that she was not. That it was a false pregnancy, simply her body fooling with her, playing an evil joke. This figment of a child in her womb would go away, disappear like some temporary derangement of the senses brought on by God or the devil for reasons she could not divine. But at four months she could feel it quickening, and by five months it had begun to move around quite a bit, to thrust and kick and stretch, so she could not pretend it was anything else. By seven months in she had begun to talk to it. *I will try to do right by you*, she said, *if you promise that you will try to do right by me. Do not die before I do. Do not come out a defective child doomed to unhappiness or an early death.*

When she spoke to the child, the fetus, in this manner, it would go very still, as if listening, considering her terms.

The night her water broke, her husband summoned the midwife named Emmalene Harris, whose family sharecropped forty acres on their property, to tend to his wife until he could fetch Dr. Thompson. His two sons were already near-grown and working their way through the state college up north, so he had to make the errand himself. He feared complications, given his wife's age and her darkened mental state.

Emmalene stood waiting for the doctor in a corner of the bedroom, flickered by firelight from a small woodstove against the far wall. She had heated a pot of water and put a basket of clean rags at the ready. She watched Mrs. Chisolm there in her bed, sweating, pale, tears in her eyes. She said a silent prayer, asking please God let this child be well. When Mrs. Chisolm cut her eyes over as if she could hear the woman's thoughts, Emmalene turned away and busied herself checking the hot water, the neat little stack of clean rags.

On a small stool in a darkened corner of the room, silent, looking at the floor, elbows on her splayed knees, sat the older daughter, Grace, so still she was practically invisible. When she blinked her eyes Emmalene noticed and startled, as if the blink itself had materialized the girl, brought flesh and blood into being, revealing her sullen presence there among them.

DR. THOMPSON LIVED just two miles south of the Chisolm farm, on the semi-rural outskirts of the small but bustling city of Mercury. When Chisolm arrived at two a.m., the doctor was awake, sitting in the dim moonlight that fell through the windows of his study, unable to sleep. He heard the shod hooves on the road, then in his front yard, and stepped out onto the front porch in his nightgown.

The man sat bareback and silent, hat crammed down on his head, skinny shoulder bones rising like bumps inside the loose cotton blouse he wore.

"Aren't you chilled in this evening, Chisolm?"

"Cold don't bother me, no, sir."

In the bedroom he took up his clothing from the day before, quietly as he could. The coin change in his pants pocket jingled and his wife groaned, turned over in sleep. He went back to his study to dress. In the yard, Chisolm was hitching big Rufus to the buggy.

He finished dressing, checked his medical bag, then stepped out, shutting the door quietly behind him. Chisolm stood holding his mule by the reins in one hand, Rufus in the other. The doctor pulled his lanky frame up into the buggy, packed and lit a pipe of tobacco, pulled an old blanket over his legs against the chill, and they began the two-mile trot out to the Chisolm place.

Rufus, his big bay gelding Missouri Fox Trotter, with a smooth gait and agreeable disposition, was good company on a night ride. The doctor could have taken his Ford, but reserved that for when he had to cover a lot of ground and make several stops in a day. He'd named the horse Rufus because noble as he was there was something of the jokester in his eye and disposition. The name seemed to fit.

He felt illogically happy to be out on this errand. The ghost of a friend's imminent death seemed to trail out of him like wisps of smoke from the pipe. He'd briefly thought to take a little cocaine to pep himself up but resisted. He knew well enough to be stingy with that stuff, save it for extreme fatigue. He felt instead an itch for a drink. Chisolm made a good batch of whiskey, aged in an oak barrel that he charred on the inside, just like the fancy distilleries in Tennessee and Kentucky, so the whiskey had a nice mellow brown color. He tested each batch by taste for proof, added branch water to bring it down to what the doctor judged was close to ninety, then strained it through cheesecloth into pottery jugs and corked them with stobbers of whittled sweetgum sticks. All in all, a first-rate operation.

He hummed another tune, the words in his head, *Let me call you "Sweetheart," I'm in love—with—you*, trotted the rig down the wide dirt highway, the man and mule close behind him in blue silhouette. "Get up, Rufus," he said, tapping the reins against the horse's flanks.

He took the narrow access road to Chisolm's farm, barely lit by stars and sheen of moonlight, through hushed and tunneled woodland, beside pastures silvered with an evening frost on the grass, a waxing moonlight on them like blued silver dust, and down into the draw over the creek. He heard Chisolm's mule veer off the road into the woods, taking a shortcut. He slowed to cross the bridge, little more than a couple of square-hewed logs supporting a narrow pallet of oak planks. The creek was quiet, low. More than once Chisolm had toppled his wagon off the bridge into the creek, taking it too fast or careless and slipping a wheel off the edge. And more than once the doctor had been summoned to peer into his dilated pupils seeking evidence of concussion, or to reset a dislocated shoulder, and thrice to set a broken arm and make sure a broken rib had not pierced a lung or other vital organ. Every time, Chisolm had been coherent enough to have one of his family place a fresh jug into the back of the doctor's buggy under a feed sack before he left. The wife would have made sure that he toted a full stomach of chicken and dumplings or cornbread and greens back to the wagon. He'd sip from the jug on the way home, suffering no grievous consequences aside from his wife's quiet indignation, half from the whiskey drinking itself and half because the rich food plus whiskey invariably gave him a case of flatulence that drove her from their bed and into the empty bedroom in the back of the house, to fulminate and toss and turn and fuss her lot as a country doctor's wife. For that reason, he had adapted by staying up, sipping late into the evening, settling onto the sofa in his office or in front of the fireplace to snooze away the rest of the night in pleasant dreams and uninhibited, flatulent segregation from the niceties of marital diplomacy.

He pulled up at the Chisolms' gallery, noted the mule already hitched to the post there. Chocked the buggy's brake and climbed down as the side door to the house's main room opened and a long rectangle of weak yellow light spilled out into the breezeway of the dog-trot house. Chisolm's long angular face peered out, then pulled itself back inside. It was a dog-trot house but grander than most, larger and kept-up, and clean. The hound that had bayed at his arrival had quit and disappeared. Once in the house's breezeway he could smell the dying scents of fried pork, stewed vegetables, fried bread, and molasses from the kitchen. He entered the house through the large common room, heard a low guttural moaning, and felt a tingle in the air of physical discomfort and alarm. Smelled the odors of labor, sweat and blood and fecal matter. Marveled that probably Mrs. Chisolm had done most of the dinner work herself before rolling into the bed to have this child. He was glad it was not her first.

Chisolm sat hunched in a straight-back chair before the fireplace, a loose-rolled cigarette burning down to the knuckles in one long bony hand. Nodded at the fire as if to the doctor, without looking up. The doctor caught the glint of a glazed jug in the shadows to one side of his weathered brogans.

He went on into the bedroom. A pot of water steamed on the small woodstove against the north wall. The midwife had hold of Mrs. Chisolm's hand, another hand on her left leg, the covers tossed away. A hand dark as black coffee against skin pale as a blinding cataract. And there, in the mussed bedding, between the poor woman's scrawny splayed thighs, the crowning head of what he hoped would be their last child.

Over in a dark corner of the room the daughter, Grace, sat on a stool looking grimly at nothing. She didn't look up when he came in. He figured her to be about ten years now. Seemed older by a couple, at least.

He walked over to the bed and spoke to the midwife.

"Get me a bowl of that hot water—you boiled it? Good—a bar of soap, some of those clean rags, and set them on that bench. Light the lantern on that table beside the bed, there."

She went over to the stove and came back in a minute with the water, soap, and rags and set them on the trunk that sat at the foot of the bed. Struck a match to the lantern wick.

He spoke to Mrs. Chisolm.

"You ready, then, madame?"

She gripped his wrist in a sweaty tourniquet. Her voice was a low whisper, her words reflecting her desperation.

"Where in hell have you been?"

"The usual purgatories."

He detached her hand from his wrist, gave her a near-placebo dose of laudanum, washed his hands and forearms, carrying on a one-sided conversation as he went to work, as if he were dressing a simple wound. Generally this helped to calm people, baffling them into a kind of confusion that settled into a calmer state.

She was a veteran. Most of the hard work already done, she was finished in fifteen minutes. No stitching required. He snipped the cord, and took a good look at the child, who'd come around to crying a bit. He didn't say anything. He looked at the midwife. She stared through narrowed eyes but kept her lips pressed shut. He gave her the child to wash, turned his attention to the placenta and cleaning up Mrs. Chisolm with warm water and disinfectant. The midwife helped him roll her off the soiled sheets and sop rags and took away the afterbirth in a pail, brought in fresh sheets, helped him get them under her. He washed his hands and forearms again as the midwife covered Mrs. Chisolm with a fresh sheet and clean counterpane. He took a lantern over to the crying child in the little crib padded with a folded quilt. It was squeezing its hands and crying well, head to one side. He looked closely, prodding a bit, peering through his spectacles in the poor light. He pulled a small notebook from his vest pocket and wrote something, put it down, and probed a bit with a blunt instrument. Picked up the notebook, wrote again. Then he drew a sketch in there on a fresh page. Looked at the child, back at the sketch, then put the notebook away.

"What is it?" Mrs. Chisolm said, propped up now against the pillows by the headboard and sleepy with exhaustion.

He heard someone come up behind him and saw the girl, Grace, looking around his shoulder at the child, her eyes pinched. Then she left and he heard her open the door and go out, say something to her father in the main room. He spoke quietly to the midwife, asked her to pin a diaper on the child.

Chisolm looked in from the other room. His long face half in shadow.

The doctor picked up the diapered baby, who was crying with some vigor now.

"What, then?" Chisolm said from the doorway.

"Well," the doctor said. "Let's have Mrs. Chisolm nurse and then we'll have a talk."

"About what?"

"Good set of lungs, eh?"

The doctor took the baby over to Mrs. Chisolm, who looked at him as if he were some kind of threat, but took the child and bared a breast and let it nurse. The baby suckled furiously and kept its milky blue eyes on its mother's face, the infinite and divinely vulnerable eyes of an infant. Mrs. Chisolm looked as if she thought it to be some kind of potentially dangerous creature.

WHEN HIS WIFE finally nursed the child to sleep and then dozed off herself, and the midwife had put the baby back into the crib, Chisolm went over to look. He loosened the diaper, gently raised the child's bottom, leaned sideways so as not to block the light. The doctor watched him but didn't come over.

"Good lord," Chisolm said. "What trouble have we gone and brought into this world now?"

"Trouble for you and Miz Chisolm," the midwife said. "But more trouble for the child, I expect, poor thing."

Chisolm didn't look her way. He gazed at the child. The doctor was quiet.

"I 'spec so," Chisolm said. He called softly to his older girl, *Grace*. The girl came slumping in.

"Get the doctor a plate like I told you. And some coffee."

To the doctor he said, "I'll leave a little something in your buggy for the ride home."

The doctor nodded and touched a finger to his brow in a gesture of appreciation.

Chisolm's jug was empty. He pulled on a barn jacket, took a lantern from where it hung on a nail beside the door, went outside, and stood on the porch. Maybe an hour till the full dawn, just a sense of its light in the sky. Against that stood the black outline of trees west of the house and the fields to the south, silhouette of the barn's pitch, and the shed. He lit the lantern and headed down the narrower of two paths into the woods behind the house, veered off that one onto an even more narrow and discreet one—no more than a game trail, at best—that led to his makings and storage. Light had begun to sift like faintly luminous dust into the trees. He could just make out the delicate shadowy patterns of the variously stubbled barks on the trunks, knots on limbs. Switch branches brushed his denim overalls like blind, limber tentacles noting his passing, allowing his pass. In a little clearing down near the creek was the squat figure of his still and the crude shed of rough lumber he'd built there with a heavy door and the padlock he left unlocked most of the time. Folks were aware of his habitual vigilance. He set down the lantern, removed the unhasped lock, and opened the door. He selected a jug from a middle shelf, set it on a broad stump near the fire pit. He went back into the shed and fetched a small pail of kerosene-soaked sawdust, shook some onto the blackened wood in the pit, put the pail up, closed the shed door. He took some gathered limbs from a small stack next to the pit, set them on top of the old logs, struck a match to the sawdust, watched the flames come up and catch the fresh pieces. He took up the jug and sat on the stump, pulled the whittled beech stick that served as his signature cork from its mouth, took a good swig, forced it down, coughed, recorked, and set the jug on the ground behind him, back from the fire. The throbbing heat of the whiskey filled his chest and drifted in blood up into his mind and opened a little door, just a bit. He let out a heavy breath, took his tobacco pouch and papers from his overalls bib, and rolled a loose cigarette, lit it with a slender stick he held to the flames for a moment, blew out the stick and set it aside, and smoked.

For the devil of him, he couldn't recall exactly when it had happened. He supposed he'd been drinking or he wouldn't have entertained the idea. They'd had no need nor desire for another child. Would have gone elsewhere, if he could. Must have been that. A late hour, nowhere to go, an urge that overrode everything else. He thought, *Ain't I old enough yet to be over that?*

Then he hoped he wouldn't ever be, just as quickly after thinking it'd be a good thing if he was.

He hit the jug again, finished the cigarette, and dropped its butt into the fire now heating his shanks and knees against the chilly dawn threading down through the fragile canopy of pine needles and sparse-leaved hardwood branches. He sat awhile. The light turned smoky in among the trees. He took a mouthful from the jug and spat it into the fire, watched the brief roaring up of the flames, took another slug that burned down into his gullet and rose unchecked now into his mind, corked the jug, rolled another cigarette, and thought, *What's done is done.*

He heard something behind him and turned.

It was his hound, ambling down the trail as if to come sit and share a sigh or two.

"You got the face of bored sadness," he said to the dog.

The dog didn't take umbrage. Came over beside his left foot and plopped down with a heavy sigh as if he were the one going through all the trouble on this evening.

IN TRUTH, MRS. Chisolm had no memory of the act of the child's conception, either. *My lands*, she said once to Jane many years later, after she'd been widowed and felt the memories of her life drifting about her mind like vapors: *I cannot recall*.

But her solution was simple, really. The doctor had supplied her with a measure of laudanum for—he stressed this—only her worst days of the nerves. And it had been a day back that late winter of cabin fever and a spitting cold rain as she hurried to gather the few most-late greens (she called them sneaky greens, popping up long after what you'd thought the last would be) from the winter garden, canning and cooking, and an argument over money at the supper table, and him going out in the weather with hat and coat to his little shed beside his still to drink and smoke and curse about things general, and she had thought he'd be gone all night or incapacitated at the least, so she had taken a dose to help her sleep.

All she remembered after that was waking well before daylight and feeling in herself that something had happened, and being so upset all she could do was leave the bed in a rage of silent tears. She rekindled the fire in the main room fireplace, then the large kitchen stove, made coffee, and sat drinking a cup while the bacon fried and grits bubbled, trying to pull herself together before he woke up, then made eggs and set a plate before him and went about her chores that morning in the relentless bitter late winter rain without a word. Feeling in her reeling mind that her body was already changing, taking itself away from her again, making another creature to push out into this unpredictable world.

THE DOCTOR FINISHED eating, set his plate and cup in the sink, and went back into the bedroom. The midwife was still there, standing silent beside the woodstove.

He asked of the midwife: "Mr. Chisolm?"

"In there by the fire. Went down to his makings but come back a minute ago."

Chisolm looked up when he entered the room.

"So just what is it we have here?" he said.

"A little girl, I believe."

"You believe."

"I need to make a telephone call to an old friend of mine in Baltimore, a specialist, ask him some questions. I'll be back tomorrow if possible, next day if not."

Chisolm said nothing, blinking at him.

"Make sure the child is eliminating waste properly," the doctor said. "If she isn't, and especially if there is any swelling in her lower tummy, you send for me right away."

Chisolm nodded.

"I don't see any distension, meaning nothing seems to be dangerously out of place," the doctor said. Chisolm stared at him, frowning, not seeming to really process this.

"All right, not to worry," the doctor said. "I'll be back tomorrow afternoon."

HE FOUND THE JUG under the blanket he'd brought along to warm his legs. Made his way back through the dawning countryside taking his time, taking a pull on the jug every quarter mile or so. When he pulled up into the driveway of his house he was dismayed at what he saw. Tired deep in his bones and joints, and a little drunk, he sat there a moment taking it in: a wagon, two blanketed mules, a runabout pickup, one ragged buggy, and a smallish gaggle of people on the porch plus two in the ragged buggy, all awaiting his arrival. A small string of swaybacked horses stood tethered to the hog pen fence down the hill from the house. He dropped the blankets he'd used to cover his legs over the jug between his feet, and climbed down bending his stiffness as if simple movement were akin to heaving against a stubborn animal or heavy load.

He tethered the Fox Trotter to the post, grabbed his medical bag.

He called out, "Somebody take my rig around to the shed and put up my horse."

A young boy jumped down from the porch and ran up.

"I'll give you a penny before you go."

"Thank you, Dr. Thompson."

The doctor leaned in close, spoke quietly. "Mind the jug there under that blanket."

The boy grinned like a lovable imbecile.

"Yes, sir."

"Don't you get into it. It'll make you sick."

The boy giggled in a strangely ecstatic way, as if something inside him had been too pleasurably stimulated, and ended with an odd hum, looking at the doctor sideways. *My god, what made this one?* the doctor thought.

He stepped up onto the porch among the sagging, ragged group there.

"How long you all been here?"

"I been here since first light," said an old woman whose goiter had swelled up to the size of a yellow squash. She had no teeth and sounded like she was talking with her mouth full. That was an odd paradox he'd noted so often that he hardly noticed anymore. But his senses were always more alive and alert when he was this tired.

"My wife tend to you?"

"She brought out some coffee and biscuits about an hour ago," the goiter woman said. "We do appreciate it. Said she was going on back to bed for a while, tired out waiting up for you since early morning."

"All right."

Also on the porch were a boy with a broken arm from sleepwalking off the porch of their home, a man with a swollen, possibly broken ankle from stepping into a gopher hole, another leaned forward clutching his chest with what was probably a heart attack, and yet another with a giant blue-and-yellow-clouded goose egg on his forehead.

And all these wretched souls came out of the womb perfectly normal, the doctor thought, looking around. *Who can say what life will make of a body?*

"What happened to you?" he said to the man with the goose egg as he started into the house with his bag.

"I hit him with the barrel of his own shotgun," the woman sitting next to the man said. The man didn't say anything, gazing in a dazed way straight ahead at nothing, looked about half conscious.

"He said I hit him so hard he's done gone blind," the woman said. "I tried to shoot him with it but it wasn't loaded and I don't know where he keeps his shotgun shells."

"Won't never, neither," the man said in a whisper, not moving his head or his apparently sightless gaze.

"Better hope I don't," the woman said. "Come home drunk again. I had the money I'd get my own gun or at least some shotgun shells for his. I'd stick him with a knife when he's like that but I'm afraid he'd get it away and stick me."

"That'll do," the doctor said.

He gestured to the old man clutching his chest. "Help him on into my office, I'll be there in a minute."

He went inside his house and set his bag on the desk in his study, a kind of anteroom to his office where he saw patients, and drew a small amount of cocaine solution into a hypodermic. He was quiet through all this so as not to wake his wife. He injected the solution into a vein in his arm, then put the hypo away and rolled down his sleeve. He stood there over his desk for a few minutes, allowing the dope to start running through him, opening his eyes good, before taking up the bag and going into his office, where the older man sat in a chair, a young man standing beside him. He put a stethoscope to the older man's chest. The older man, his stiff hair shorn in what looked like the feathers of a ruffled white hen, stared ahead and sieved a light breathing through his open mouth.

"What happened?" the doctor said to the young man.

"He just kind of sat down in the yard while we was on the way to the barn this morning," the young man said. "I had to help him up."

"Where you been, Doc?" the old man said in a whisper.

"Down at Chisolm's, delivering a child."

The old man said nothing for a moment, then whispered out, "Ain't she a little long in the tooth for that now?"

"I reckon if Chisolm can still make it happen and she can still accommodate it, it'll happen," the doctor said.

"Heh," the old man wheezed. Then he said, *Oof*, like laughing hurt him.

"Take it easy. You got arrhythmia going on in there. Means your heart's not beating regular. I'll give you something just to calm it down."

"All right."

"Is he gon' live?" the young man said.

"Of course," the doctor said. "Just how long is always the question, isn't it? I've seen young men your age die of a bad heart, too. Seen old men with bad hearts live on and on."

He administered a hypodermic and gave the young man some pills.

"These here are nitroglycerine tablets. Make sure he keeps them on him and if he feels a pain in his chest, put one under the tongue. If he knows he's going to be doing something strenuous—hard work, I mean—he can take one a few minutes before and maybe ward it off. Take an aspirin every morning."

"What if he just gives out like today?"

"Make him go to bed till he feels better. Cut out the bacon."

"That's about all he eats," the young man said.

"Just a new idea going around. Vegetables, cornbread, a little lean ham. Easy on the chores. Plenty of rest. No conjugal relations."

"What?" the old man said.

"Fornication."

"Oh."

"Or if you do, take one of those tablets before that, too."

"Heh. I ain't like old Chisolm down there."

"Equipment not standing like it used to, eh? Well, that's the way it goes. Chisolm's younger than you."

"Sometimes it just gets kind of thick," the old man said.

The young man snickered.

"Well, just enjoy that, if you can, means you're still alive," the doctor said.

"What was it?"

"What?"

"A boy or a girl them Chisolms had."

The doctor didn't answer for a moment, then said, "Baby girl."

"Healthy, then?"

"I believe so."

"Well, God bless 'em."

"I'll pass that along."

Then he helped the young man help the older man out. The man with the goose egg on his head looked paler, and the goose egg larger, and he signaled for the man's wife to help him into the office.

"He can make it in on his own," the woman said.

"Suit yourself," the doctor said. "If he dies, you know, the sheriff just might charge you with murder for knocking him in the head like that."

"Wouldn't be nothing he didn't deserve," she muttered as the doctor closed the door to his office behind him. He sat the man down, examined the big bump.

"I'll have to drain that off, if I can," he said.

The man said nothing.

"You got a concussion, at best, but I'm worried you got bleeding still going on in there."

The man still said nothing. Then he said, slowly, "Just tell the sheriff she was lying. I dropped a ax head on myself splitting firewood." Then he closed his eyes and stopped breathing, still sitting upright in the chair.

"Well, damn," the doctor said. He checked for a pulse, fingered the carotid.

"You need to come in here," he said to the woman still sitting on the porch. She looked at him hard for a moment, then got up and followed him in. She looked at her husband sitting dead in the chair.

"Is he gone?" she said.

The doctor nodded.

"He said you were lying and that he dropped an ax on his own head chopping firewood."

"Well," the woman said after a long minute. "You don't need no help around here, do you? Cleaning, what-all? I got a daughter can do it, won't cost you much."

The doctor stared at her in near disbelief. Then he said, "Got all the help I need right now. I'll ask the coroner if he can use anyone."

"I appreciate it," the woman said, and left the office, climbed up onto the seat of a buckboard behind a swayback mule. The doctor had the young man, who had not left yet with his ailing father, help him carry the dead man outside and lay him into the back of the woman's wagon. He unwrapped the reins, traveled them over the mule, handed them to the woman, who looked as if she didn't know what they were. Then he went back up onto the porch and motioned to the woman with the goiter. Before he closed the door behind them, he said to the rest on the porch,

"She was just mad-talking. He dropped an ax on his own head, splitting firewood, by his own admission. You all know how it goes, long married."

All on the porch nodded and murmured. One said, "Lord, yes."

"Well, the rest of you figure out the order amongst yourselves."

He wasn't tired anymore when he was done with them all, so he went into town and sent a telegraph to his friend from medical school, Ellis Adams, now a urological surgeon at Johns Hopkins. Then waited an hour and called him, long-distance. Described the Chisolm baby from his notes and drawings, asked some questions. Then went home again. No patients waiting this time, thank God.

His wife, Lett, was in the parlor drinking coffee. He sat down and she brought him a cup, sat with him. She was tall, like him, with long brown hair she kept pinned up nicely. A locket cameo beauty carved from ivory, come miraculously to life. But she looked tired. Beautifully so, but tired. And so was he, now. Exhausted.

"I guess you didn't sleep much last night, either," he said.

"No." She set her coffee cup down and tapped on her wedding ring, a habit she had when bothered. "Ed, have you thought anymore about setting up a clinic in town? Or joining someone? Not everyone makes house calls anymore, you know."

He sipped his coffee. It entered his blood as what it was, some powerful drug.

"I don't know what to say, Lett. I've told you it seems unethical to abandon a practice, especially this kind."

"Well, find someone to take it, then. As I have suggested before."

"And, as I have explained, the youngest doctors—the ones who don't like house calls—don't want this kind of practice anymore. And the older ones are already settled."

"Well. Ed."

"Yes."

"If you come home from a late-night call and I'm not here, you can figure I've gone to Mother's for the night. I don't like being here on the edge of town in this big house by myself when you go out. It didn't bother me so much for a while, but it's begun to. I wake up, find you gone, and can't get back to sleep."

"How is getting up, getting dressed, and driving or taking a buggy into town, waking up your mother—just how is that going to help you sleep, Lett?"

"It's not all about not being able to sleep, Ed. It's feeling left alone."

He noticed her hands were shaking just the slightest bit. She saw him notice, clasped one over the other, and went to the window, facing out.

"Did you sleep at all last night, Lett?"

He was gazing at her tall slim figure there, her lovely neck exposed and half in shadow of diagonal light, and suddenly he felt a fear for her.

"I'm scarcely ever gone more than a few hours, often less."

She gestured with one hand, as if helpless against her frustration.

"I could give you something to help you sleep," he said.

She turned then, looking so on the verge of tears he was startled.

"Laudanum, are you saying? No, thank you."

"No, Lett. There are herbs."

"They don't work for me." She looked at the floor, shook her head.

"Come along with me, then. At least sometimes."

She turned back to the window and seemed to stiffen.

"You know I don't like being around sick people. I'm ashamed of it but it's true. I guess I shouldn't have married a doctor," she said, trying to laugh it off. But her laughter was momentary, false, and he could only gaze at her as tenderly as possible, knowing that her feelings for him had been weakening for some time. Detecting the loss of love from one he'd hoped would always give it.

HE DROVE BACK to the Chisolm place the next afternoon, in his Model T Ford. Went inside the house and examined the child, asked Mrs. Chisolm a few questions, then went out to his car, gathered up a douche apparatus, and went back inside. Ida Chisolm seemed to recoil from it.

"Do you have one of these?" he said to her. She shook her head, like a horse pestered by a fly. "Well, you can have this one. She must be kept very clean—inside, I mean. You want to try to keep her fecal matter—her poop—from getting into her other parts. It's all kind of together in there, with this child. Let me show you." She didn't move. "Come on over, now. This is important. And when she's old enough, she must be taught to do it herself, and frequently. Otherwise she will have frequent problems for sure."

"What kind of problems?"

"What I believe, from what I can tell and what I've been told, is that without it she could have frequent infections, and you don't want me over here every other day having to treat that."

Warily, the woman approached and watched, listened to what he said. When he looked up at her for a moment, he saw her blinking back tears.

"It will be all right," he said.

"So you say," she said.

"All right," he said after peering at her, trying to figure her state of mind. "Now, listen. I know we normally don't let infants sleep on their backs, if we can help it. But it would be good if she could sleep with her hips slightly elevated. It might mean checking on her more often, I know. But it will help avoid the possibility of the kind of thing that would lead to infections. And during the day, when she's in the crib, same thing. And when she's upright, being held or whatnot, not a problem."

She said nothing, looking blankly at the child lying there in her crib, at the little diaper the doctor had folded and placed beneath her bottom.

"You understand, Ida?" He said her first name to get her attention.

She only nodded. And he went out.

CHISOLM WAS in the work shed sharpening edges on a disc harrow. He stepped out and the doctor met him there just outside the shed, in the shade of its eave. The doctor removed his hat, ran a hand through his hair, inspected the hat as if for flaws, then put it back on.

"Child seems all right," he said to Chisolm. "Seems healthy, to me. Doesn't have everything she ought to have, but there does not appear to be an obstruction and as long as she's able to eliminate waste and y'all keep her clean, she should be all right." He looked at the man. "I've explained that to your wife." Chisolm looked back at him curiously. "We'll see how she comes along in time, but I believe she'll be all right. She's nursing well."

"She, then."

"Yes."

Chisolm looked at him a long moment, studying him the way he did, taking the words in.

"Doesn't need anything special, then?" he said. "No medicine or special food?"

The doctor shook his head.

"I'll be honest with you, though," he said.

Chisolm said nothing, waiting.

"The truth of the matter is that if something is going to go wrong, it will likely go wrong in these first weeks or even first few months. If she doesn't soil her diaper often as any child ought, or especially if she goes even a day without that, as I said, you send for me quick. Keep an eye out for any swelling in her lower tummy. Or something kind of poking the skin out in an odd way. You can expect me to be checking in pretty often for a while. I won't charge you for it. Let's just call it a learning experience for everyone, but especially me, as a doctor I mean."

Chisolm just nodded, his eyes on the doctor's as if expecting more. Then he looked away.

The doctor yawned and rubbed his face with his hands.

"Blame me if it doesn't seem I've treated half the county in the last few days. I had a passel waiting on me when I got home this morning, then went to town to call a friend who knows more about this kind of business here than I do. Went home hoping for a nap but I'd hardly lain down before a boy rode up hollering his father cut himself bad at the sawmill. Had me a bit of a nap under a sweet gum beside the road between there and here. I thank you for that gift of spiritual aid in that regard."

Chisolm nodded, managed a grim smile.

"You need another?"

"I'm plenty good for now, thank you. Sir, I believe your product is as good as anything bottled in Kentucky. You are an artist."

Chisolm almost grinned. "Anytime you're in the neighborhood, Doc, just help yourself." Then he said, "I guess I got one question."

"Shoot."

"How is it a child comes out like this'n?"

The doctor shrugged his shoulders inside his jacket, like he'd got a chill. He was overtired.

"The way I see it, most everybody's lucky nothing goes wrong during a pregnancy. I sometimes can't believe how often nature gets it just right. I've seen some things you wouldn't believe. Most that come out wrong or odd die soon after birth. Sometimes I can be pretty sure, when I come back to check on them, that what happened was not a natural death."

Chisolm looked at him for a long minute, but the doctor kept looking out over the field.

"Anyhow," Chisolm said, "you figure this one's a girl just because, I reckon, it's clear she ain't a boy."

"Best I can tell," the doctor said, "she's just a girl who did not fully develop. Something stopped that in the womb, for whatever reason. It happens. No one's fault. It's rare, but at this point I do not think it's life-threatening." He paused. "There's many a case of a child being *both*, to one degree or another, but that's not the case here. I'm told this is most likely a condition you see only in female children, anyway, and not boys."

Chisolm looked at him.

"Both, you say."

The doctor raised his eyebrows and gave a nod, took his hat off to look it over again, brows furrowing down.

"Can't be a nothing," he said. "Come out able to be one or the other, and you have to wait and see which one wins out. Sometimes it just stays both."

Chisolm looked at him, taking that in.

"Well, I reckon if a thing like that can happen to a child, we got damn lucky."

"All things considered," the doctor said, "I'd have to agree."

"And nothing to do about it."

"I don't believe so, no. But, in time, who knows? If you can, you might put a little away toward it whenever you can, just in case."

They stood there another long minute. Then the doctor gave Chisolm a light pat on the shoulder. "She'll be a little treasure for you and Mrs., I don't doubt it," he said.

Chisolm nodded, and went back into his shed and began filing at the disc blade again. The doctor left and made a couple of house calls in the general area. The afternoon grew chilly, late November coming on. When he returned home at last light the house was empty, but a small fire flickered in the hearth, and there was a tin plate on the stove's warmer, covered by a clean cloth. A note from his wife on the kitchen table. She'd gone into town to visit her mother, might stay overnight, not to worry.

He went into his study, where he'd left the jug from Chisolm, poured himself a measure into an empty coffee cup, lit a small lamp on his desk, and wrote in his journal. A tree frog sang out its loud, long, piercing song just outside the window on the porch, and even its near-deafening note, coming from an inch-long operatic amphibian soprano, somehow brought up a corresponding silent note of melancholy.

AS SOON AS the child got a little strength in her neck, her mother enlisted the older daughter, Grace, who carried the infant around like a broken third arm in a makeshift sling. She brought her to her mother when she was hungry and would step outside and walk fast, then run to someplace on the farm she could hunker down, hide out, curse or weep as the mood might fit her. Occasionally she would take a little homemade corncob vine-stem pipe she'd fashioned with a paring knife and puff on a bit of tobacco she'd snitched from her father. It was a small rebellion but there was a measure of satisfaction in it.

Later on, when winter had passed and the baby was able to crawl around like a quick little hobbled dog, Grace got her out of the house as often as possible. They wandered as far as the child's ability and bobbling curiosity would take them, Grace only picking her up when she veered too close to an animal or machine and turning her like a windup toy in another direction. She grew out a full head of fine dark brown hair that Grace pulled up into a tiny little bow on top of her head. Quite cute, her older sister had to admit.

But she never lost her conviction that this motherhood business wasn't ever going to be for her.

She stepped from the privy into the gray-blue light of a windy March afternoon, gusts buffeting the wooden door she held on to, kicking up dust in the yard, rattling the leafing, bony limbs in the trees, and rippling the surface of the cattle pond down in the pasture. The door to the house opened and her mother's arm swung out, tossing a wadded diaper over the edge of the porch and into the yard. Grace looked at her duty lying there, steam rising like scant smoke from its folds.

The doctor's Ford pulled to a clattering stop in front of it, as if it were a traffic sign of the oddest sort. He was in the habit now of stopping by at least once a week. She watched him get out, step around the car on his long, just slightly bowed legs, look down at the steaming bundle, then over at Grace standing in the open door to the privy. He was hatless, hank of carelessly debonair hair on his forehead, hands in pockets as if studying something worthy of thought. She just looked at him. His casual relationship with the world, his bookishly handsome, relative ease, infuriated her. He had the audacity to give her what looked like the faintest smile, as if he were amused. Grace was not.

She followed him inside the house and stood in the doorway to the living room as he examined the baby, pinned her fresh diaper, then followed him as far as the kitchen doorway to listen while he spoke to her mother.

"Four months now," he was saying as they sat at the table. "If anything serious were going to develop, I believe we would have seen signs of it already."

She looked at the doctor sitting there, his oddly aristocratic features, no gray in his hair. It struck her he might be younger than she'd thought.

"Grace, mind your manners and put on a pot of coffee," her mother said.

She slumped over and got the pot, rinsed it at the pump out back, put in new water, and brought it back inside. Loaded some coffee in it and set it on top of the stove. Threw another chunk of wood in the stove furnace. At one point a lull in the conversation caused her to glance at the doctor. She started when she saw he was looking at her, a quizzical if bemused look on his face. She frowned and went back to the doorway and stood just outside it, as if not listening.

He went on to say that Mrs. Chisolm should continue to make sure there was no odd swelling, and that he would continue checking in regularly if she wouldn't mind.

"I thank you," her mother said, though her tone held something of suspicion and a trace of resentment as well, no doubt at having to feel beholden.

Grace went back in when the coffee was done and poured the doctor a cup. He smiled up at her.

"Thank you, Miss Grace."

"Welcome," she mumbled, furious at herself for blushing.

He said he thought he would take a little stroll into the woods behind their house and then be on his way, if they wouldn't mind. Her mother gave herself a wry smile and said of course, to make himself at home. The doctor smiled in an odd way back at her, a bit of mischief in his eye, then took up his coffee cup and went out the kitchen door.

"What's that all about, then?" Grace said.

"He's one likes to walk in the woods, I guess."

"Oh, I thought maybe he just needs a little sweetener in his coffee."

"Don't be impertinent," her mother said. "He's not charging us for any of this, whatever it's worth."

"Why not?"

"I don't ask."

Leaving, later, when the doctor rounded the corner of their long drive toward the road, she was standing just off it in the shadow of a ragged pine tree, watching him pass. Without looking her way he lifted a finger from the steering wheel in a little acknowledgment or wave, to which she responded by lifting her middle finger toward his car as it raised the dust on its way down the drive.

Ellison Adams, M.D.
Johns Hopkins University School of Medicine
Baltimore, Maryland

Dear Ellis,
A busy winter it was here with ague and the results of physical violence bred and borne by folks cooped up a bit too much with their chosen enemies. I'm sure you would find it all most amusing.

Since there have been no complications (and I have to say I expected there to be some, but it seems you were right so I must have described it well enough), it has been some time since I've written to you concerning my young patient with her interesting if apparently manageable urological condition. As you expected, there's been no apparent danger arising from blockages, fistulas, or other developments in that direction, etc. An interesting case, and a very fine and otherwise normal child in the making as it turns out.

The mother seems to have found her ways to cope. Her older daughter takes on most of the child caring duties whenever she's not away in school. Curious girl, never says much. I get the feeling she's like some wildcat tethered to that family and her duties as if to a tree by a pulled-taut chain. Only question is will she give more trouble than she gets.

Speaking of coping, my Lett seems to spend more time in town with her family than here, these days. Not really but it seems so. Feels like I see our housekeeper young Hattie more than I do my own wife. I had not considered how difficult (and unamusing) it might be for a refined city girl to be married to a man who for some reason ends up an old-time country doctor. I suppose she expected me to end up in research, like you, or at least some sophisticated urban practice, coming and going like a banker, instead of mending the cracked limbs and skulls of simple farm folks who often enough show up at the door bloody and smelling of animals and dirt. I believe she is profoundly disheartened by the sight of a man or woman with the dental apparatus of a jack-o'-lantern.

Of course do please keep your more refined and intelligent ears open whenever possible to any research developments that would apply and let me know posthaste should something relevant be in the works. If such a case/condition as I have on my hands here is indeed as rare as you suspect, then I wonder if Young et al. would be interested in some kind of pro bono examination, for the purposes of advancing science, as we say. If you should manage to get anyone's attention on the matter, please let me know directly. Your colleague Dr. Young will, I believe, continue to make great strides in this field, in time. Please maintain your friendship with this man and do not let the horse's ass in you come out at some kind of social gathering or whatnot, as we know this Dr. Young is a bit of a prude and campaigned against prostitution when he served in the war, etc. etc., as if contracting a case of the clap could somehow be worse than having one's entire apparatus blown off or to pieces by a German artillery shell—but, pardon, I stray afield. In other words also be discreet as possible concerning your other habits, if you will, oh Great One. My regards to Mary Kate and the children, by the way.

Spring has arrived, in any case—gusty, always thrilling to me. The songbirds are in a riot of pugnacious pleasure. What I would do to have this season exist without end. Except, what did the poet imply, that having our pleasures always in-hand we would no longer appreciate them? Possibly even our recognition of them would cease to be anything remarkable at all.

Yours, etc.

Eldred The Terrible & etc.

Weanings

Ida Chisolm weaned her new one at little less than a year old and the baby took to her mush of peas and sweet potatoes with the same toothless puzzlement, then gluttony, as any child. Grace, whenever she wasn't at school, went about her babysitting duties in silence. At eleven years she had the demeanor of a disgusted, life-strangled sixteen-year-old. As if to speed up and thereby shorten the period of being harnessed to the task, she worked hard to train her little sister on the chamber pot, then the outhouse, and taught her to clean herself. But soon enough recognized a problem and complained about frequent accidents and once the doctor confirmed the incontinence it was a matter of either getting the child to run to the outhouse or to drop her drawers (the loose diaper she had continued to wear, in any case) wherever she stood in the yard, or pasture, or at the edge of the woods, by the barn, wherever. Since she was just a toddler they allowed it, since she did not like soiling herself and wanted to go like everyone else. She tried. A good-humored, even cheerful little child. She seemed intelligent enough but not dangerously impulsive, so Grace let her wander by herself around the house and yard barefoot (except in winter) as freely as a child at least a

year or two older. It became a familiar sight to the family and the
sharecroppers and tenants, this small scrawny creature baring her
bony bum and relieving herself whenever and wherever like one
of the animals in their care.

Watching this from the front porch at churning, or from the
back porch washing dishes in the pump sink, or emerging from
the privy, Grace indulged in what little humor she had in her
system, smiling a tight smile and muttering to herself in a low
chuckle, shaking her head and going back to work, keeping one
eye loosely on the child. Jane was indeed like some kind of herky-
jerky windup toy that never wound down till sometime in the
evening right after supper when the winder just stopped and
clump, down she went. Clean her and put her to bed.

When she got a break from her babysitting Grace would sneak
out to the barn and go around it to smoke a cigarette from the
Luckies she now kept hidden behind a loose chink in one of the
foundation posts. Got to where she liked them so much she began
sneaking one after supper, too, watching from shadows for when
the washbasin was unoccupied, then hurrying to wash up, brush
her teeth, before going to bed without a word to or a glance at
anyone. They were all used to that.

When little Jane noticed a rag doll in the Sears catalog, Grace
put one together for her using material from a flour sack and filling the shape with hard corn kernels cracked with a hammer. She
let Jane help draw on a face with India ink, then stitched over that
with blue thread. They made a tiny skirt for it and drew a pair of
slippers on its shapeless feet.

She'd thrown her own similar doll into the bushes along the
road one day years before, suddenly embarrassed and disgusted
with herself for still carrying it in her school satchel. Now, young

as she was, she felt a twinge of lost childhood and tried to steel herself against it, turning her thoughts once again to getting away. But she could not harden herself entirely anymore against her feelings for this little girl, her baby sister and the only one in her household she could enjoy even a little bit being around. With her yellow hair and blue eyes, she felt like a changeling left at the door of this cantankerous woman and gloomy man, yet here was this child, this odd one, a defective, dark like their parents but with blue eyes even bluer than hers. She did not want to love her, or as she sometimes referred to her, *it*, but she thought, *I have to love something*.

She sat on the porch one afternoon during the autumn Jane would turn three and watched her wander out into the yard and over near the shed across the drive, stop, squat, and instead of what Grace expected from that, saw her reach down and pick something up, hands working like she was winding something around them as she walked, stopped at the edge of the porch, hands raised, eyes wide open with the secret hidden in them.

"Well, what is it?" Grace said. She was looking on this strange and beautiful child, big eyes so expressive, as if wiser or more knowing than possible.

Little Jane opened her hands and a tiny garden snake no bigger around than a night crawler and no longer than the length of a knitting needle popped up and curled around her hands as if it were the strange birth of an extra, wild, writhing digit. Grace stood up as if called to military attention, not knowing whether to go knock the snake from the child's hands or trust to luck it was a harmless one.

"Put it down, now," she said as calmly as she could. But Jane closed her eyes and laughed and ran past her into the house and in a moment she heard her mother shriek and holler to "get that thing out of this house right now!"

Later, she looked on as their father gave Jane a lesson on which snakes were safe and which were not. He drew pictures of the poisonous snakes' broad, triangular heads, and brought out an old rattle from one he'd killed in the yard, shook it for her. "You hear that," he said, "you stop, stand real still, figure out where it is, and you back away. You see this here cottonmouth moccasin, you run," and he described and drew one, told her their coloring and shape. Told her about coral snakes: *Red touch yellow, kill a fellow; red touch black, friend to Jack.* She liked that rhyme enough to mimic it back to him, making him smile a rare smile.

He said, "Anyway, you see one of those snakes, you hightail it out of there. And if you can't tell, don't chance it."

She asked if she could have the rattle to keep on a string around her neck.

He seemed amused by this but said he thought not, as it might attract another snake.

"All right," she said, handing the rattle back. Her father put it away in the little box on the mantel where he kept it along with a bear's tooth and the tiny mole skull Jane herself had found one day, just roaming around the yard.

When they left, Grace went to the mantel, took out the rattle, and made herself a necklace of it by poking a hole in the open end and lacing through it a length of pale thread. She made it long enough so the rattle would be hidden by her blouse. She hooked a finger under it and gave it a little shake, and something about the sound made her heart beat a little faster.

Little Jane heard it one day and was excited. "You made a rattle necklace!" she said. "Papa wouldn't let me."

"I know."

"He said it might make a real snake come after me."

"I doubt that," Grace said. "You want it?"

Jane seemed to think about it, then shook her head with a mysterious grin.

Her mother asked Grace one day what she had on that thread around her neck.

"Nothing," she said.

"I can see there's something on it, there under your blouse. I can hear it making some kind of little noise when you move around."

"Nothing but the rattle of my little old heart," Grace said, and ignored the look her mother gave her.

LEAVING THE CHILD'S care to her older daughter had made it a little easier for Ida Chisolm to avoid her dark thoughts, though not entirely. When she had a little break she sat on the front porch, dipped a bit of snuff—which she knew was smallish sinful but did it anyway, a soul was corrupt at birth and adding a little vice wouldn't change the equation much—and spat into the bare dirt of the yard doing the best she could to empty her clamorous mind. Crows banked about the grove of pine and hardwood down by the cow pond and flew back up on fluff-cranked wings into the pecans near the barn, settling in their gnarly limbs like black flittering shadows into the foliage of clouded thoughts she could not and did not bother to plumb. Late fall blackbirds swept in waves to the oaks at the yard's edge, and their deafening, squawking, creaking calls, the cacophonous tuning of a mad avian symphony, drew the grief-borne anger from her heart, into the air, and swept it away in long, almost soothing moments of something like peace. The occasional fluid murmuration of migrating starlings, a wondrous sight when she was a child, could evoke in her all over again a strange sense of foreboding.

She said nothing to anyone about her feeling that this child Jane's condition could've come from the sinful way in which she was conceived. No matter a man and woman be husband and wife. If the wife doesn't even know it's going on, it's a sin and an abomination to the woman and the punishment would not be a death but something to linger, to remind you of what you had done or allowed done, either one. And in God's eyes does it really matter who was to blame, and who could say she did not bear her share of the blame, putting herself in such a state that he could do what he did without her awareness, much less consent? Being a man, he considered their long-ago vows consent enough, and that thought sent her out to the woodpile to chop kindling till she could see again, so blind she felt in her rising and inexpressible anger. When she had spent her rage, kindling chunks around her as if the woodpile had exploded and left her standing, she buried the ax in the block and stalked off out the back yard and down the main trail in the woods to the fishing pond. She stood there looking at the smooth brown surface of the pond, arms straight at her sides, and thought she could go back up, fetch a heavy piece of mechanical scrap and a rope, tie it about her waist, and walk into the water until submerged and will herself to fill her lungs with the silty water. She let her mind imagine the scene, the moment. Then, in angry tears again, she stripped off her clothing, leaving on her shoes, and waded in to her neck, dunked herself, and swam out deeper. She held her breath as long as she could, then blew it out, her body sinking deeper, until in a panic she pushed herself back up to the surface, broke out of the water, and bobbed there, treading water. She slung hair from her eyes and saw her husband on the bank where she'd entered, his arms limp at his sides, watching her. She watched him, feeling like a wild animal caught in the open by a strange human creature, until he turned and walked back up the bank on the trail, out of sight. Only then did she swim in and put her clothes back onto her wet, clingy body, feet squishing in her sodden shoes, feeling at least a little bit mollified, as if his having witnessed her act was at least a warning, an act of emotional revenge. She was washed clean in body, if not entirely in mind.

IN THE FALL of 1918 there came news of the flu epidemic. Several cases down in Mercury left people alarmed, and when a local child seemed to have come down with it, officials closed the school and Grace was free to perform her babysitting duties full-time.

Ida Chisolm took advantage of Grace's presence to disappear into the woods and gather a large basket of echinacea and ginseng root. She slipped off to a neighbor's farm to beg some fruit from their pomegranate tree and, not finding them home, scuttled away like a desperate thief with several pomegranates tucked into the folds of her apron. She set into a constant, haranguing administration of tea from the herbs and doses of a syrup she made from the pomegranate seeds stirred into drams of her husband's precious apple brandy, which Grace and Jane resisted, grimacing, but she put her own grimacing face into theirs and told them in a cold voice to drink it or die. "I will not have death visit this house again until it is mine own," she said in her ominous way. She looked up to see her husband watching her from the other room, looking wary and maybe even a bit worried by what must seem her obsessive manner. *Well, let him think I'm crazy*, she thought. *Somebody around here has to practice good common sense.* She got up and went over to him, took up the tin cup he was using to sip whiskey, and poured a measure of the syrup in there, too. Looked him in the eye. "Drink it," she said. He shrugged and did as she said.

They did stay healthy, and she looked at them all in defiance for their lack of faith. The school reopened in late fall but she forbade Grace to return just yet, saying she didn't trust the ones saying the worst was over. Dr. Thompson, during one of his visits, said he couldn't disagree with her on that.

"I'd rather lose a year of school than risk the sickness myself," he said. "I've seen people with it, and I've seen them die of it. Children do seem to be less at risk than young adults. If I were you," he said to Sylvester Chisolm, "I'd wear a mask whenever I went to town to trade."

"Mask?" Chisolm said.

"Gets close and crowded in the cattle auction at the stockyard, doesn't it?"

The doctor went to his car and got his bag and from it brought a square surgical mask with string ties. He gave it to Chisolm. Ida Chisolm watched all this as if witnessing some kind of introduction to a ritual, her shoulders hunched as if against bad luck or a jinxing.

"Wash it good, tie it above your ears and then behind your neck."

Chisolm looked askance, took the mask by one tie string between finger and thumb, and examined it.

"I'll think about it," he said. He went to hand it to his wife but she drew back and shook her head.

"This is not your regular ague," the doctor said, leaning forward and putting on his serious face. "This one is killing people. Not so bad here as in town, and not so bad in town as in big cities. But if you get it, you're in trouble all the same."

And then they heard, not two weeks later, that the doctor's own wife, who had been spending a lot of time in Mercury proper with her family and, it was said, going to society parties and such, had become a victim of the illness. Dr. Thompson tended to her along with the regular hospital doctors and nurses in town, but it did no good.

"You see what good newfangled medicine does for a body, now," Ida Chisolm said.

Mrs. Thompson was buried in the cemetery on the east side of town after a service at her family's church, and after all the people who'd come to the funeral were done, Sylvester Chisolm went over, Ida Chisolm following, reluctant, little Jane nearly hidden in the folds of her voluminous skirts. Then Jane broke from her mother and ran to her father's side. Ida felt a chill in her heart as the doctor reached to take the child in his own arms. He smiled and pushed a strand of her hair behind her ear.

"I'll be all right," he said to her father. "Thank you for coming today. It's good to lay eyes on this little angel at such a time."

"Say you're welcome," Chisolm said.

"Okay," she said.

"You need to say it," he said.

"It's all right," the doctor said. "She said it with her eyes. Why don't you bring her along sometime when you go to town? I'll have our Hattie make a pie. And she can play with her little boy."

Ida Chisolm tried to speak in protest but only a nearly silent croak emerged.

"What's his name?" Jane said.

"His name is Mister. He's the same age as you."

"All right," she said, with the kind of kerplunk finality of a child.

"Bright little thing," the doctor said. "I always wished Lett and I had had children, but now I suppose it's best we never did."

"Is Mister your little boy?" Jane said.

The doctor and Chisolm laughed at that, and little Jane laughed with them. Then the doctor looked over at Ida Chisolm glaring at him from where she stood a few feet away.

"I appreciate you all came," the doctor said, looking past her to where Grace sat in the bed of their buckboard. Like her mother she wore a black dress and black bonnet that hid her face. "The Mrs. seems upset."

Chisolm said, looking over at her, jaw set, "She did consent to come along, but I'm afraid that death does not become her."

THAT EVENING, the doctor sat in his study with a tumbler of Memphis bourbon on ice. Earlier in the stealthy departure of dusk and standing on his porch he'd heard the calling of a young mockingbird down in the virgin woods behind his house. On the randy hunt, he supposed. Wouldn't be long lonely, not down there. Had half a mind to walk his trail through them all the way down to the lake, as if following the looping flight of some dreamed night bird, in dry moonlit undergrowth, step from the canopy to come upon open water and a calling loon. Though he feared it would take him too deeply into his sadness to escape. He ate a tin plate of supper left in the stove warmer by the young woman Hattie he'd hired to keep his house and cook when it became apparent that he and Lett were living a practical separation. He'd come home once too often to no supper, no fire in the hearth or cookstove, a house with dust balls fairly rolling along the baseboards like little animated creatures. This Hattie, the midwife Emmalene's daughter, with her illegitimate child, he'd taken pity on her and admired what seemed an admirable dignity about her, advanced for her young age. He'd had a patient one day who'd observed her child Mister playing in the yard by himself and then said something about colored people not caring for their family. Sometimes he was astonished how often he forgot people's cruel ignorance, people who'd never been anywhere but the little hamlets where they were born, raised, and would die. Not that he hadn't known plenty of so-called sophisticated people with the same attitude. He'd said, "You know that the smartest thing about you, Heck, is probably your pecker." Even Heck had to laugh at that, being treated as he was for a case of gonorrhea.

He left the plate in the sink and stood in the doorway to the bedroom and looked at his empty bed. He could see, out the window there, smoke rising from the chimney in the cottage he'd had spruced up for Hattie Harris, down the hill at the woods' edge. A former slave cottage, was the irony there. The chimney smoke trailed off above the trees of his woods, sloping down the long wooded decline to the hidden lake, dissipating to nothing. There was no birdsong. Some respite between the noisy late afternoon and the last ephemeral moments of dusk. The heavy presence of his wife's absence—not just gone from home but no longer a presence in the living world—was suddenly unbearable, and he wept, silently, standing there, let his tears blur those things before his eyes. Like the vision of a weary newborn child. He stood there until his eyes stopped leaking and dried themselves, stiffening trails down his cheeks he could feel tightening the skin. Such a mortal feeling, this small thing.

DURING JANE'S FIRST few years, her two much older brothers would come home from the state college in the summers to help out, wiry and Indian-brown like their father from working the experimental farm up there. Jane was happiest then, with these grown-up brothers she hardly knew teasing her and playing jokes on her, Sylvester, Jr., tickling her (*Don't do that to HER*, their mother said), and all the conversation around the table. Her father seemed better able to avoid drinking when his older sons were around.

Now they were grown and gone, with families of their own, and it was just her, Grace, and their parents. Sylvester, Jr., and Belmont married and took their wives all the way out to Wyoming, impossibly—unimaginably—far away, to work on a ranch and look for a piece of land to buy and ranch for themselves. Sylvester, Jr., wrote a postcard back:

It's a big place. Has to be. Takes ten times as much grassland to graze a cow here as back home. Winter is hard, hard, hard. Summer is heaven but spring (around June) brings mosquitoes that make ours look like mites. Saying is, mosquitoes that could stand up and mate with a wild turkey, ha. Work is constant, and people are very tough. Belmont and I are saving everything we can and hope to buy a good sized spread in a few years. If you want to see us, you need to come out. Much love from your sons and brothers. S.S.C., Jr.

"We'll never see them again," her mother said, dropping the card into the stove and clanking the lid back down. "Got away when they could, didn't they?" Her father said nothing, as if he hadn't even heard.

Days seemed longer then, on the farm. At dawn everyone rose

and set to the chores, she and Grace milking, her mother getting breakfast together in the kitchen, her father checking the stock for losses or injury or sickness come in overnight. The sourceless light in distant trees, in the dust raised by their feet in the yard. Jane helped her mother scatter cracked corn for the chickens and check their nests and hideaways for eggs. Before heading to school, Grace cleaned up from breakfast as her mother began to plan the noon and evening meals, the dog-trot silent save for the sounds of her working the kitchen or sweeping the floors or churning laundry in the grassless, immaculately swept yard, hauling water from the pump on the back porch in a heavy bucket, heating it in the big black pot over a fire, stirring the dirty clothes with a long, stout hickory stick. There was the bustling of the noon dinner meal when her father came in, ate, then went back out to work, the clanking and scrubbing of cleaning up, the long hot still afternoon, her joy at Grace's arrival home from school, then preparation for supper, and finally the rustling descent of quiet voices and bodies slowing into the evening until everyone slept.

Soon enough she was given the job of feeding the poultry and pigs herself. The pigs had their large pen, below the work shed, and when she wasn't kept busy with something she sometimes slipped away and watched them, their strange aimless waddling, and then sudden activity, frightening the shoats into loud squealing races around the pen as if some predator were after them, but really it was all in their minds. She came to understand that it was play. She didn't want to eat pork after that, and became even thinner, for that was their daily meat except for the occasional venison, rabbit, or squirrel. And there was really no avoiding it entirely, since nearly every vegetable they ate was simmered with fatback for hours.

She fed what little table scraps there were to the two dogs, but otherwise they hunted and scavenged. They knew not to get after the chickens, somehow, some sense of self-preservation. There was the hound and the shaggy thin-shouldered mutt with a long snout and a natural smile, with black fur around one eye and white around the other. This one she took for her dog and named it Top. *How'd you come up with that name?* they said. *He's Top Dog*, she said, and they laughed, even Grace and her mother. The hound had no interest in following her but Top followed her everywhere. He would allow Jane to gaze at him and he would gaze right back at her. He didn't smile, just looked attentive and expectant, as if he could feel what she was feeling about him. Most dogs when you looked at them, strays mostly wandering through, would look away. Her father said it was the wild still in them somewhere deep. But Top was more like a person that way, not afraid of her, at least, and sometimes if she didn't pay him enough attention he would come over and rest his snout on her arm or leg and sigh, then look up at her with just his eyes, and if she was distracted and didn't pet him, then he would give her a little kiss-lick on her hand or forearm, then press his snout onto her arm or leg again until she scratched him behind the ears or rubbed the top of his head or his back. Sometimes he would roll onto his back and allow her to place her ear against his furry chest and listen to his heart beating, so fast, even when he seemed just as calm as could be. She figured a dog had to get in all his heartbeats in a hurry if he wasn't going to live as long as a person might.

She loved the taste of cool buttermilk more than anything in the world. And her favorite after buttermilk was butter on hot biscuits, and after that, butter on hot cornbread, and after that, fried chicken, and after that, apple pie and the rare treat of homemade ice cream, and after that, and later on, fried bream from their own pond. Especially the crisp, salted tails.

Between the ages of four and five, she began to make sure she was the last to sleep. It made her feel safer to be the last one awake, watching and listening to the world settle into the evening quiet and dark. The steady breathing, snoring, sleep-mumbling of the others made her feel more awake and alive, and that was a kind of safeness, too. An owl hooted down in the woods and she hoped no one would die. She studied the pale palms of her hands in the darkened room. The skin there gave off a light as soft as starlight on birch bark. How private, the palm of one's hand. How intimately one knows it. So she may have said, had she the words.

She was a guardian over the slumbering household in her sole awareness of it, and in that comforting role she could finally let go and sleep herself. Although one night, when she was just dropping into that long dark nothing where for an unknown time you ceased to exist, and from which may never come back, it was so hard to get over the idea of that—for every night she said her prayers, *If I should die before I wake, I pray the Lord my soul to take*—she heard the low growling of something, a growl of something that sounded massive, slow, and fierce passing just below the window of her room. Some unspeakable monster. Her heart seized and she shouted out. Grace sat up in her bed, looking around for whatever was the cause of it, and her mother and then her father came running from their beds across the breezeway. Her mother came to her bedside, while her father remained in the doorway open to the breezeway and glittery moonlight slanted on the unpainted boards there. Her father took a lantern around the house to look for tracks. But there was nothing, they said, there had been no beast.

"I didn't hear a thing," Grace said. "I was sound asleep till she started yelling."

"Why would you imagine such an awful thing?" her mother said.

"It could have been a bear," Grace said.

"Not only would we've heard that," her father said, "we sure would've smelled it. Nothing stinks quite like a bear."

But Grace surprised her by lying down beside her until she could go back to sleep. She even teased her with a lullabye she made up: *Hush, little girl, now, don't be a' feared, wasn't nothing but an old bear you hee-rd.* That got her giggling and soon she relaxed and went to sleep, and when she woke up Grace was still there, snoring lightly on top of her bedcovers in her nightgown. She watched her till she blinked her eyes awake. Grace looked over, grumpy again, muttered something to herself. Then said, "How could you know what a bear is when you've never seen or even heard one, far as that goes?"

"It was you said it was a bear," Jane said. "Have *you* ever seen one?"

"I've seen worse," Grace said.

"Like what?" she asked, fascinated.

"Haven't you?" Grace said, being mysterious. "In your sleep?"

"No."

"You will."

But her only nightmares would be about the nameless beast she had heard, her sleeping mind imagining it in all kinds of forms, none of which she was ever able to recall upon waking.

Light of the Gathering Day

By late spring of the year she would turn six, a more complex awareness of her difference had begun to shape itself in her mind like the root of some strange plant down deep in the woods. She had moments when she felt like a secret, silent creation, invisible, more the ghost of something unknowable than a person, a child, a little girl. More than once she felt the light slap of her mother's hand against the back of her head, the voice saying, *Snap out of it, have you gone deaf and dumb and blind, now?* For a second it was as if something just as ethereal as herself, a harsh and spiteful guardian angel, had snatched her back into the world against her nature, then whooshed away again on invisible wings.

She began thinking about what it would be like to go to school. She couldn't go the following year because of her late November birthday, but she began to wonder what it would be like, among strange children—and adults—who did not know about her. Would her mother or father tell them and would that make everything all right? She had played a game of checkers one day with Mister, the doctor's housekeeper's son, out on the doctor's back porch. They'd been watching the doctor's new peacocks in the yard, but Mister got bored and suggested checkers. She said, "When did he get those peacocks?"

"I 'on' know," Mister said. "Recent. It's a strange bird." They watched the birds, several of them, peck about the yard and stand every now and then to fan their tails. "Said he just liked to watch them. Mama says he's been lonesome since his wife died."

He was a skinny boy, with his hair clipped close to his head and baggy clothes that'd been handed down from his cousins.

"They sure are pretty," Jane said. She could see their deep, shiny blue neck feathers gleaming in the sunlight.

Mister went to get the board and chips. She was a bit sketchy on the rules, so when Mister made one of his pieces a king she insisted that he allow her to make one of hers a queen.

"Ain't no such thing as a queen in checkers," he said. They were on the back porch just off the kitchen, and Mister's mother Hattie kept a close eye on them.

"If you get to be a king, then I get to be a queen," she said.

To which Mister replied, "That ain't how the game works. You got to get all the way to the top. And they call these pieces 'men' and that's why it's a king when you get it there. Plus, you stink."

"What?"

She'd become so accustomed to her accidents that unless she was in public she sometimes didn't even attend to them right away.

Then Hattie came out where they were and told him to hush, he was being rude.

"Well, she does," Mister insisted, and that got him a light whack on the noggin and a scolding, and by that time Mister's words had sunk in and Jane had become acutely self-conscious and smelled herself. She got up and ran inside the house to the doctor's indoor privy, stripped off her diaper, cleaned herself, ran water in the tub, and scrubbed the garment with soap, rinsed it, squeezed it as dry as she could, washed her hands, then put it back on, cold and wet against her skin beneath her skirt. Then she rinsed the tub good and turned off the water.

Mister called from outside the locked door, "Why you taking so long in there?"

"Hush up, Mister," she heard Hattie whisper, and then the sounds of her pulling him out of the room over his protests. She waited on the front porch until the doctor came home from the emergency call he'd made, and asked him to take her home.

"Are you all right?" he said.

"Yes," was all she would say in reply. But after that she didn't want to play with Mister, and would demur when the doctor offered to take her to his house for a visit. Sometimes she would ask him if he would just take her on a drive in his car or a ride in his buggy, since she didn't want him to think she didn't like him anymore. If he had other patients to see she would wait outside until he came back out and took her home again. If there were other children about she would stay in the car or buggy and decline their offers to come play.

Her parents and other members of her family had got to where they never said anything to her about her "problem," except to tell her quietly to go change herself if she forgot about it, especially before a meal or if someone was dropping by for a visit.

But now she thought about it quite a lot, through the winter and into the spring. How she was different. It descended more deeply into her mind that she was the only one made the way she was made. That she was strange. She became accustomed to that flushing sense of shame that could come on and heat your face and make your scalp tingle and make you want to cry.

Summer came early, and then came on hard in June. It was

very hot. She took to wearing light dresses and leaving off her diaper, and staying outside in the shade most of the day, hopping behind a bush or tree when she felt something coming on, instead of out in the open as she had when she was younger. She kept with her a catalog page she would tear a piece off of, use, and discard. And she would feel that flush of shame whenever it happened, and her mind would bristle with the sense of that strangeness. Ever since the day playing checkers with Mister, she had taken to washing her own diapers down at the creek instead of letting her mother or Grace take care of it. She would not put them in her mother's boiling pot for sterilizing washed undergarments until all the others' had been removed.

She was past her sixth birthday that November before it occurred to her that no one had even mentioned the possibility of attending school the next year.

She went to where her mother sat mending a shirt on the front porch.

Her mother looked up as she stood there.

"What's the matter?"

"I guess I won't be going to school next year like the rest."

Her mother stopped her mending, though she looked down at it for a bit before meeting her daughter's eye again.

"No," she said. "I don't see the sense in putting you through it." Then, more to herself, she said, "Most girls, I'd say it's a waste of time, anyway." She looked a long moment at Jane again and said, "We will have to figure out something that you can do."

Her mother and Grace taught her simple sewing, her mother offering single-word corrections now and then, while Grace did the hands-on teaching. Jane's hands were small and clumsy and she pricked herself, her bottom lip trembling when she tried not to cry. *Be patient*, her mother said, and she tried, and got better. The idea was it might be something useful in life when there was no more mother, no more father, nothing but the farm, which would probably be sold by her older siblings. It was understood that Grace would have to make do on her own soon enough, as well. Either get married or go to find work in town.

She got better at sewing and soon even enjoyed it, applying a child's blind concentration to the task, from mending seams and sewing patches into quilts, up to eventually using the machine to make simple smocks and skirts and then dresses. She liked the rhythm of pumping the machine's treadle to keep the stylus going and guiding the material through. She had to stand to reach it with her foot. Everything else disappeared from her mind. She was more like her father than her mother. He did not mind work, easily focused on a task.

Perhaps as a consolation for not having school to look forward to, she was given freedom to wander about the whole place as she wanted. She walked the path through the woods that were charmed with their strange stillness and the scents of various plants and rich earth beneath moldering leaves. She walked the path down to the beaver pond, which was so much prettier in its wooded canyon than the cow pond sitting in the open and surrounded by hoof-cleaved muddy banks at the edge of their south pasture. She came out and sat on the hill above those woods and watched, at the juncture of field and woods down below, a pack of scruffy stray dogs that she imagined were the wild dogs she'd been cautioned about. They skirted the field in a silent little troop, tongues lolling, then disappeared into the undergrowth again, as if they'd been a ghost pack not really having been there except in her own mind.

HER FATHER TOOK her fishing one Saturday afternoon when the bream were on their beds, down at the beaver pond. They walked the trail slowly, her father guiding the tips of their two cane poles through the tree limbs and saplings and shrubbery along the trail, and sat in the shade over a bed and pulled out more than a dozen of the broad, snub-nosed sunfish, wriggling. They were bluegills and bigger ones her father called shell crackers. The tug on her line ran a current from the line and pole straight through her body, a long-lined static shock, and she soiled herself in excitement. Her father only laughed a little and told her to toss her undergarment aside and lift her skirt and go for a little cool wade down the bank at a clear and shallow spot. When she hesitated, he said, "It's safe there, go on." Her mother had forbidden her to go down to the pond by herself and said the water was dangerous, as if she had a morbid fear of it herself. Her father came over, found a stick, and told her to beat the grass near the edge before stepping through it, to scare off any snake that might be resting there. She whacked at the grass, waited a moment, hesitating again, looking at the smooth brown surface of the water. "Go on, now," her father said again. She carefully took a step in, ankle-deep. The cool water on her skin, the cool mud of the bottom squishing up between her toes, was delicious to her senses.

"Now, how's that?" he said.

"It's grand, Papa," she called back, and when she came out again he gave her a little one-armed hug, an expression of sentiment so rare in their household that it sent her senses singing all over again, and brought the beginning of tears to her eyes, which she hid by walking away and picking wildflowers on the little hill above the pond and bringing them back to him.

"That's good," he said. "Your mama can set them on the table for our supper."

That evening they had a big mess of crisply fried bream and her father showed her how to nibble on the crisp, salty tails, which Grace said was disgusting but they ignored her. The delicate white meat peeled easily off the fishes' thin bones and you could pull the whole skeleton and head away, which seemed in its simplicity almost a miracle.

"Why haven't we done this before?" she said, and her father said he guessed he'd just got out of the habit, and they would have to do it again soon.

"I think your mama got tired of them," he said.

"Well, tired of cleaning them, maybe," their mother said, frowning at being called out.

As her father rose to go be by himself, and Grace and her mother began to clean the table and wash dishes, she sat looking at her own, with its two beautifully symmetrical, cleaned fish skeletons lying there in a thin film of congealed grease. It occurred to her what a very strange creature a fish was, a thing that lived in the water, underwater. And somehow breathed water, which would kill a body fool enough to try it, though she'd once wondered if she could sift it carefully through her lips and make that work, and when she'd mentioned it to her father, he'd blanched and said, "Don't ever try that."

Now in this moment she wished she had paid more attention when her mother was cleaning the fish, scraping out their insides, their small and delicate organs, had gazed on the mystery of them. And she wished she had asked her mother for one of the heads, so that she could peer closely at those gills, what they had instead of lungs, her father said, with their strange, blood-filled filaments that were apparently the secret to their magical abilities to live as they did.

She wondered what happened to a fish that was born without them. If it just floated to the surface of the water and died.

HER FATHER WOULD point things out to her. He knew the names of most trees, the oaks, elms, sycamore and sweetgum, the beech, pines, hickory, the maples, redbud, dogwood, the hollies, magnolia, swamp bay, cherry, cypress, pecan. Some shrubs, the buckeye, sweetshrub, huckleberry, sumac, snowbell. Flowers, lily of the valley, wisteria, joe-pye weed, jack-in-the-pulpit.

Of the mushrooms roosting in the loam and on the bark of trees live and rotten, he would only say some knew which ones you could eat but that he'd had an uncle who thought he knew them and died after making a mistake one day. "Stay away from them," her father said.

When she would go into the woods with her mother it was for the express purpose of gathering edible plants and herbs for use in food dishes and medicinal potions. Chicory, dandelion greens, primrose root, wild strawberries, garlic, and wild onion. Teaberry, beechnuts, sassafras, blackberries, blueberries, rose hips for tea and jelly. She showed Jane how to prepare them, and when they were in the kitchen preparing for a regular meal she would call out the names of this one or that, and if Jane was unable to recall their uses and method of preparation, she would sometimes come over and pluck a single dark brown hair from Jane's head and say, "You don't want to be going around bald-headed for not knowing your lessons, do you?"

When she walked alone in the woods barefoot at midday after the noon meal she tried remembering the names of the trees and shrubs and flowers. She was fascinated by the mushrooms and their dry or slimy tops and delicate stems and gills beneath their caps. She liked to pop her toes against the ones that burst into orange dust that bloomed in the breezeless air. But it was the quiet, modest ones that were most interesting. If they didn't want you to see them, you would not. They lived out their lives in shade and dampness, quivering when you passed and going so still if you happened to notice and squat down to take a closer look, to touch. One day she came upon a strange one that was not at all modest, growing straight up and tall with a small cap on its top. She broke it off at the base and took it home to show her father, but her mother saw it first and snatched it from her hand and threw it into the hog slop bucket.

"But what is it?" Jane said. "I've never seen one like it."

"If you see another, you leave it alone," her mother said, oddly angered.

"What's it called?"

"It's called a stinkhorn," her mother said, "and aptly so."

When she asked her father about it later, during one of their walks, and asked him why it grew straight up like that when all the others were short and round or flat like fat leaves growing from a tree's bark, he said some called it the devil's horn and some called it dead man's finger. "There's different shapes of it from just what you found."

When she next saw Dr. Thompson she asked him about the stinkhorn and her mother's reaction to it.

"Your mother was upset because she's a modest woman and it so happens the stinkhorn mushroom resembles a part of the male anatomy or body, the part that is used in reproduction. In making babies."

"Sure is a big'un," she said.

The doctor said nothing, but rubbed his mouth for a moment and seemed to grip his jaw, then removed his shaded spectacles and rubbed the lenses on his shirtsleeve.

"Well, in fact," he said, "there are varieties of the plant that resemble the complementary part of the female anatomy as well, in quite a lurid fashion."

She didn't know those words, complementary, lurid.

"Like mine?"

"No," the doctor said. "Not really."

"It's what I'm *supposed* to look like, then?"

"Not exactly," the doctor said. "It's just people using their imagination. For the most part, anyway."

He told her that he would explain it to her in more detail when she was a little older.

"What's wrong with now?"

He fiddled in his vest pocket for his pipe and took it out, but only held it out from him and looked at it as if to examine it for flaws. Then he looked sideways at her.

"Soon enough," he said. "When the time is right."

She walked off, perturbed, but then came right back.

"I need you to tell me why I'm the way I am, why I'm different, or how I'm different. Why can't I control myself?" She had learned this discreet term well enough over the years.

He looked at her a long moment, his eyes squinting that tired squint, a mote of some kind in there that was more than a speck of dust, more something in his mind than his eye. Then he nodded, said, "All right, then."

They sat on the ground and he told her as best he could about what she did not have that most girls and women had. "First, there's no 'why.' It's just how you're made. Inside you," he said, "I believe you have just about everything, if not everything, that any other girl has. But on the outside you don't have everything they do. Everything is kind of tucked up inside you, hidden away. And one thing you do not have is the little muscle that allows you to control yourself. It's a squeezing muscle, see. And when you need to go potty, if you *have* the little muscle, then you can squeeze it and stop it until you get to a privy or bathroom or a good-sized bush to hide behind, you know."

She nodded, serious. She was trying to form a picture in her mind of her insides, and make that match up somehow with what she'd been able to tell about herself from what she could see on the outside. It was like trying to imagine some very complex mushroom.

"What you have on the inside is just as complex—I mean it is just as much a wonder of a miracle of the human body—as anyone else. But it didn't get to finish putting itself all together, didn't get to finish itself up and get everything right, before it was time for you to be born. Or maybe I should say at some point, for some reason, it just stopped making itself into what it was supposed to." He paused, looked at her looking back at him, her brow bunched down. "That's about as best I can explain it to you at your age, Janie. I hope that helps a little bit. It's not anyone's fault, certainly not yours, and it's not anything to be ashamed of. It's just a difference, is all. And the only thing is that it causes you to have to live your life in a special way. To have less freedom to go to school and such as that. But it does not mean that you are not a normal little girl. You're just a little girl who has to deal with more things than most little girls. And that will make you strong. It already has."

"Can you fix it?"

"I hope one day someone can. But right now I don't know.

Well, I know they will one day. I just don't know when. I know they work at figuring these things out all the time."

Jane nodded, still trying to put together some kind of picture in her mind that made sense. She was coming up with something, although she had no idea if it was a fantastical idea or something close to what the doctor knew.

SHE WOULD HOLD a mirror beneath herself and stare for a long time, studying herself there. She had seen her mother naked, and her sister Grace, too, but not really up close. It was not the kind of thing she could ask to *examine*, to use the doctor's word.

But she longed to do just that. If she could only look closely at Grace, and then again at herself, it would satisfy such a curiosity. So she got up her courage one day and asked Grace, bluntly, if she could see her down there.

"I mean take a real good look," she said. "An *examination*."

Grace looked offended, even baffled.

"Find you some girl your own age, if you want to play doctor," she said before heading off toward the barn and her smokes.

Sometimes she was frightened, in a heightened way, briefly, as if some panic were about to take hold of her, and she would run, just run, until she outran it, or wore it out, and she would find herself way out in the middle of a pasture, with a curious, half-startled cow looking at her, stopped in its cud-chewing, like she was some kind of creature it had never seen before. Then she would notice the other cows, all turned to look at her, their chewing interrupted, some with long pieces of grass hanging from their mouths, their big brown eyes on her as if in wonder about how she'd suddenly appeared in their midst, a tiny creature from some other world. They'd wait to see what she would do. She would think in that moment she could do anything. She would move slowly to pluck a long piece of Johnson grass and chew on the sour end of it, let it hang from her mouth. The cows would take notice. She would stand very still. When she moved again they would startle, as if she had suddenly become human again.

Then, calmed, she would walk in the woods by herself.

She loved most being in the woods, with the diffused light and the quiet there. Such a stillness, with just the pecking of ground birds and forest animals, the flutter of wings, the occasional skittering of squirrels playing up and down a tree. The silent, imperceptible unfurling of spring buds into blossom. She felt comfortable there. As if nothing could be unnatural in that place, within but apart from the world.

There were innumerable little faint trails her father said were game trails. Animal trails. Their faint presence like the lingering ghosts of the animals' passing. There was a particular little clearing she believed she had discovered, only her, filled with yellow sunlight on clear days, its long grass harboring primroses and wild sunflowers. A meadow she considered to be her very own, her place. The eyes of all the wild, invisible animals watching her. Time was suspended, or did not exist. She could linger there as long as she liked and when she returned from it no time had passed at all since she had stepped into the clearing and then awakened from it. That's what it was like.

The meadow did not exist if she wasn't in it.

THE SPRING AND summer storms were terrifying and thrilling, with sudden gusting winds, thick waves of rain, bone-jarring thunder, lightning that made everything for an instant like the inside of a vast glass bowl of bright blue light, or crackled across the sky as if to crack it open to the heavens, or *boomed* so near so sudden, leaving smoking trees in the woods or the edge of a field. There was a wooded area her father left open to the cattle so they could hide in there during storms. The rain flooded the flat yard, creating rivers where before there seemed no natural depression in the ground. Wind howled around the house in long, bending moans, moving against it like a flooding river, so that she feared it would rip the whole thing from its columns of foundation stones. And always, after, the yard and the fields beyond were littered with stripped branches and leaves, arboreal detritus and debris, and often, in the yard, some animal drowned from the sheer volume of water in such a brief time, a stray housecat caught out in it, or a bird, or a possum.

She would sit alone on a branch in a hickory nut tree near the pig pen, watching the hogs, sows, and piglets. Beyond that the cattle grazed in the pasture beside the pond, in their massive, slow, ponderous bodies. With their stupid, wary expressions. They startled easily.

She'd seen the hogs mount the sows in their pen. The hogs seemed almost to try to tender up the sows before they got to it, bumping the sows' behinds with their noses, rubbing up beside them, bumping their heads gently, almost like a kind of kiss. The boars' big pink things with the curled tip would come poking out. She went a little pop-eyed first time she saw that. They did *not* look like stinkhorns. And when they would mount the sows, the hogs didn't seem to move much, every now and then pushing against her bottom, shuffling their comically tiny hind feet toward her in a little two-legged dance. And the sows stood as still as they could, just kind of staring ahead, their ears canted forward, and then after the hog got down they would kind of stand next to each other until another sow or boar came up, curious, and broke the spell.

When she asked about it, her mother seemed surprised and shocked, but the others only laughed at her questions.

She had seen dogs going at it, too, of course. A female would stray from a neighboring farm and have a small pack of males trailing along, nosing her. The female always seemed a little sullen, as if to say, *I suppose I'm ready for this, although I'm not sure about it*. She would be evasive without actually running away. The male had always to follow the female around, patiently impatient, attentive, until the female would stand still long enough for him to mount her. Then it was quick, with great purpose, the male's eyes wandering off either in pleasure or distraction, she could not tell. The female's eyes kind of sideways like she was thinking and not able to quite figure it out.

She had never seen their hound or Top doing it. What she didn't realize was the hound was too old, stupid, and lazy, and Top, having been a stray, had been fixed by whoever he had first belonged to, before he was run off or ran away on his on.

Birds fluttered themselves together while on a branch in a tree and then fluttered apart and looked a little bewildered. The birds did not truly understand their compulsions at all. She thought maybe they would actually forget they had done it pretty much just right after doing it. *Birds are the most distracted creatures in the world*, she thought. She could figure that much. Bird brains. The rooster, too, hopped onto the backs of the hens, who seemed to bow down for him and lift their tails, and he clawed and grappled and flapped his wings and pushed himself at them, and you couldn't really see much because of all their feathers, just the thrashing around. If they let that hen keep her eggs they would have chicks.

She was never able to come upon cats going at it. They were as secretive and mysterious about this as they were about anything else, if not more so. Although a female in heat seemed truly tortured by the condition. She did not want what needed to happen to actually happen but if it didn't happen soon she was going to lose her mind. But somewhere, sometime, it always happened, for the female would disappear and no longer be seen creeping through the yard yowling in a low growly way, shoulders hunched. You might hear them down in the woods, screaming like tiny panthers. And then later there would be kittens.

She spied on Grace and her mother, when she could, after their baths, while they were dressing. If they saw her they stiffened and turned away or shut the door. Then she would take the shaving mirror from the wall over the pump sink out back and, down in the woods, set it on the ground, pull up her skirt, and *examine* herself. She hadn't been able to tell enough about Grace or her mother to see much difference, but she could tell she was different, all the same. Well, she'd long known she was different, but she wanted to know more.

When she asked the doctor to tell her more, at first he looked a little exasperated, then said he would try to show her.

He came back the next day with a book in which there were drawings of the female genitalia. He let her study it. She asked questions about some of the details, and he answered her bluntly. She looked at it for several minutes, the drawing. Then she closed the book and said, "I'll be back in a minute," and ran off for the shaving mirror, book in hand. Down in the woods, squatting over the mirror, she looked back and forth between the image there and the drawing in the book. At this point, she was mostly just fascinated by seeing what she was seeing. She didn't feel a shock, or anything bad, just then. She closed the book, returned the mirror to its place, and went back out front where the doctor was waiting. She handed him the book and thanked him.

"Clear enough for now, then?" he said.

"I guess," Jane said. Then she said, "I want to go to school like everybody else."

"I know."

"Help me figure out how to do it."

"All right. Let me think about it for a couple of days."

He started to go, then turned back.

"You know, Jane, there will likely be teasing."

She just looked at him, tears welling up that she blinked back. She nodded.

"I already know that," she said.

Mrs. Ida Chisolm
Rt. 1, Old Paulding Rd.

Dear Mrs. Chisolm,
As per our conversation regarding daughter Jane's (and your) concerns about managing her incontinence as she begins her public life at the Damascus school, and if you feel the necessity of taking extra measures to insure her mental comfort and avoid accidents, I would recommend that the child refrain from eating and drinking after the evening meal. A little extra time in the privy first thing in the morning. A very light breakfast (absolutely no coffee, as this is not good for children of her age in any case but coffee is a diuretic

and would increase the frequency of urination and possibly bowel movements as well), a very light lunch. She should sip a little water during the day so as to avoid dehydration. She should have a healthy snack when she gets home and partake heartily at supper. Make sure she drinks plenty of water in the afternoons. I would not give her iced nor hot tea.

I'm sure she has told you that I went over all this with her myself. She seemed to understand. Such a wise little girl you have there, as you well know.

She is a healthy child, all things considered, and this regimen should not cause her any more than some initial, mild discomfort, to which I believe she soon will become accustomed.

Yours truly,
Ed Thompson, M.D.

AND SO SHE willingly took up the routine. At home they had a double privy with a wall in between, so she would go there first thing in the morning and stay, stomach growling, until she felt she was entirely empty. She hardly even noticed the coming and going of others on the other side. No one spoke to her, interrupted her concentration on becoming an empty vessel, her body an empty, hollow chamber of flesh, dry and clean as the inside of a cleaned-out fish. And then she would step back out into the yard, feel the dust on her feet and between her toes, as if she had stepped out onto the surface of the moon, which was sometimes still there pale and wan just above the tops of the trees.

Her dresses were sewn to be loose and hang from her shoulders in a way that would not cinch her waist and accentuate her preventive undergarment. There were no secrets, really, in such a small world as their little school, but there was a kind of natural discretion. Her mother gave her a vial of inexpensive perfume to dab onto her wrists and her undergarments to disguise—at least for a moment, for a getaway—any smells in case of an unavoidable accident. Even young Jane sensed the sad futility of this gesture, although she would wear a bit of perfume most days for the rest of her life.

Despite the constant faint but cloying scent of this perfume, the smells peculiar to a school classroom fascinated her almost to the point of being mesmerized. Pencil lead, waxy crayons, writing-tablet paper and the paper in the schoolbooks, all of them used and handed down from children years and years before, the chalk used on the blackboard, the rising and then fading smells of lunch the students ate from their paper sacks, lunch boxes, or (for some of the poorest) pails covered with a kitchen towel, the boys' hair oil and the girls' bath powder, the dung from the horses and mules that some of the older children would ride to get there and then tether outside the building to a hitching post. All of it combined into a medley of smells that would always mean "school" in her memory.

It was a small school that took the community children all the way from first grade to high school graduation, and there were not many enrolled, so the environment was relatively intimate, like some great, overgrown family, in a way. The children seemed to know and understand one another like siblings, whether lovingly, or with hostility, or with the purposeful ignoring of this one or that.

She established herself in the little world there, and was accepted well enough, easygoing as she was, and thick-skinned by virtue of her family's ways in general and her mother's often harsh tongue. She could tell that Grace was keeping a distant eye on her but she stayed just that: distant. Early on, she caught some teasing from the other children during recess, saying, *She wears diapers.* The principal and high school teacher, Miss Deen, who had taken it on herself to supervise the younger children's little playground, reprimanded them.

"You should not make fun of anyone for being who she is," Miss Deen said to them in her calm and level but somber voice. She was a tall and sophisticated woman with a long face and square jaw and glinting sharp green eyes who had grown up in the capital in Jackson, then married a local farmer she'd met at the state agriculture and teachers college.

"You there, Steven," she said, at which the boy immediately blushed a florid pink. "Should we all laugh at you for your disgusting habit of picking your nose and eating the product thereof? You, Morgan, shall we laugh at you because you secretly like to nibble the lead from your pencil? Do you know that will make you feeble-minded? You, Marjory, should we suggest that you wear diapers because of the time you laughed too hard and wet yourself right there in your seat? You, Bobby Land, because you soiled yourself being afraid to go alone to the privy?"

All fell silent in a pall of embarrassment. A couple of other children had come up and giggled but when Miss Deen turned her hard gaze upon them fell silent again. None was more appalled than Jane. She willed Miss Deen just to be silent and let it go.

"I am sorry to have embarrassed anyone," Miss Deen said. "But perhaps y'all have learned a lesson about making fun of other people for the ways in which they are not perfect human beings. As we none of us are."

Jane both loved her and was angry at her for making more of it than had already been made. She'd rather have fended for herself.

She saw Grace, shaking her head, go back into the schoolhouse.

The other children didn't tease her so much after all that, and then after a while not at all. Jane had a dignity about her that the others had come to admire and respect, though some of the other girls did seem to quietly resent her, as if thinking she was a little stuck-up. But that wasn't it. She was in fact in a bit of a fog by midday, usually, the effect of having not eaten or drunk anything since the night before.

But no matter how much the other children seemed to begrudge a respect for her, to feign unawareness of her mysterious need to wear diapers (and who could tell how much they might know or think they knew through rumor?), and no matter how out of it she generally was, she was all too aware of her difference. How *that* was what really communicated to others that sense of strangeness. This was enough in itself to cause a gathering of something like sadness in her mind, a heaviness in her chest. There was no getting away from this awareness, a strange self-consciousness, as long as she was around others. And so it wasn't very long before she began to question whether this business of schooling, of trying to be like everyone else, was actually worth the trouble. The odd mingling of a sense of sadness and embarrassment.

She had even caught Grace looking at her more than once with what seemed, possibly, a genuine sympathy. That was almost harder to take than what she sensed in the others.

And besides, she found it hard to concentrate, being hungry and thirsty all day. And tired of pretending to eat a lunch when she actually only picked at a bit of cornbread or biscuit she carried in a napkin in her pocket like some crumbling talisman, to ward off any overly curious attention. She knew it was safe to eat her lunch—nothing would happen before she got home—but she was too anxious about it all.

On the last day of school before the Christmas holiday, she let Grace walk on ahead without even trying to keep up or asking Grace to slow down. She cut through the woods, around the house, and came out in the pecan grove, the spindly gray branches ugly against the austere sky. A loneliness she didn't even know how to name welled up in her so swiftly that she didn't realize she had tears in her eyes until she felt them cold on her cheeks, and for the first time since she was very small she let them come, blurring her vision, pushing the hurtful feeling from her heart. When it was done she went on to the house. Her mother, standing on the back porch as if watching for her, didn't speak but looked as if she understood everything. And so Jane went to her room to be alone until time for supper. And they left her alone, no doubt knowing.

Ellison Adams, M.D.
Johns Hopkins University School of Medicine
Baltimore, Maryland

Dear Ellis,
I have a regular supply of very decent homemade spirits and the occasional quarter of venison from Chisolm. He feels the need to pay me for my attention to the girl but I persuade him otherwise with the argument of acquiring valuable medical research. She is now seven years old, and seems practically immune to the kinds of infection apparently common in some such cases. Your diagnosis has not faltered at all.

Her disposition is generally bright, if also somewhat prodigiously contemplative. A fairly solitary and independent little sprite. I have driven up, looked around, finally asked, and no one will know where she is nor seem too concerned about the not knowing. And then she will appear, as if from thin air, behind me, standing there looking up at me and smiling. We talk. It's rare that anything she says prompts me to request a thorough examination.

In any case, I figure we are out of the woods in terms of any potentially dangerous complications. I will keep a close watch when it comes near time for puberty, of course, although—again—if it is indeed what you believe it to be, I shouldn't have to worry about that.

It was a disappointment to her, the attempt to attend our local school. I don't know exactly what happened, and it didn't seem the teasing was excessive. She was melancholy for a while after, but seemed to recover entirely by spring. Still, I cannot help but think that she hides a deep emotional burden inside her little child's chest. I don't see how she could escape it. My god, Ellis, the child pretty much picked up reading in just three months there. Such a waste.

I am considering taking it on myself to bring her up there for a thorough examination by Young, if you could help me arrange it. She is plenty old enough now to undergo surgery, if it were advisable. I know you think my own examinations and communications are probably sufficient to diagnose as you have: that this is not an operable condition, at this point in time, and that most likely even sphincter construction is unlikely. But, if the girl and her family are willing, I would rest easier knowing for sure, after examination by an experienced specialist in the field. If not your people, then at least let one of the urologists in Memphis take a look. It is only a little over 200 miles from here, as opposed to the near 1,000 to you.

In any case, I will be in touch about the potential visit/examination. Please continue to send any news of developments, but I will try to make this examination happen as soon as possible. The girl is such a delight, truly, that I hate to think ahead and imagine her living a long life of isolation and shame, which is sure to come on her if there is nothing to be done about her condition once she is older.

My best to Mary Kate, when you see her. Tell her the one she should have married wishes you all well. I do so miss Lett. Her family keeps fresh flowers at her grave in town. She is in their plot, as you know. As for me, burn and scatter the ashes in my woods if I go first. It's in the will.

Yrs,

Ed

PRETENDING TO BEGRUDGE it but seeming to enjoy it once they'd get started, Grace sometimes helped Jane with her reading in the evenings, bringing home books from the school library, and corrected her handwriting efforts. The teachers had let her borrow the books, knowing she had a little sister at home who wanted to learn. There was the Bible in the house, of course, but it was incomprehensible. No one read from it, much less aloud. The pictures of paintings inside it were interesting. More helpful was the Sears, Roebuck catalog, with its pictures of the items described there for sale. There was always a new one in the house, and an older one in the outhouse. Sometimes she would take the newer catalog to her father in the evenings and ask him to read her the description of something in there for sale. It was all a kind of schooling, anyway.

When Dr. Thompson learned that she wanted for reading material, he began bringing books when he visited.

"I don't know why I didn't think to, before," he said. "Lett was a reader. I am, too, of course, but she read novels, made-up stories. I like some of them but it's the rare one I like a lot. I thought I'd bring some by, you see which ones you like, we'll start to get an idea of which ones I ought to give you."

"You don't have to give them to me for good."

He shrugged, said, "I don't care much about hanging on to books after I've read them. Most of them, anyway. Better to give them away to others who might want to read."

"Well. Thank you." Then she stood on her tiptoes and kissed him on his bristly cheek. The doctor stood there a long moment, something like a look of amused wonder on his face. Then he smiled to himself, got into his car, and drove off.

Inside, Jane looked at the books he'd given her. One had her own name in the title, *Jane Eyre*. It seemed a little bit dense, but would be interesting to her later on. Another was *The Adventures of Tom Sawyer*. It was an old battered copy and about boys, so she thought it might have been his own book and he was just tired of reading it. She set it aside, too. The third one was old, also, but not so worn. It was a slim little book with a faded red cover and the title on the spine: *A Simple Heart*, by Gustave Flaubert, an odd name. She set to reading it that night, and couldn't stop. She finished by candlelight. She was in tears over poor Félicité's sad but beautiful life, her broken heart and her loneliness, her love for her mistress's children, and fascinated by the way she began to lose her mind, and filled with wonder at the spirit of her beloved parrot hovering over her at her death.

She lay awake late into the night, the candle finally guttering out in its holder, and in the dim light left in the room from a bit of moon she passed into sleep without even feeling it coming, and dreamed heavily, and though she couldn't remember anything particular when she woke the next morning, she remembered that the dreams had been kind of heartbreaking, and thought that she may have wept in her sleep. The odd thing was that she didn't feel sad in their aftermath. She felt something like a lightened joy. She felt the damp of her tears on the pillow, and turned it over so that her mother would not see.

SHE BEGAN TO HELP her mother out in the kitchen, preparing meals. She wasn't allowed to cook anything yet but she was shown things, so that she would gradually learn that and be able to take over from Grace—and maybe even her mother—after Grace left home. No one knew when that would be, although when she was angry Grace was threatening to leave any minute. She made no secret of her desire to get off the farm.

As her mother and Grace began early preparations for supper, Jane helped shell peas and butterbeans, rinsing them and leaving them in water for their mother to boil all morning with salt pork while Jane sucked her thumb, which was sore from prying apart the butterbeans' tough pods. If there was to be a chicken fried, her mother would walk calmly among the nervous yard birds, casual as if just strolling through, and then would snatch one by the head and give it a quick twirl to snap its neck. Then she would dip it in scalding water, pluck and gut it, chop off its feathered head and hard yellow feet.

Jane took the bucket in which her mother had tossed the head, feet, and guts down to the hog pen and tossed them straight onto the bare earth there, where after a momentary silence for comprehension the hogs, sows, and shoats set upon it, bawling, brawling, squealing from lust and the pain of swift and intense battle. Yet another, if negative, reason to dislike the eating of their meat.

Back at the house her mother had carried the plucked and headless hen back to the porch and pumped a little water to wash it, then carried it inside, cut it to frying pieces, dipped it in egg and milk, dredged it in flour, and dropped it piece by piece into the broad pan of hot lard on the stove, and set it piece by browned piece aside to drain on a sheet of newspaper on the counter.

Jane would be set to peeling potatoes to boil and mash for the meal, or washing greens in a small tub on the back porch. Looking out over the yard, she would recall the remarkably casual, vivid slaughter, each arcing flop of the hen's unceremonious exit from this world, each rise and quick chopping blow of the little hatchet through its neck into the oak stump, and somehow feel apart or invisible, a strange presence locked in her own consciousness, like no one else's in the world, apart from all others, her fingers tightening in recollection of this or that casually violent action, and it sent a current into her spine up into the base of her neck, the tingling of it coming out her eyes in invisible little needles of light indistinguishable from the light of the gathering day.

Grace in the Wilderness

❧

Anyone could tell something was up with Grace, these days. It was her last year of school. She seemed distracted, more than usual, and even more silent. Jane spied on her when she wasn't aware of it. She was distracted and strange, like one of the chickens when it got what her mother called "broody" and wouldn't leave the roost or just wandered about if her mother shut it out of the pen and henhouse, like it didn't know what to do with itself and was ornery.

Finally Jane said, "Grace, you have a secret," and Grace surprised her by seeming to snap out of it: "Yes, I do, and that's the reason it's none of your business."

That didn't stop Jane from pestering her, whispering when they were alone, "Tell me."

"I'm working on my ticket out of here, that's all I'll say."

Several times, she'd been late coming home from school, and when their father and mother questioned her about it, she tried to ignore them. But one afternoon she came down their drive toward the house, a bit of a spring in her step, and found them waiting on her. Jane was spying from inside the screen door. Her parents, like two still and silent buzzards on a limb, watched Grace approach.

"Where you been, then?" her father said, his voice and eyes level.

"With friends," she said.

"Which?"

"Just some of the dumb girls at school, is all."

He looked at her long and steady and said, "Better be the truth, girl." Then he said, "I want you here right after school's out, every day, to help your mother and your little sister with chores around the house. Like you're supposed to." He got up and walked over toward the hog pen. Her mother sat in her chair and continued to give her the glare.

"I don't care if you don't believe me," Grace said to her.

"That is one thing I know for sure," her mother said before rising and going on inside. She saw Jane squatting there, in her spying position, and pulled up briefly, gave her a look, and went on.

At supper there was silence. Jane watched Grace furtively, and watched for any telling looks between her mother and father, or between one of them and Grace, till her mother told her to eat her supper and stop dawdling. In the quiet after that, a sound seemed to arise in a small but regular way with Grace's movements, like occasional hard grains of rice dropped into an empty gourd. No one said anything. But when their father finished eating, ahead of the others, he stood up without a word, walked around the table, took out his pocketknife, and opened it. He lifted the thread from Grace's neck, to which she had attached the rattlesnake rattle, held the rattle in his palm for a moment, then cut the thread and removed the rattle from it and took it into the other room. When Jane peered around through the doorway she saw him throw both thread and rattle into the coals there, and then stoke them with a small handful of kindling on top of which, after a moment, he placed a solid chunk of dry oak. And then he went out.

That Friday, Grace came home from school on time, helped

her mother put on pots of greens and peas to slow-boil, scrubbed the kitchen floor, then quickly cleaned up after throwing out the scouring water at the edge of the yard. Jane followed her at a safe distance, pretending to work but mostly watching. Something was up. Grace put some lotion on her hands, arms, neck, and face, and, after wandering with Jane awhile to let the scent of it dissipate, told her mother she had forgotten her homework at school and needed to go back so she could do it over the weekend.

Her mother stopped cutting slices from the ham she'd taken from the smokehouse and looked at her, the carving knife in her hand.

"I'll take Jane with me," Grace said. "The walk will help her sleep tonight."

"She sleeps fine," their mother said. Then after a moment she nodded and said, "Don't dawdle. We'll eat in a couple of hours."

They walked slowly, as Jane tended to dawdle. Grace grew impatient enough to grab her by the hand and pull her along faster.

"Why're you in such a durn hurry?" Jane said.

Grace looked at her, then stopped. She leaned down to put her face at Jane's level. The seriousness in her look made Jane back away.

"What?" she said.

"We're not going to the school," Grace said.

"But you said we were."

"And if Mama or Papa asks you if that's where we went, you just nod and say, 'Yes, sir' or 'Yes, ma'am,' and nothing else, you hear me?"

Jane looked at her, not comprehending.

"Why?" she said.

"Because I said so," Grace said. "This is real important."

She went over to the side of the road, reached behind a tree there, and came out with her school satchel.

"So, see? We went to school and I got my homework." Jane looked at the satchel, then at her sister.

"See?"

Jane nodded. They went on. A little farther, they cut off onto a trail. When Jane lagged behind, distracted, Grace caught her up again. When they reached a little clearing, Grace took her by the hand and guided her to a spot about thirty feet away just behind a thick dewberry bush.

"You stay here at the edge of this where you can see through but not be seen. Don't make a sound and stay real still, okay? Whatever you see going on with me and this boy, you just watch and be quiet."

"What boy?"

"Never mind that. Don't get scared, I know what I'm doing and you don't have to be afraid. I just need you to watch it so you can say you've seen it if I ask you. I won't have to, though, all right?"

Jane just looked at her from where she sat on her rump. She put her arms around her knees and looked off into the woods, then back at her sister.

"Okay, but why?" she said.

"Just hush and do what I say. And you listen here." She knelt down and got her face close to Jane's. "You don't say a word about this to anybody unless I tell you to. Do you understand me, Jane?"

Jane was a little scared—it was really more of a thrill than a scare—but nodded.

"Don't be scared. It's like I said."

"What are you going to do with the boy?"

"You'll see. I'll explain it to you later. Now, can you do this?"
Jane nodded.

"Are you sure?"

She nodded again. Grace's eyes looked positively wild. It was thrilling.

Grace looked long and quietly at her, then ruffed her hair with a hand and said again, in a whisper, "Be *real* still and *real* quiet. I'll come get you when it's time to go."

Grace walked away and into the clearing and stood there as if she had turned into some kind of picture of herself, and it would have or could have become just that if not for the birds that began to move again, inside the bush and from tree limb to tree limb, fluttering and alighting, hopping to the ground to peck and then flying up again to a branch in the bush or a tree. Jane could see through a little seam in the thickly leaved shrub. She knew it was a dewberry because of her mother's teaching, and knew the root was good for an upset stomach. The berries made a good jelly, too. A couple of squirrels played a game of chase around a big pine tree nearby, their claws scrabbling on the soft bark, and chittering. It was hard for Jane not to laugh out loud at them. But she stayed still and quiet. She became part of the bush, her feet and bottom rooted down with its roots. Her hair its leaves, her eyes its berries. Then she saw something and the boy came into the clearing and she went still in her mind as well. Grace didn't move as the boy came up to her. He was a tall boy with coal-black hair, and skin browned from the sun, and bright brown eyes. The two of them stood there like that for a little bit, looking at each other. She could see them breathing hard, their chests moving out and in, up and down. Then they took off their clothes, Grace just lifting her dress above her head and dropping it to one side and unhooking her bra and dropping that, too. She wasn't wearing any underpants. She didn't take off her walking shoes. The boy took off his shirt, which was just a dirty T-shirt, the same way Grace had taken off her dress, and his overalls fell to his feet. He *was* like a stinkhorn there. They grabbed each other and kissed for a minute, the longest kiss Jane had ever seen, as if they'd fallen asleep kissing except they were moving their hands over each other like they were looking for something in different places on their bodies. Then Grace's hand stopped and Jane saw she had ahold of him and she thought, *Don't break it off.* It didn't break off. They knelt down to the ground and he got on top of her. She helped him put it *in* her and they started pushing against each other. It was a little more like the dogs than the pigs but face-to-face, and she realized, later, that she hadn't thought people would do it differently. The boy's black-haired head was buried into Grace's shoulder and she saw Grace look over and make eye contact with her. She soiled her diaper, it took her so by surprise, Grace looking at her with this look on her face, her mouth just barely open, like to say, *You see and you keep quiet.* And then the boy raised his head and she thought he was going to look at her but he was just arching his head back and closing his eyes, and he pushed harder at Grace, who seemed to be looking over at her again but now it was like her eyes weren't focused, and she heard the boy kind of grunt-groaning and then heard him heave a sigh. They lay there like that, him on top of her, for a little while, Grace stroking the boy's back with her hands. Then they got up, him shiny and floppy now. They put on their clothes without saying anything. The boy looked at Grace for a second, then nodded like he was embarrassed, and trotted away from where he'd come. Grace had put her bra back on and slipped into her dress and was adjusting and smoothing it. She took a rag from her pocket and raised her dress and stood there a minute with it pressed to herself where she peed from, then rubbed with it vigorously, took the rag over to the opposite edge of the clearing, and tossed it into the woods there. She went over and picked up her satchel where she'd set it down. Then she looked back at Jane, and crooked her head as if to say, *Come on*, and Jane got up and went to her and together they headed back home, hurrying, Jane struggling to keep up, until they got to the bend in their driveway, where they stopped to catch their breath. Grace wiped perspiration from her face with the hem of her dress, checked herself down there for something, crooked out her thighs in a funny way like she was monkey-walking, felt of the insides of her legs, and, seeming satisfied, said, "Come on," and together they walked up to the house. Grace tossed her satchel onto the porch and Jane followed her through the pecan grove to the barn, where Grace pulled a loose brick from a foundation post, came out with a packet of cigarettes, shook one, kind of flattened and crooked, into her hand, lit it with a match she took from a box in her dress pocket, and leaned back against the barn wall, smoking it like she was finally able to take an easy breath. She pushed her thick blond hair away from her forehead and blew out a big plume of blue smoke. "You all right now, little sister?" she said. Jane nodded. Grace kind of laughed and looked away, shook her head. "What a body will do just to get a little something she wants," she said. She looked at Jane again. "We just went to the schoolhouse and got my books, you remember now?" Jane nodded. "But don't you forget what you saw." Jane nodded again. It was the most curious arrangement. But also it was simple enough. Grace smoked, in silence, and Jane watched her as if there might be some significance in that, too, somehow.

"Why were you doing that with him?" she said then.

"You'll find out," Grace said. "Maybe."

She whispered, "Were you trying to make a *baby* with him?"

Grace gave her a sharp look, then ground out the cigarette with the sole of her shoe. She picked up the butt and stripped the paper from it, tossing the tobacco into the grass and rolling the paper into a little ball she flicked farther away.

"Maybe so. Maybe not."

"*Isn't* that what makes babies?"

Grace narrowed her eyes. "Now, how would you know that?"

Jane felt herself blush. She looked away, shrugged. Grace laughed then.

"I guess we do live on a farm, don't we?" She laughed again, louder, even slapped her knee.

"What?" Peeved at being laughed at.

Grace stopped laughing, wiped her eyes. "Oh, sister. Whether I make a baby with that boy or not, I figure I'll get what I want from him. And what he'll want from me: gone."

"Gone where?"

"Away."

"But *why*? And why would you want to make a baby with that boy?"

"I don't, dummy."

Jane stomped her foot. "I don't *understand*."

"I don't expect you to." Grace looked at her, lips pressed together in irritation. "Look," she said then, "I want that boy to give me some money so I can move to town." She got close to Jane's face, serious. "He doesn't want a baby, he just likes doing that to me. If I tell him we made a baby, he'll give me money to go away." She stood up straight again. "I know his family has money."

"But I don't want you to move to town."

"Grow up a little. I can't do everything in my life just for you. This is for me."

Jane had been about to cry, but she held herself together. Then she said, "I don't think I'd ever want a boy to do that to me."

Grace looked at her a long moment.

"I don't think you'll ever have to, hon."

"Why not?"

"You don't have the right 'equipment.' You know that, don't you? I don't have to tell you that."

Jane didn't say anything to that, though she blushed and blinked her eyes.

"You know who that boy was?" Grace said.

Jane shook her head.

"His name is Arlo Barnett. You remember that. Just remember that, and you remember what it was we were doing. Could you describe it if someone was to ask you?"

Jane nodded. Then she buried her face in her hands in mortified embarrassment.

Grace said, "You just hold on to that, in case I need it."

Jane nodded again, face still buried in her hands, burning with self-consciousness.

"So, anyway, you can see there's not really a whole lot to it," Grace said. "No different from some animal, in the end. Probably do you good to remember that about it, anyway." She shook another cigarette from the pack, lit it, blew the smoke from the corner of her mouth. "You ought to go clean yourself," she said to Jane then. Jane got up and ran toward the creek.

Always she would be haunted by the memory of seeing the boy on top of Grace, his white butt cheeks going at her like the big churning wheel on their hay baler. And never forget Grace's face while he was doing it, eyes locked on her own, looking straight to where she was hiding beside and just behind the dewberry bush, right through the leaves that seemed to quiver in the stillness, as if they were about to burst into white-hot flame.

Sensual Matters

Dear Ellis,

I've decided I suppose the impetus is the girl's decision not to
attend school—to arrange for an examination, if for no other reason
than to find out if there is the possibility of sphincter construction
or repair, which would at least allow her to be in social situations
without embarrassment. There is no reliable urologist around here.
I will be speaking with her, and of course with her parents, in the
coming days. I understand it is a slim chance of good news. And will
make sure they understand that.

It's not that I think a life with romantic love—full on or
chaste—is necessarily something anyone and everyone should pur-
sue, and in my opinion many I've known would've been better off
following their solitary natures. But it seems wrong not to have the
option. Her family trusts me and knows I have consulted with you
on this a number of times, but I worry, still. I don't want to have
been mistaken and would very much like to be corroborated by such
an examination by a specialist—I hear the men in Memphis are
good, among the best.

I wish we could travel to Baltimore, but that's quite an under-
taking for a seven-year-old child, without her parents. It would be

good to see you again. It would be a shame not to see one another again before we are old. You should consider a visit down here, in any case. Get out of the city for a while, have a little country vacation. We could go fishing or even quail hunting if I could rustle up someone's dog. Let's think on it together, though we are what seems almost a world apart.

Yrs,

Ed

A LITTLE LOST in the here and there, birdsong in the trees of the warm afternoon, invisible but for one silent flicker in its undulating flight from one line of trees to another, the air beginning to take on weight it would carry hard into the summer. When Jane awoke from this and stepped through the screen door of the house, she saw the doctor's Ford coming around the bend in the drive. She went down off the porch to greet him and they stood there talking for a few minutes before he surprised her by asking if her sister was at home.

She said, "Grace?"

"You have another sister?" He grinned at her.

She went into the house but no sooner had the screen door shut behind her than she saw Grace looking like she'd just tugged on her nice yellow dress, it being a bit askew on her frame, a small brown valise in one hand and a blue umbrella in the other.

"Where're you going?"

"To town," Grace said. "I'm done here."

She brushed past Jane.

"Your friend the doctor's going to give me a ride."

She walked out, nodded to the doctor, went around to the passenger side. She plumped herself down in the passenger seat and upended the valise to stand between her knees, the blue umbrella cocked onto her shoulder like a rifle.

The doctor looked at her, raised his eyebrows, then nodded to Jane.

"You want to go live in town now, too?"

"No," Jane said, before she realized it was a joke.

"I'll speak to your mother and father before we leave," the doctor said.

"I don't have all day," Grace called from the car seat.

"Be just a minute," the doctor said.

Jane and the doctor walked out to where her father and mother were weeding the cotton field with hoes. They stopped and came over.

"Ma'am," the doctor said, touching the brim of his Stetson. "Where am I to drop the girl off?"

"Search me," her mother said. "Said she's got herself a job working at a dry cleaner's. Somebody she knows of somehow."

"Well, I guess she knows how to get there, then," the doctor said.

Jane's mother turned and went back to weeding.

"Well," her father said. "We knew she was going, and told her to wait till the weekend, I'd take her on in myself, if she was so set on it. I reckon she couldn't even wait that long to get away."

He took his hat off and wiped his brow and face with a handkerchief, looked at the gritty sweat that came off onto it, shook it out, folded it back into his shirt pocket. Then he said, "I thank you for taking her. I suppose she's going to do what she wants, no matter."

They shook hands, then her father walked back into the cotton rows and set in to chopping weeds again like nothing had happened.

On the way back to the house, Dr. Thompson rested a hand

on Jane's shoulder and said, "Your sister can take care of herself, I have no doubt."

She looked up at him and thought to make a comment, but recognized something of self-pity and resentment in it, beyond the puzzlement, and buttoned it.

He turned the crank and got into his car. Grace sat in the passenger seat as still and silent as someone with a gun held to her head but who seemed entirely unconcerned about the danger of the situation. He patted his jacket pocket as if to check for something, waved to Jane, then made the turnabout in the drive and headed out.

Grace isn't even wearing a hat, Jane thought, watching them go. The dust raised in the hot still air by the car's wheels like the dusting away of Grace herself into what it was said people came from. She had never thought literally of that before. A human being made out of dust from the earth would never hold up, and a human being made from mud would be nothing but a crumbling mold creeping about swamps to keep from drying and whisking away in the wind, like the dust she stood watching drift and settle back onto their driveway, no longer disturbed.

IN MERCURY after dropping the girl off at the dry cleaner's, he posted his letter, stopped by Hellman's speakeasy for a beer, then on a whim he'd never indulged before stopped by a popular whorehouse on Ninth Street to have a drink with the men there, thinking he might think on one of the ladies there. He'd been disturbed in that way by Grace's demeanor and didn't know what to do about it. He got caught up in a poker game that was interrupted by a fistfight between two young men named Bates and

Urquhart and escaped the brawl quick as he could. It put him in a better mood, though, those boys fighting over a girl. He headed back downtown to Schoenhof's to pick up a sack of oysters fresh from the Gulf, plus a sack of crushed ice, then at a bootlegger's for a pint of bourbon and a case of Pabst Blue Ribbon beer. He put several beers and the oysters into a broad bucket in his car's trunk, dumped the ice onto them, and headed out.

Driving home, he took a long swallow from the bourbon and relished the new calm in his blood. About halfway there he started thinking about the girl Grace again. The way she'd sat there in his car's passenger seat, he'd swear to God he could smell her the way a stallion scents a dripping mare, and he'd wished he had a drink right then. And how he was sure he saw her, from the corner of his eye, looking him over with a frank stare like she was sizing him up in a way she never had before. He smoked hell out of his pipe most of the drive, and neither said anything much.

"There's a canteen of water for you there under your seat," he said once over the clatter of the motor and wheel noise.

"Thank you."

"I presume that medicine I gave you worked out all right."

"Just fine." Then, "I don't like you wouldn't take my money."

"I don't like how you got it."

When he'd dropped her off he offered to carry her valise and she said no, thank you, it didn't weigh anything.

"Anything in it at all?"

"Just a few personal items," she said with a half smile that taunted him to say more.

"So you just got the one dress you're wearing, then."

"I'm going to be a seamstress," she said. "When I need a new dress, I'll make it."

"Makes sense."

"So where you headed, then, Dr. Thompson? Going to have some fun?"

"Just a little business."

"Busy-ness," she said, smiling.

And with that she closed the car door and walked toward the door of the shop, letting her hips move casually in the yellow summer dress she wore, and when the afternoon light shone through it, good lord, he was right. Nothing at all underneath, and the shadow of her young little bushy hair in the gap between her slim legs below her hips.

Now, driving home, he muttered to himself, "I am nothing but a sad case of horny old low-minded pitifully lonely son-of-a-bitch."

Out of a low-frequency guilt and the need to somehow expunge it, he went on past his house and back to the Chisolms', pulled into their yard honking the Klaxon. He got his lanky bulk down from the driver's seat and wobbled a bit before getting his feet back and checking to see that the tub with ice, beer, and oysters hadn't bumped out along the way. Everyone came over and crowded around. First the doctor took a brown bottle from the ice, flipped the crimped top of it off with a church key, held it out.

"Taste of cold beer, Chisolm?"

"By god," Chisolm said. "On ice, is it?" Chisolm hesitated, then took the beer and drew a long swallow, his Adam's apple bobbing, then held it out in front of him looking at it, blinking like his eyes were smarting in the sunlight. The doctor extracted another bottle from the ice and uncapped it.

"Mrs.?"

Jane's mother glared at him and set her lips. He shrugged and drank, himself.

"What're those rocks in the ice for, or did you just put them in there to steady your bottles of beer?"

"No, ma'am, these are *oysters*, straight from the Gulf of Mexico, come up on the train to Mercury for Schoenhof's Restaurant."

"*Oysters*," Mrs. Chisolm said, twisting her mouth around the odd word. "What is it?"

The doctor lifted his chin and looked at her. Yes, he was a little tight.

"Let me show you."

He produced from his belt a small dagger-looking knife and grabbed one of the rocks with his left hand, and went to prying at one end of the rock with the knife in the other, and the oyster parted like a mouth with a sound like a suction cup coming off the sink bottom.

"This is called shucking them," the doctor said.

"Shucking!" Mrs. Chisolm said. "That's what you do to an ear of *corn*."

"Well, they use the same word for this," the doctor said.

He handed the top half to Jane's father and said, "You can use that for an ashtray." He wiggled the tip of the dagger gently underneath some kind of jelly-looking gray-white blob lying in the bottom half, and next thing you knew he put the lower half up to his mouth and slid the blob out onto his tongue and was chewing the thing, his eyes closed, and then he was swallowing and smiling.

"What in the world?" Jane's mother said.

"What is it?" Jane said. "You ate it!"

"I did," the doctor said. "It's delicious. It's a mollusk, from the sea. You harvest them from the ocean bottom and keep them on ice so they don't die and eat them fresh as you can."

"You mean that thing you just ate was alive?" Jane's mother said. "My land, that's horrible."

"Looks like something that ought to come from inside something," Jane said.

The doctor cocked an eye at Jane, amused. "I guess that's kind of what it is, then."

"Oh, for heaven's sake!" Jane's mother said.

"As I said, it's delicious. And perfectly safe, mostly. These are, anyway. I ate several before purchasing this sack. Try one. The Indians down on the Gulf used to practically survive on these things and a few fish."

"Mostly safe is not near good enough for me," Jane's mother said. Then, under her breath, "Indians."

"I'll eat one if Papa will," Jane said.

Her father looked at her, eyebrows raised. Then he nodded at the mound of oysters. "All right, shuck me up one of them."

"I'll not witness it," Mrs. Chisolm said, and went into the house. She stuck her head back out the screen door and called out, "Won't be on me if you all get sick and die."

The doctor took an oyster from the pile and shucked it, handing the bottom half to Jane's father, then did the same and handed one to her.

"Okay," the doctor said, "just tip it back into your mouth. And chew it, now, don't just slide it down."

Her father did as the doctor said. His face became serious as he held the thing in his mouth for a moment.

"Go on, chew."

He looked sideways at the doctor, then began to chew. His eyebrows went up again, and then he swallowed.

"What, Papa?" Jane said. "What's it like?"

"I can't really say," he said. "You'll just have to see for yourself."

She tipped the shell up and slid the oyster into her mouth, held it there a moment looking like she thought it might explode, then she bit into it, and the doctor watched her eyes get big with what he knew was the actual explosion of salty juices bursting onto her tongue and cheeks and the cold strange taste overwhelming her palate. And then it was down.

She stood there very still for a moment, then looked at her father, then the doctor. They were all standing there with big grins on their faces.

"What?" she said.

"Well, how'd you like it?" her father said.

"I do like it," she said. "But sure does seem like you'd have to eat a whole big bunch of them things to make a meal."

Her father smiled and the doctor laughed out loud and reached for another and began to shuck it.

"Sure enough," he said. "But the ocean's full of them. All over the sandy floor of the big Gulf of Mexico. And every other ocean in the world, far as I know. Let's have us a bounty."

But she and her father would have only a couple more each.

"Keep some, then," the doctor said before he angled himself into his car seat to go. He put several into a small croaker sack and put some ice in with them and set them down onto the ground at their feet. He took a couple out, shucked them, and set them on top of the sack with their tops loosely covering them. "Don't like them raw, I tell you what, they're even better battered and fried."

Her father shook his head.

"I don't think I could get the wife to touch them," he said. "Otherwise I might try that."

"Well, you get a notion to try one that way, just come on over to the house this evening. I might just fry some up myself. Or get Hattie to. Course, they say a raw oyster'll put the lead in your pencil."

"What's that mean?" Jane said.

The doctor grinned, touched his hat, turned his car about in the yard, and trundled off toward the road. Then he stopped, put it in reverse, backed up. Chisolm came over to the window.

"I need to talk to you about something. Not tonight, but in the next day or so," he said.

"All right."

"It's about little Jane," he said. "I want to have an expert take a look at her. I'll tell you more when I come back by." He smiled. "When I'm a bit more sober."

"Good enough, Doc," Chisolm said with a grim smile of his own. He backed away from the car and the doctor drove on.

THEY WATCHED HIM go till he was out of sight and they could only hear the car speeding up and its wheels bumping on the rutted road.

"Always something new in the world," her father said.

Jane grabbed one of the shucked oysters from the top of the sack. The young tenant Lon Temple and his even younger wife, Lacey, leased eighty acres on their place and Jane had been looking for an excuse to try to make friends with Lacey, since she seemed so young for a farm wife.

Ice-cold oyster in her hand, she ran down to show it to her, keeping her hand clapped on top of it, the sticky wet coolness of it against her palm. She knocked on the door of the cabin, then knocked again, and in a minute Lon Temple came to the door and stood there looking at her. She was surprised, thinking he'd be in the field like her father and mother had been. He was a shortish, square kind of man, square face, small eyes, and a small mouth. She'd always thought he looked a little peevish. His young wife Lacey she couldn't tell much about from spying because she wore a bonnet outside most of the time.

"I wanted to show Lacey something," Jane said. She lifted her hand, revealing the oyster, and held it toward him.

He just looked at the thing in her hand.

"Lacey can't come out," he said. "She's not feeling well."

"Oh. Can I help?"

"She don't need no help but what I can give her. What the hell is that thing there?"

"It's an oyster. You eat it, *raw*, like this. Dr. Thompson said it'll put the lead in your pencil."

Temple looked angry then.

"What the hell?" he said.

Then he shut the door.

"Mean little son-of-a-whore," Jane said to herself, echoing words she'd heard her mother mutter about him. She looked at the oyster, and popped it into her mouth, chewing as she climbed down the porch steps. Even then she had to stop for a moment, the sensation of it was so strange.

She went back up to the house and stood there in the yard, then walked in a kind of daze back to the pecan grove, found some leftover nuts in their smooth brown shells, held them in her hands, rolled them between her fingers and thumbs and into her palms, savoring her tongue's memory of the new strange thing, the taste of it lingering even in her teeth. The light began to fail and fall about her like a weightless, silvery, disintegrating rain. She felt flushed by it down to the very tips of her toes.

All things of this nature, apparently unrelated—torrential

storm, the burst of salty liquid from a plump and ice-cold raw oyster, the soft skins of wild mushrooms, the quick and violent death of a chicken, the tight and unopened bud of a flower blossom, a pack of wild scruffy dogs a-trot in a field, the thrum of fishing line against the attack of a bream, and peeling away the delicate frame of its bones from the sweet white meat of its body, a smooth and hard oval nutshell rolled in a palm, the somehow palpable feel of fading light—were in some way sexual for Jane. Not that this was how she would or could have expressed it, especially at that age. She felt it inside herself, though, as deeply and truly as a lover. She fell into the grove's rough, tall grass and into darkness, some charged current running through her in pleasant palpitations of ecstasy.

Mortality

Eldred O. Thompson, M.D.
North Poplar Road
Mercury, Miss.

Dear Ed,
*I have, as I hope you know, been taking careful notes from your
letters, concerning your monitoring and examinations of the
Chisolm girl in your care. Recently I put them together in the most
assimilated fashion I could and sat down with colleagues—and
even managed to get the busy Dr. Young into the meeting. We had
your notes, your drawings. We met quite a while, for meetings
in this place—a good half hour or more. I must tell you that Dr.
Young and the others—and I concurred—concluded that it is
highly improbable anything can be done here to correct the girl's
condition, at this point in time, given what we know about what's
possible, surgically. I will say that Dr. Young raised an eyebrow at
me and told me that he thought, and certainly hoped, and had good
reason to think, that we or others to follow us will soon have the
knowledge, skill, and means to correct her particular condition, but
it is impossible to know, just now, exactly when. Dr. Young did say*

he was certain that a young woman he examined in the past few months has a condition almost if not identical to your Miss Chisolm's, down to the length of the common channel, and he chose not to—could not with any degree of confidence for success—operate. I would imagine that, if there is anything definitive to learn by having someone in Memphis (I recommend Davis) examine her, it would be to find out whether or not sphincter work is possible, at this point. We doubt it.

You take care, now, Ed. Living alone, there, you take care not to over-indulge in your favorite vices. I would complain and urge you to work a little bit at marrying again but there is a part of me, as you know, that feels like you have always been the loner kind at heart, and that if you could get a bit of relief from wanton urges now and then you'd be fine. But, I know, small town, etc. etc. I do wish you had some closer poker or drinking buddies than those backwater snobs in your town. Take a vacation and come see us. Or hell, just hide out in a hotel and I'll take you out on the town incognito.

Yrs.,
Ellis

HE TUCKED THE LETTER into his jacket pocket and took a walk down the path into the woods behind his house. Walking through the yard was like walking through some kind of medieval court, given all the peacocks standing around watching his passage as if he were a strange and sacred cow in their midst.

He'd already persuaded the Chisolms to let him take Jane up to Memphis to be looked over there. Lied and said it wouldn't cost anything, that they would consider odd cases for the value of learning more about them in order to treat others down the line.

He rounded a corner in the trail and heard something and just did see the spritely forms of half-grown children bounding away through a thicket like so many frightened deer. A rare sighting of the species *Urchinus trespassus*. Although he knew very well his woods were regularly roamed by boys from nearby farms and even the northernmost neighborhoods in town. He'd seen their roughshod forts and campsites. That was all fine with him. In his better moods he'd pretend they were his own wayward, half-wild children, conceived in a sylvan, satyrical dream, mythical forest creatures not to be tended like the mortal child. He didn't like knowing the little bastards shot songbirds with their air guns, but he had done the same as a boy. It was rare he heard the rifle or shotgun of a true poacher, and if he'd heard it regular he would've called the sheriff, but so far that hadn't been the case. There were deer and hogs and turkey in here, he knew, and, he suspected, an ivorybill, maybe a pair. He only hoped some fool boy or man would not shoot one or both of those birds. He heard the call of a peacock deeper in the woods and thought, *Or them.*

He crossed the creek where it was shallow and narrow and walked through a little glade and then up a long, sloping hill. At the top there was the old gazebo he'd built just after he and Lett married. They'd loved to come out here, have a bottle of beer and a picnic. It was high up. You could see out over the woods. Just a glimpse of glinting light on the lake a quarter mile west, at the end of the property. He knew those same boys (and their parents) trespassed to fish there all the time. By now most knew he didn't spend much time in his own woods. They probably considered it public property, for all they cared. And he practically did, too, he supposed. As long as he knew he himself had access, and no one the right to tell him otherwise.

He sat in the now-neglected gazebo and remembered those

Sunday afternoon picnics. No one could reach him there, with
her, even if they came calling, even if someone was a-dying and
a-crying, *Oh, my lord!* he would not know it. He put the world out
of his mind and enjoyed the time alone in a little paradise with
his sweetheart, before she began to go sour on him. On them.
Nothing is forever, it was true. He could be sitting alone here now
with her alive and no longer even caring to come out here with
him, to enjoy such days. *Which is better?* he wondered. *What is the
difference, given enough time?*

ACROSS THE YARD from the front porch, to the right of the drive
that came to the house from the road, was the large shed where
her father would do everything from work on farm machinery, to
smith horseshoes or mend tools, to grooming the horses or mule
before turning them out to graze for the evening if they'd been
worked. In the part where he had worked for years on machinery,
the earth was red clay discolored and redolent with oil and grease,
and packed hard, and the smell of those things combined was
for some reason one of the most delicious to her, even more than
those in the barn. What she wished almost more than anything
was that she could fix a tractor, or repair a broken wheel, or even
hammer out a wheel rim or horseshoe on the anvil. That's what
seemed like real *work* to her, even as a child, not sweeping a porch
or churning milk or washing and hanging clothes or cooking over
a hot stove. Men's work seemed like freedom.

Just down the two-track drive, closer to the road, was the one-
room general store her father operated for the tenants, sharecroppers, and neighbors who didn't want to travel to the larger one in
Liberty a few miles away. It had a simple board counter where her

father set his money box when he went up there, shelves on the walls for dry goods, canned goods, crackers, tobacco and matches, flour and sugar, canned coffee, and such as that. Heavy sacks of feed were stacked in one corner. Leather for tack repair hung on the wall space just behind the board counter. A tall potbellied woodstove sat in the center of the room, placed in a sandbox, and sometimes a customer would sit next to it for a bit sharing a smoke or a sip with her father, usually in the late afternoon. He didn't keep regular hours there, but people would just walk or ride up and wait outside it till someone saw them there and went to tell her father, who would come serve them if he could get away from work. If he couldn't get away, her mother or Grace (before she left) would get the key and go tend to it.

Jane had taken to following her father or mother or Grace to the store when someone came up. She stayed quiet and out of the way but she was studying what went on as intently as a bird eyeballing a worm, pulling up close when the money was exchanged, and jumping to get a product when someone asked. And without anyone noticing she had learned not only the inventory but about money and how to count it, too, all from just watching and thinking, and when there was something she didn't quite understand she would keep her mouth shut and watch more closely the next time. So pretty soon when she would run to get a sack of meal or tobacco or sugar or coffee or what have you, she would plop it onto the counter and call out the price, and when the customer would put down his or her money she would call out that amount and in a flicker call out what change they had coming back, leaving her father or mother shaking their heads in wonder, or Grace glowering at her in irritation. "How'd she figure all that out?" her father would say, and her mother would say, "Well, you know when she gets quiet, watch out, 'cause she's thinking and she's going to come up with something to surprise you, I'll tell you that."

So when she would see someone coming or pulling up to the store she would run to her father so fast, so light on her feet, it felt like she hardly had to touch the ground to get going, half flying to where the key hung on a nail in the mantel, saying, *Customer!* At first her father hadn't wanted her to tend the store by herself, she was too young despite her talents, but soon he gave in and got her an old apple crate to stand on and let her mind the store whenever she wanted. And since she was pretty much the only one who cared anything about it, and who didn't have anything really to be interrupted by it, she became principal storekeeper. So much so that her father took to just leaving the cash box on the mantel near the key so she could grab it, too.

And when people would come in, black or white, they always greeted her with respect, some with a bit of humor, "Hello, young lady," or, "Hello, Miss Jane." And she would pipe up, "What can I get for you, Mr. Everett?"

"I'll be durned if I don't think more people been coming by the store since she started keeping it more often," her father said, laughing a little bit. He said to her, "You remember what I said, though, about strangers or rough-looking types. You don't open up for them, you hear?"

Sometimes a neighbor man, vaguely familiar, would not tell her what he wanted and only ask her to get her father. "I can get you anything you want, sir," she would say. And the man would act as if he were deaf or stupid, until she went to get her father, and he would tell her to stay put or go to the house, he would take care of this one.

Later she'd come to realize the man was there to purchase liquor. There was a locked cabinet at the very rear corner of the store that she was never given a key to.

The only time she didn't run out to the store to meet a customer was when she had just had an accident and had no time to clean up, and she hated that.

She liked to go into the smokehouse after the meat had cured and stand beneath the big bodies of meat hanging from hooks attached to fence wire that was secured around the joist beams. The sides of bacon, roasts, hams, and rib slabs turned so slightly in the thin strips of light that leaked between the board siding that she may have imagined it, as she did the spinning of the earth itself as she stood stock-still in the middle of the yard, causing her mother to call out from the breezeway, "Jane! Come in this house and cool your forehead. Have you gone feebleminded on me?"

There was a small two-room storage shed that contained odd discarded objects the family no longer used. Jane was told to stay out of there, might be snakes or wasps or things that could fall off of shelves and knock her in the head. So she did, though sometimes she tried to see through the windows. The panes were too dusty for her to make out much. One day she went in against the rules and saw a dust-covered little red wagon high on a shelf, and wondered why it was up there and she'd never been allowed to play with it when she was younger. And then her father told her it had belonged to her older brother William Waldo, who'd died of the fever just a few years before she was born, and that her mother had made him put it up on that shelf and wouldn't let anyone so much as touch it, much less play with it.

"Why did she want to keep it, then?" Jane said.

Her father gave her a long look, blinking his eyes, and shook his head. He looked away. "She loved him best," he finally said. "You have to keep that in mind when she's acting ornery. Losing that little boy broke her heart."

She kind of nodded.

"He was just three years old, going on four," her father said. He leaned down to tug on her blouse where it had gotten twisted a bit. Then he looked her in the eye, his gray eyes there but hardly seeming to really look at her. He was seeing something else. Maybe the dead boy William Waldo. Then he said, "That's when a child is most precious, you see. Kind of between being a baby and a little boy or girl. It's when they seem like little angels. It's the hardest time to lose one. I do believe." He patted her shoulder and went off, leaving her there feeling something she hadn't felt before. Only later would she identify it as grief. The gift of it given from her father, and her mother, too, to her.

THEY WOULD MAKE the trip to Memphis after all, she and Dr. Thompson. She did not know that he had been vacillating on the idea for some weeks, only that he up and said to get ready for the trip. Her mother and father seemed tense and didn't want to discuss it. She was so excited about taking the train ride to Memphis that she felt little or no apprehension about the fact that they were going to see a doctor up there, someone who would supposedly know more about what was wrong with her than Dr. Thompson himself. She doubted that. But the trip sure sounded like fun. She'd never been farther than to town, and never been on a train.

They rode coach to Jackson, then switched to the Chicago train for the ride to Memphis. Though the ride would be relatively brief, the doctor got them a private compartment anyway, so that she wouldn't have to worry about accidents. The rolling countryside to Jackson was pretty, the bright and rusty leaves fluttering down from the trees along the railway. On the northbound to Memphis the land flattened out once they veered close to the Delta. The doctor got her a soda pop and some peanuts and had himself a beer as they rode, throwing the peanut shells out the window and making her laugh and join in like a game.

In Memphis, they caught a streetcar to what the doctor said was the medical college. It was a big, square, red-brick four-story building. Jane had never seen anything quite like it. But then they'd seen lots of big buildings, hotels and civic buildings, on the way there through town. Her neck just about got a crick from looking right and left every block.

There was a woman sitting near them on the streetcar who looked back at them with a sour expression and got up to sit somewhere else. Jane saw her say something to the woman she sat down next to, and the other woman turned to look at them, too. The doctor stuck his tongue out at them and they looked horrified, but they stopped looking then. Everything seemed so loud, from people's voices to the car's bell, automobile engines and horns, and even the smells were loud, of exhaust fumes, the strange burnt smell of the sparking streetcar wires, all kinds of food cooking, and the savory smoke coming from restaurant kitchens and street vendors. It was like they were in a foreign country. The doctor seemed to be enjoying watching her experience it all more than he enjoyed being there himself.

They climbed the big white steps up into the hospital. It smelled sharply of what he said were sanitary chemicals, soap, and lots of human odors. Not a place where she would feel so self-conscious about herself. They went straight into an examination room, which felt like a different *world*, something weirdly not like regular life.

She'd never been in a room that felt so starchy clean and white, with gleaming metal tables and bright light. She half expected to be packaged up as a specimen and shipped to the future or something. Then a tall man, even taller than Dr. Thompson, but thinner, wearing thick spectacles on a small nose, with a balding head and a crewcut, came in and said he was Dr. Davis. There was a nurse with him but he didn't even bother to introduce the woman, who wore a blank expression beneath her white cap and said nothing, just did what the doctor said like she was some mechanical person instead of a real one. Her hands were cold and Jane looked at her, momentarily startled by her, and the woman didn't even seem to notice.

Quickly, they had her on the table and in the stirrups, the sheet up, cleaned her good, and then she heard Dr. Davis murmur the usual words about cold, some discomfort, and so on, and she felt him using what she called the metal duck thing to look inside her. She flinched but soon calmed and turned her head to the side to see Dr. Thompson, who was watching the doctor. When he saw her looking at him he came over and held her hand. He patted it.

"Won't take long," he said.

Indeed it didn't. Dr. Davis, out of sight behind the sheet and using his bright light and reflector, used some kind of blunt instrument to poke and probe her here and there inside, seeming to take care not to hurt her, to be gentle. Then he pulled everything out, stood up, told the nurse Jane could get dressed again, and went over to a sink to wash his hands. Dr. Thompson took a fresh diaper from a bag he'd carried and handed it to the nurse.

"If you wouldn't mind, madame," he said.

The nurse suddenly turned into a human being, broke into a big smile, and said, "Not at all, Doctor!" Almost startled Jane into peeing on the tabletop.

Then Dr. Thompson went out with Dr. Davis and they stood

talking in low tones in the hallway. The nurse went back to being a mechanical person, putting the fresh diaper on Jane, gathering up the instruments, and putting the sheets into a hamper in a corner, and then she left without so much as a glance at or a word to Jane. *I guess she must be used to the likes of me*, Jane thought.

As they were leaving, Dr. Thompson said he was going to take her out on the town.

"What did the doctor say?" she said.

"Tell you in a bit," he said.

They went to see the Pink Palace mansion, where the doctor said a strange old lady lived by herself, which was amazing. They went to the river bluff to see steamboats tied up and going by. They went to the zoo, where Jane was disappointed they didn't have any monkeys, but fascinated by the tiger and elephant, more so by the tiger, until the doctor told her that elephants were very smart and had long memories and were sad and cried when one of their loved ones was killed or died.

After the zoo they ate at what he said was a famous barbecue place before going to their lodgings. She didn't want the pork ribs, so she got the smoked chicken that fell off the bone, and was afraid she might never love fried chicken as much again after that.

They were staying at the old Hotel Peabody, a huge five-story building with an enormous lobby, and Jane had a room all of her own, right next to the doctor's room, with a door that adjoined them. He told her how they were going to tear the old hotel down, and that was too bad because a lot of interesting, important people had stayed there, and it stayed open and served as a hospital when the city was struck down by a yellow fever epidemic in the late 1870s. He said it was similar to what had killed her older brother William, before she was born.

"Now, if you need anything, or get scared in the night, you

know I'm right through that door, you just come on in and wake me up."

"Okay, but I'll be all right."

"I know you will." He gave her a kiss on the forehead.

"When are you going to tell me what that doctor said?"

"Tomorrow, on the way home."

She sat up for a few minutes, wondering why he wouldn't tell her right away what the other doctor had said, although she knew in her mind and heart what he had to say, and why he hesitated to say it. That there was nothing they could do for her. She alternated between a kind of nameless dread and a forgetfulness borne of her fatigue from the day.

The sounds of people and cars and wagons on the street below went well into the night, and the soft glow from streetlamps cast shadows on the room's ceiling. It was the tallest ceiling she'd ever seen in her life, as if the room were meant to be a place for enormous people, giants, but then how would they get through the regular-sized door? She was thinking about people who came in through the door at a normal size but started growing then, becoming huge, giants, and as she passed through that image into sleep her body felt heavy, massive, so much so that she was unable to move, and sleep overcame her and moved through her like death.

Death Insurance

It was not quite the end of childhood, but something between that and whatever would come after. After Grace left, she'd been essentially alone on the farm. The Harris sharecroppers' children were either nearly grown or gone. The young tenant Lon Temple and his even younger wife had no children yet. She wanted to make friends with young Lacey Temple but she seemed hard to approach, somehow. So Jane was the only child around, and hardly ever went anywhere, the Chisolm girl who had something wrong with her, something mysterious, and who kept to herself with her family. Strange little bird.

She still had the thought, though, that maybe she could make friends with Lacey Temple, now that she was a little older herself. She walked down one afternoon, hoping to catch her alone. Lacey was sweeping her small front porch and wearing her bonnet, and when she looked up, startled, Jane saw a deep purple bruise on her cheekbone. Lacey set her broom aside and hurried into the house. Jane knew better than to follow. When she went home she commented on it to her mother, who stopped what she was doing and turned to give her a grim look.

"I knew that young fellow had a temper but I had hoped he wouldn't be the kind to do that."

"You think Lonnie hit her?"

"Well, how else do you get a bruise like that?" her mother said. "And who else do you think would or could've done it?"

Jane said nothing. She'd seen her father slap her mother that one time. They were at the dinner table, just the two of them, supper done. Jane watched from the breezeway through the screen door. In the middle of one of her mother's rants her father stood halfway up from his seat, leaned over the table, and slapped her across the face, and she looked shocked but she went quiet and just sat there. In a minute they both began drinking their coffee again in silence, and the slap hadn't left anything more than a red mark that disappeared soon after.

"I wouldn't bet against that he knocked her down with a blow like that," her mother said then, turning back to finish stirring her cornbread batter and pour it sizzling into the hot greased pan on top of the stove. The smell of the browning batter was delicious enough to distract Jane from her thoughts, but only for a moment.

"Papa ought to say something to him about it," she said.

"Your papa is not the kind to interfere in other people's affairs."

"What if he was to really hurt her, I mean bad?"

"I reckon the sheriff would come calling if it came to that," and then she said no more on the subject.

That weekend, late Saturday afternoon, they had a visit from her uncle Virgil McClure, her mother's younger brother. Sometimes when he came by it was just for family matters and he would bring his beautiful wife Beatrice, with her abundant black hair, full lips, beautiful pale skin, dark brown eyes, and their two children, Little Bea and Marcus. But this afternoon he came alone, wearing his narrow-brim Open Road Stetson, and his business coat, and carrying the leather briefcase he used in his job selling insurance for the Rosenbaum firm down in Mercury. There weren't all that many ways to get out of a farming life, but Virgil had the smarts to start selling insurance on the side and got good enough to do it full time. No one disrespected him for it.

He sat and had a cup of coffee with her mother while they waited on Jane's father to come in from the pecan grove, where he had been up on a ladder all day pruning and trimming. Spring would be coming soon and they hoped for a good, heavy crop this year, as the year before had been a light one. Jane loved the pecan grove, the way you crossed through a narrow strip of woodland between the cotton field behind the house and the view opened up to the beautiful gray-barked trees with their crazy limbs splayed against the sky and how they leafed out in spring, their long, narrow leaves so green in the spring and summer, like precise clippings from larger leaves when they browned, shrank, and fell in the fall. You could walk around the field and woods but she liked taking the path through them. She loved walking through the grove after harvest and searching for pecans they'd missed and cracking two together in her palms to get the sweet nut meat from those that hadn't rotted in the rains. She helped gather at harvest, and her father had explained to her how the catkins were the male flower and the little spiky new flowers were the female, and how they had planted two different kinds of pecan trees so that the differences between them would combine to make a robust crop. The wind would blow the pollen from the catkins to the female and the nut would begin to grow in the female flower, on the new growth. It was fascinating to Jane. It made the trees seem alive in a whole new way. They made their fruit, working together. It wasn't just some accident of nature. It made her wonder anew about the strange miracle of creation, how the world came to be, and all the beautiful and strange plants and animals and insects that made it alive.

When her father came up onto the porch and into the house from the grove, he seemed surprised.

"Didn't expect you today, Virgil," he said, and Jane noticed her mother shut herself down in the secretive way she sometimes did when she wanted to hide something from you. Jane went silent and tried to turn her ears toward their talk the way a dog or cat would when it heard something curious and interesting.

Uncle Virgil had a quiet, soft voice and an old country way of not moving his jaw or mouth much when he spoke so that his words somehow always seemed private and friendly. Intimate, like he was chewing softly on the words. Even when he was speaking of hard matters, such as a death or someone in trouble, he spoke in the same even voice, and somehow that carried a kind of authority, his expression consistently one of earnest interest, not like he was amused but like he took it all in stride as part of life. He had briefly been sheriff in the county and had been good at it but did not run for reelection, saying it saddened him too much to see all the hard things a sheriff has to see. But the experience had made him more even-tempered than he'd been before.

"Well," he said then, glancing at Jane's mother and straightening his gaze onto her father. "I had me an idea. I don't know as you'd like to spend the money, but it's a pretty good arrangement and likely to help everybody out should there be an accident."

Her father just looked placidly back at Virgil, waiting, seeming neither impatient nor overly interested. He could be a patient man when his work had gone well and he wasn't itching for a drink.

"What I'm talking about is something more and more farmers

are doing these days, and that's taking out accidental death and dismemberment policies on their tenants and sharecroppers."

Her father still said nothing, although he leaned his head just slightly to the side and his eyes registered a combination of wary curiosity and heightened interest.

"I take it you want me to continue on," Virgil said.

Her father nodded, only then taking off his field hat and setting it on the table beside a cup of coffee Jane's mother had set in front of him on a saucer. He brought the hot black coffee to his mouth and took a careful sip, set it back onto the saucer. Virgil did the same with his cup. Her mother occupied herself with mending a tear in the shoulder of a shirt she had in her lap.

Virgil took some papers from his briefcase and set them on the table.

"Now, these here pay you, the one paying the premiums, if one of the people you take out a policy on should die as result of an accident here on the farm or anywhere else, or if they lose a hand, arm, part of an arm, or a leg, even a finger or two-three. Anything that affects their ability to continue to work for you."

"How much is it for each policy?"

"Here's the price of the monthly premium, you can see it's not much. You could pay for it easy out of their rent if they're tenants and their crop if they're sharecroppers. You just got a little less, but if something should happen to them, well, then you get paid this"—and he pointed to some figures on the papers—"for a death, and this"—he pointed again—"if it's a dismemberment. It's more than enough to carry you over till you find someone else to lease the land or sharecrop it."

Her father looked at the papers and figures, blinking a couple of times, seeming to study them and to think.

"It's an investment, Sylvester, if you think about it. Against potential catastrophic loss. You do have to put some money in up front, but after that you can figure it out of your profit from these sections, just like you would any other expense. Now, I know for a fact you've had it happen before. Accident, I mean."

"That fellow name of Whitehead. Saw blade caught him in the leg right where the big artery sits, he bled out on the spot."

"That's right," Virgil said. "Nothing anybody could've done. And you had to hire help to finish his crop. And still gave his widow a share of the profit."

Her father nodded, still looking at the papers. He took a sip of his coffee, glanced at his wife, who got up and poured a bit more in to reheat it.

"And not to mention the poor Stephens woman helping her husband pitch hay and catches him right in the neck, that must've been a good ten, twelve years back."

Her father nodded, sipped the fresh coffee.

"Ten," he said.

"Now, if you look here," Virgil said, pointing, "for just fifty cents more each premium, you get enough to cover a lost crop, should you not be able to get anyone in there to take it over in time, and still have money left over. I'd say it's worth it."

"And this all goes to me, something happens?"

"'Less you want to give something to the widow, or help out the disabled man, which of course some do, some don't."

"Let me think on it a little bit," her father said.

"How many you got here on the place now?" Virgil said, although even Jane knew Virgil knew the answer to that. He was a good salesman, even to his own kin.

"Got the colored 'cropper Harris, and the young tenant Temple."

"Each doing eighty."

"Right. I do my forty in cotton, tobacco, and corn. Ten acres in pecan trees. Rest in cattle pasture and the woods here behind the house. I keep it for hunting, fishing, and just pleasure, you know."

"Well, you don't have to cover everybody. I'd say the tenant, maybe. Maybe just Harris himself, not his sons." Virgil scribbled some numbers on a pad. "This premium every three or six months, your choice. Feel safer, protected from some fool accident, or one couldn't be avoided, for that matter. Happens."

"Happens," her father said, nodding. "And what about myself?"

"Wouldn't be a bad idea," Virgil said, scribbling again. "I can get you a discount on yourself, I'm pretty sure, you being the owner and taking responsibility for them that work your land." He scribbled a little more.

Her father studied the new numbers a minute, nodded, went to the jar in the kitchen cupboard, and gave Virgil some bills and coins.

"All right, then," Virgil said. "All I'll need is for you to get their full legal names and dates of birth. You can tell them it's like a liability policy on the whole place, as it is, practically speaking. This is completely legal, and as I said more and more common. Makes good sense in the farming business, all things considered. I can set up everything here, and you can fill out that information about these men when you get it, and I'll come back by next week and get the papers."

Then they both signed, and Virgil and her father stepped out onto the porch after Virgil had said good night to Jane's mother.

Jane slipped out the kitchen door and crept through the breeze-way to spy-listen on them there.

"I'm recalling that business up in Scooba," her father said.

"Well," Virgil said, "that was an unfortunate case."

"I wouldn't want anybody thinking I had anything like that in mind."

"No reason anybody would, you got a spotless reputation."

"Drinkin' aside."

"Well. You got a lot of company in that, I'd say. Now, like I said, this is becoming more and more common among your farmers."

"Folks know I'm a good businessman, always aboveboard."

"Yes, they do."

"Anything was to happen, I'd hope nobody'd think anything underhanded gone on here."

"No reason to think that. Besides, that thing in Scooba—I wouldn't call a fellow dying of poison spasms exactly an accidental death. They got away with it for so long because that doctor up there was involved in it."

They were quiet for a long moment.

"Well, Virgil, I reckon this is good business."

"It is, Sylvester. You don't have to think twice about that."

"I generally think three, four times about most everything."

"Well. That's why people respect you."

"I mean to keep it that way."

"I don't doubt it."

"Want a little snort before you go?"

"I would, but Bea wouldn't approve."

"You stay on her good side, don't you?"

"That's good business, too."

"How come you all don't call this kind of thing 'death insurance,' since that's what it is, wouldn't you say?"

"That would be bad for business," Virgil said.

The men chuckled together at that. And then there were no more words at parting. She heard Uncle Virgil descend the porch steps, make his way to his Ford pickup, and the pickup coughed and rattled and creaked on down the drive out to the main road. She heard her father descend the steps, walk across the yard to his little store, and then come back. When she heard him sit in his rocker and pull the stobber from his jug, she stole around and sat on the porch boards beside the chair.

"Want me to roll you a cigarette, Papa?"

"Here you go, girl," he said, handing her a tin of Prince Albert and his little rolling machine. She rolled up a perfect one for him.

"Can I light it for you?"

He handed her a box of matches. She struck one, held the match to it, and sucked lightly on it.

"Mind you, don't take it into your young lungs."

She handed him the lit cigarette, held the warm smoke in her mouth and then puffed it out.

"I won't," she said.

"I don't want you to take up smoking like your sister Grace."

"I won't."

"You do, I'll tan your little hide."

They watched a mockingbird come down from his perch and peck at Top's head as he tried to cross the yard toward them. The dog ducked his head, then leapt up to try to catch the bird in his jaws when it came at him again. They watched this dance until Top made it to the porch and the bird quit and flew off. The way Top looked at them then, the look on his face, like he was both happy and confused at the same time, just made them laugh again. The dog, embarrassed, went underneath the porch instead of coming up onto it with them.

"Oh, come on up, Top," Jane said. "Come on up here."

But they heard the dog sigh hard through his nose and flop down in the dirt.

"Sometimes that dog acts like he knows as much about what's going on as we do."

"He does, Papa."

"Dog's supposed to have it easier than that," he said.

ON A SPRING AFTERNOON when it was near harrowing time, before planting, Jane walked up on her father having what appeared to be an argument with young Temple down by the shed. She slowed and stayed back, behind the tractor pulled up near the shed for repair.

"Well, then, you do like I did," she heard her father say to Temple in his quiet, hard voice. He never raised his voice but he had a way of leveling and hardening it that let you know he was angry and meant business.

Temple said something she couldn't understand, half mumbling. He had his hat off and was nearly crushing the brim in both hands in front of his waist. He kept looking down at the hat, off at the field, and then giving her father brief looks, askance. He caught her peeping from behind the tractor before she could duck down and his face reddened. Now she was caught spying and couldn't sneak off.

"You do like I did and like anybody would do that wants to make a better life," her father said. "You save everything you don't have to spend to live on. You find any way you can to make a little money during the winter, you can't be too proud about what it is, neither. When you have a good year, you put as much back as you can and don't just spend it. And when you can, you buy yourself some land of your own."

Temple mumbled something else. Jane couldn't see him now, kept her head down behind the tractor wheel fender.

"You can't resent them that has more than you if you don't put in the honest effort to make your own way. And you might try and fail by plain bad luck when others make out all right trying no harder, but there's nothing to be done then, either, but to try again. Let me tell you, son, I've known failure, and I could fail tomorrow, any farmer or cattleman could, and you know that. So don't come to me complaining about a fair, agreed-on trade which is me giving you a chance to make a start. Everybody starts humble. If you didn't like this agreement, you shouldn't have signed on to it."

Temple said nothing. Jane peeked up. He was looking down, but looking angry, too.

"And you can pack up and go now, too, if that's what you want," her father said. "I'll find a way to finish your crop, if that's what you want to do. But if you walk away from it, it's not your crop anymore, you understand? You don't get your rent money back. You've had the land while you've worked it."

Temple said something, looked her father in the eye kind of sideways, and seemed like he said he didn't want that.

"Well, then," her father said. And both men stood there another minute, her father looking steadily at Temple and Temple trying to meet her father's eye but unable to for more than a moment at a time.

And then Temple said something, and held out his hand, her father took and shook it once, and Temple went on back walking toward his place. Her father turned and Jane ducked down, then peeked up to see him go into the shed, taking his hat off and running a hand through his graying hair, shaking his head.

Two days after that, a Saturday, Jane was walking in the woods looking for a sweet gum tree that might be leaking some sap she could nibble. Top kept dashing off to chase foraging squirrels. She heard the tractor muttering its way in a field and looked up to see she was on the edge of it, and it was Temple on the machine, having stopped to tinker with something. Her father let him use it when he could. Temple looked up and saw her there, and she ducked back into the shrubs and trees and made her way toward the trail again. In a while she found a tree with a leaking seam, gathered a little of the gum on the end of a twig, and rolled it into a ball she put in her mouth to nibble with her front teeth. She sat there and Top came to lie down beside her. But in a moment he stood up and gave a low growl and she saw the fur on the back of his neck stand up. When she stood up and turned around she saw it was Lon Temple standing among some oak saplings not far away, looking at her.

"I want a word with you, girl," he called out just loud enough for her to hear, and she froze. Top growled. She could still hear the tractor idling off in the field.

It took a moment to get her voice. She put a hand on Top's bristling neck. "All right," she said.

"My wife said you been coming around snooping at our place. Far as I'm concerned, even though we rent from your daddy, my place is private property. You ought to respect that, keep it in mind."

Jane flushed with embarrassment, afraid he was on to her sometimes spying on them, but then realized he was probably only talking about her seeing Lacey in the yard with her bruise.

"You hear what I'm saying?" Temple said. "I ain't saying nothing nobody wouldn't say about their property."

"I haven't been snooping," Jane said. "It was just that once and I was only coming down to be neighborly."

He stared at her.

"We ain't neighbors," he said. "We're tenants."

Temple spat, as if to spit that word out of his mouth, then turned and made his way back up the hill through the woods and out of sight.

She was trembling. The man scared her. She stayed there, squatting and holding Top, sound seeming to disappear into the noise in her mind. She stayed until she finally calmed and then she and Top started home, first walking, then running down the trail.

"What in heaven's name is the matter with you?" her mother said when they burst into the yard. She was taking clothes from the line and had a bunch of them draped over one arm, a basket for pins crooked onto the other.

"Nothing," Jane said when she could. "Top and me thought maybe there was a bear."

"A bear!" her mother said. "This close to the house? Did you see it?"

She shook her head. Then her mother shook her head, too.

"Imagining things again, are you?"

And Jane knew she was talking about that quiet evening when she was little and heard some terrifying beast walk growling by the house beneath the open window and burst into tears, but no one else had heard a thing. And now she was old enough to wonder, what if she had only imagined the beast, and if so, where had that come from? Why and even how would a small child carry something like that in her imagination if it were not already there when she was born, and for some reason? And if it were not to make sure the child learned to keep in her heart a certain measure of fearfulness, in order to keep herself safe, what other reason could there be? There was something frightening about Lon Temple that seemed to bring up a similar feeling in her.

But these were not the kinds of things she cared to try to discuss with her mother. It was perhaps something she could bring up with Dr. Thompson. But she couldn't imagine how she could bring it up without feeling silly, like a little girl with an overly rich and foolish imagination.

IT WAS JUST under a fortnight after her encounter with Temple in the woods when she came home from a long walk down by the fishing pond and saw Dr. Thompson's car parked in the yard. He was sitting in her father's rocker on the front porch, smoking his pipe, a glass of water on the little stand beside him. She stopped still in the yard, that same kind of fear she had thought she might discuss with him suddenly there, inside her. After a moment, she walked on up.

"What's happened?" she said.

He puffed his pipe, but it had gone out.

"Something got to be wrong before I can come by, now?"

"Well, no."

"But it's kind of odd, me sitting out here on the porch by myself."

"Yes."

He nodded as if to himself, tapped his pipe out against his boot.

"Temple's wife is in there with your mother and father," he

said. "There was an accident. You might better wait out here with me awhile."

Her heart did a double bump in her chest.

"Tell me."

He looked at her, as if trying to figure her state of mind.

"I haven't even told you and you're pale as a ghost."

"I can tell it's something bad."

"Well, it is. Young Temple was killed today."

"What do you mean?"

"It was an accident. He fell off the tractor and was cut up badly by the disc harrow. Died out in the field. Didn't come in for lunch and his wife went out looking, found him there, tractor run up against a tree at the edge of the field and faltered. He's down at their cabin, laid out on the floor there. His folks will come to take the body for burial."

"How did it happen?" she said then. Her mind keening with the memory of their encounter, how she had hated him then as much as she'd feared him.

"Seems he was drinking. He smelled strong of it. I believe he got into your papa's makings."

She sat down onto the porch beside Dr. Thompson and they sat there awhile. Soon they heard the breezeway door to the kitchen open and Lacey hurried past them in tears.

"Miss Lacey?" Jane called, but all she could get out was a whisper.

Lacey Temple didn't hear, her head down, walking slowly now toward the cabin where her husband lay dead.

"Boy wasn't but twenty-three years old," Dr. Thompson said. "And she's not but, what, eighteen or nineteen, maybe."

"I don't know, really," Jane said. She was watching Lacey Temple make her drifty way down the lane almost as if she were a bit drunk herself, wobbly.

"Still, not even twenty years of age and a widow. I need to talk to your mama and papa for a minute before the sheriff and coroner arrive, soon enough. I expected they'd have been here by now." He got up and went into the house.

When she heard a car coming down the road and then turn into their drive, her father and Dr. Thompson came out onto the porch and went to meet it. They spoke to the two men in there, one the sheriff, and the other man in a dark suit must have been the coroner. Then the doctor went in the car with the coroner down toward the Temple cabin while her father and the sheriff walked that way and veered off toward the pasture where Temple must have been discing when he fell off and was killed. The four men came back around the same time and stood talking around the sheriff's car for a few minutes, and then the sheriff and coroner left. Dr. Thompson said some words to her father, then got into his car and left, too.

Her father came over and told her to tell her mother that he had to go see Virgil in town and would be back as soon as possible.

"You take a plate of dinner down to the Temple girl, see if she'll eat," he said to Jane. "Your mama's got one fixed in the kitchen." Then he got into his cattle truck and left.

She stayed on the porch. She didn't know what to feel anymore. She smelled supper cooking in the kitchen. She went inside just as her mother was covering a pie tin with a clean kitchen towel.

"You take this down to her," she said.

"Mama," Jane said, "I don't want to."

Her mother stopped and gave her a long stern look that didn't need words to convey its meaning.

"But what if she won't eat? How could she be hungry right now?"

"All you can do is try," her mother said. "Go on, now. What's the matter with you?"

Jane shook her head and didn't answer. Couldn't.

She freshened herself up and then walked down toward the Temple cabin, careful with the warm edges of the tin, using the towel so as not to burn her fingers, careful not to trip and spill it. She felt wooden and clumsy. When she got up onto the porch she set the tin down and knocked on the door. There was no lamp on inside although light was fading and shadows already deep inside.

When there was no answer, she called out, but in a fainter voice than she'd meant to. When Lacey Temple didn't reply she grew worried, turned the knob on the cabin door, picked up the tin, gently opened the door with her shoulder, and went in.

It was just a two-room shotgun cabin with a little kitchen area in one corner of the front room, a small dining table with a couple of chairs in the other, and a sitting area against the other wall by a small fireplace. She stopped still when she saw, in the shadows, what had to be the body of young Temple lying on the floor over by the fireplace, covered with a bloodied counterpane. She felt a coldness run through her, and sick, as if she might vomit.

"I can't bring myself to wash him," she heard Lacey's voice say then, coming from their little bedroom in the back. Then she saw the ghostly figure step into the shadowed doorway. She no longer wore the bonnet and her pale face glowed softly in the faint light left in the windows.

"He'd been out there in the sun long enough the blood had dried hard and I don't want to hurt him cleaning it off. I know he won't feel nothing but I can't do it."

Jane could hear the crying in her voice. She worked hard to find her own.

"My mama fixed you a plate of supper. I'll set it over here on your table."

She started for the table and was setting the tin down when Lacey spoke again.

"I'll not touch that, you can take it back."

Jane set it down anyway. She could hardly grip her fingers on it and feared she might drop it to the floor.

"I told Mama you probably wouldn't want to eat."

"I'm not hungry but I would not eat it anyway," Lacey said. She took a step toward Jane, and Jane could see now that her face had not only grief in it but anger. Jane thought she might strike her.

"I'm so sorry," and then she sobbed, overcome by emotion she couldn't begin to understand.

"What have you got to cry about?" Lacey said.

"I don't know."

Lacey stepped even closer and Jane felt herself let go, let loose, expecting the blow. She wished for it. She wanted to fall to her knees. She needed something to happen to her, something that in some odd way would make sense.

"You think I don't know she or your daddy, one, put something in that whiskey he was drinking? I could tell. He wasn't right. He drunk before but he was different."

And a whole other kind of shock came into Jane then.

"What are you saying?"

"Don't you know he took out that insurance policy on Lon, and on Harris, too? And he stands to make good money on my Lon's death here?"

Jane froze at the words and tried to make sense of it.

"That just doesn't make any sense, Lacey. My papa wouldn't do that."

"Lon said you seen them arguing. Your daddy theatening him."

"But it wasn't like that. It was—well, I don't really know what it was, but it didn't sound like that to me, Lacey, I promise."

"Well, that's what Lon told me he said. Wanted us gone. Lon might have had him a temper but he didn't lie to me."

Jane was speechless again, hearing these words. Lacey stepped closer, close enough that Jane could see her ruined eyes from the crying, the crusty trails of tears on her pale face. She worked her mouth and blinked her eyes. Then she looked straight at Jane.

"What happened between you and him in the woods that day? Don't lie to me. I know he seen you in there. He told me."

"What did he tell you?"

"Said he told you to leave us alone."

Neither said anything for a long minute.

"Did he touch you?" Lacey said. "Did he try to hurt you?"

Jane shook her head, and shook it again. "No. No, he didn't, I swear it."

"And did you tell on him for it? Tell me the truth."

"I swear it, Lacey, I didn't tell a thing."

"What did he say to you?"

Jane felt the tears coming to her eyes again and tried to stop them. When she spoke her voice was clouded with them.

"Nothing, Lacey. He just told me to stay away. Like he just didn't like me. Or us. Like he was mad about y'all being our tenant."

Lacey stared hard at her for a long moment, her eyes moving back and forth on Jane's.

"You tell your daddy and your mama that money ought to go

to me. All of it. I'm the one took care of my husband day in and day out. I'm the one now left with nothing. A widow, at my age."

Jane said quietly, "Okay."

"Now you go on, and take that plate of supper with you."

"It's good food, Lacey. There's nothing wrong with it."

But Lacey only stared at her, saying nothing. She looked over at the body of her husband on the floor beneath the counterpane by the fireplace, then turned and went back into the bedroom.

Jane stood there. She felt a fearful chill, averted her eyes from Lon Temple's covered, still form, grabbed up the plate, and hurried back up the hill to her house.

"She wouldn't take it," her mother said.

"No'm."

"Why didn't you just leave it, case she changed her mind?"

"Mama. She thinks Papa put something into that whiskey Lon was drinking."

Her mother's face went hard.

"Or even that maybe you did."

Her mother's head jerked back and her eyes went sharp.

"What, now?"

"That's what she said. She said it was because of the insurance."

Her mother seemed to gaze, stricken, at something above Jane's head for a minute, then she shook her head and turned toward the counter and leaned against it on her hands. She shook her head again.

"It was my idea, to get that insurance," she said then. "But good lord, it wasn't me or your papa did anything to that boy. He stole whiskey and drove that tractor drunk and fell out. He was bound for a bad end, anyone could see that."

And she stayed there like that as darkness fell and didn't move to light a lamp. Jane left her in there and went back out onto the porch and sat in her father's rocker. In a bit the tree frogs and crickets began to whir and sing. A dog barked, sounded like from a nearby farm, and Top came around the house, barked back once, then went under the porch to settle. Bullfrogs traded notes in their offbeat basso chorus, peepers like playful notes in response.

She couldn't get the image out of her mind, the shape of Temple's body beneath the bloody counterpane. In that dim room.

When her father finally drove up some time later, and the scents from the early supper her mother had made had all but faded as she apparently had not bothered to keep it warm in the stove, she waited for him to reach the porch, then stood up.

He stopped and stood there facing her in the dim light of a half-moon just beginning to rise over the trees.

"What is it, girl?" he finally said.

"Nothing, Papa."

He stood there looking very tired, then went inside, and she followed. Her mother was there beside the fire in the main room working on a quilt. She looked up at him, then at Jane.

"Jane tell you what the Temple girl said to her?"

"No."

She told him.

"Are you going to give the girl any of that money?" Jane's mother said then.

He looked away at the room's back wall for a minute, his long, grave face half obscured in shadow.

"I'll give her some," he said. "I'm the one paid the premiums, to protect his crop." He went back outside. They heard him on the porch, and then descending the steps and walking across the drive toward the work shed.

What Jane had never told anyone was that she had gone down there once in the late afternoon and, before she reached the house, heard them in their bed. She couldn't see in the window, but she heard the sounds they made and was embarrassed to be so stirred by them. And when the sounds died away she took off her shoes so as to sneak away in the gathering dusk as quietly as possible. It had felt low-down, like stealing something from them. But in her heart she had planned to try spying on them again, this time in the dark, when she might get into position to see something. She wanted to see again what she'd seen with Grace and the Barnett boy, and maybe understand better what she was seeing, now that she was older and smarter. So she had crept down several times in the evenings just after supper, sneaked away from the house and went down, and found a place behind a cedar tree whose lower limbs she could spy through, and waited, thinking, *They're a young couple and they must be wanting a baby*. Several times she gave up, as it was taking too long for them to go to bed, and once she was petrified when Lon Temple came out onto their front porch to smoke. But it was always after dark when she went, so she wasn't discovered. It wasn't long into this routine that one evening she saw Lacey light the lamp in their bedroom and then turn it down low, but Jane could still see as she removed a towel wrapped around herself and got into their bed, a bit of a raw-boned girl but fleshy enough in the bottom and legs, and then she noticed Lon Temple standing in the bedroom doorway looking at his wife. She watched him drop his overalls and remove his shirt and get into bed with her. Jane felt the electricity of seeing what she wasn't supposed to see, what no one but this couple was supposed to see. To *be*. She was violating a great privacy, something sacred between the two, but she could not take her eyes away from watching them in the act, which was like what she had seen between Grace and the Barnett boy except that it was tender and slow, and Lacey seemed so vulnerable. It was almost shocking to see Temple act so gently with his wife, as he had always seemed only a man of anger, a man with a temper, impatient. But now he was touching her tenderly, touching her breasts, and with his hand down there, and she was closing her eyes and parting her lips, and she was guiding him into her, and then for a little while Jane was as lost in the act as they were, so that when they finished, and kissed, and pulled themselves apart, she was flooded with feeling as if she had been there with them, that somehow she had embodied them both and experienced what they had. Then she was overcome with shame, a feeling that she had stolen it from them somehow. When in a moment she was brought back to a clear consciousness of herself she saw Lacey sit up in the bed, pull her knees to her breasts, and begin to sob, while Lon first tried to comfort her but she wouldn't accept it, and so he rolled away and snuffed the lamp, turning the room into darkness. In a horror of guilty wonder Jane, barefoot, moved away as quietly and quickly as possible toward her house—just in time, as her mother called out to her from up there. But ever after that she would worry that she had done something terribly wrong, that by watching what she was not supposed to see she had interfered with their effort to have a child, and that Lacey somehow knew and that's why she was crying. *My wife said you been coming around snooping*, Lon had said to her in the woods. And Jane had the awful thought, *Now I have become the monster outside the window, the one who cannot do what normal people who are not monsters can do in loving each other, and I have stolen something human away from them.*

THE NEXT DAY a buckboard with an older man and a younger man came rattling by the house on its way down to the Temple cabin. In a little while it came back up, with Lacey sitting on the seat beside the older man, in full bonnet, and the younger man in the back with Lon Temple's body still under the same counterpane.

Her father stepped off their porch and approached the wagon, which stopped and waited on him. She saw him speaking to Lacey, who would not look at him. The younger man in back was looking at her father with his mouth half open, as if he was thinking of something he might say but couldn't come up with it. The older man looked at her father briefly, then turned his eyes straight ahead again. Then her father held a brown envelope up to Lacey, who sat very still for a moment. Then she took it from his hand, tucked it into her lap. The older man tapped the reins against his horse's backside and the buckboard continued on up their drive and out of sight. Her father watched them go, then came back to the house. He didn't say anything to Jane, and went inside.

In the kitchen he was telling her mother that he planned to let the Swede, a bulky older neighbor who'd given up farming his own small place but still looked strong as a horse, take over half of Temple's place on half shares, and let Harris take the other forty acres, if he felt they could do it. Otherwise, she and Jane would have to help him finish it out if they could. Might have to hire a hand.

"Did you give her all the money, Papa?" Jane said. She set a plate before her father. He gave her a puzzled look.

"I borrowed against that policy to give her something," he said. "The payment won't come right away, takes a while."

He picked up his knife and fork.

"I wouldn't give her all of it, in any case." He looked directly at her. "I would not have bought the policy just for that. Don't you see that doesn't make any sense?"

"What are you going to do with the rest?"

She had no idea how much it might be.

Her father ate a forkful of peas and speared a cut of ham.

"I don't know," he said. "Not like there's anything you can call extra cash these days."

Then he said, "You might need it someday."

"Me?"

He looked at her.

"You might not want to end up spending your whole life on this place, girl."

"Where would I go?"

Her father didn't answer right away. He left off the cold peas and ate the ham with a chunk of cornbread, washed it down with tea.

Then he said, "That would be entirely up to you, now, wouldn't it?"

HE FELT THE DEATH of that young man, the weight of it, more than any of them knew, more than he would let on. Now that he had the insurance money coming he realized he hadn't truly thought out how he would feel on receiving it, blood money it was, no matter how you looked at it, no matter how much that . . . boy . . . brought it on himself with his temper and his foolish behavior, reckless. And thought, too, how it could happen to anyone, and how many times had he been on that tractor or on a mule-pulled rig with those same blades rolling behind him, and him with a snootful of mash? But now here he stood, about to get his hands on a stack of cash money, and he could feel it bring up in him the lesser part of his nature. Greed, pure and simple. But it wasn't just greed for himself, now, was it? It was for them all. And for young Jane. He stood at the edge of the cattle pond, looking at nothing, but turned to look back up at the house and saw her there, playing in the yard with her hoop and stick, chasing the hoop around like she was the little tyke she used to be. Death could move and frighten the young, he figured, but it didn't affect them the way it did their elders, who thought about it every day, and feared it.

He heard the thunk and thwack of the kindling ax out back of the house. Speak of the devil. He could picture his wife back there, working in a blind fury. Where she went when her own mind wouldn't let her be. He wondered idly if one day she would ever, for whatever reason or none, take it to him, in his sleep or as he simply walked right in through the front door. He almost laughed to himself, imagining that.

The Infernal Voices of Reason

When the crash came in '29, the farm soon felt the effect of it. Before it was over, they'd see prices for cattle and crops drop so badly that for some years they would live mostly on the garden, their own corn, the hogs and chickens. Chisolm increased the croppers' percentages in an attempt to help them survive—to keep them from giving it up and leaving everyone all the poorer. He could see the worse times coming by 1930, so he scraped up the money to increase the product of his distillery, and this helped. He declined to charge more in hard times. Charged less for the younger batches. He managed to keep the little store he'd used to supply his neighbors and sharecroppers, even though it did less business. He even gave a little credit every now and then, taking the man's word that he'd pay him somehow, when he could. He sold only the occasional cow, not nearly as often as he used to.

He'd always believed that a man could prosper at least modestly if he worked very hard and all the time. And so he worked even harder. And since he knew that if he was drinking he would not work as hard, he tried not to drink. Not too much, anyway. If you were drinking, you did not get to bed when you should.

You could not get up as early as you should. You would not think clearly for much of the day. You would not pay proper attention to your animals. You would not spend time in the winter and on summer evenings mending harnesses, repairing machinery, taking stock of your stores and planning ahead.

So he would try especially hard not to drink in these times, or not too much, even though trading more of his makings kept the temptation high. Generally, when he worried, he drank, and now he worried more than ever. When he felt overwhelmed, he couldn't help it and would drink. His moods became darker and he spent more of his time in front of the fire or on the porch, drinking and smoking one cigarette after another, going over and over what had occurred between him and this person or that, cursing them for making things more difficult for him or cursing himself for letting them do so. If his Mrs. bothered him when he was so engaged, he was quick to tell her to mind her own business and leave him alone. "You don't think you are part of the problem here?" he said. And to himself he cursed her for being nothing but an ornery burden. Hardly even a decent cook and taking in no sewing to speak of these days and not even bothering to peddle butter and eggs for a bit of spending money, so what was a man to do all on his own with nothing left but a bitter, worthless woman as a partner in this world?

He had no more money in the bank to speak of, it was all in land and cattle. Even the money from Temple's death was gone. When the banks and even the wealthy merchants stopped lending to farmers and cattlemen, and beef prices continued to drop along with the prices for crops, things began to shut down. He had done well enough by being careful, parsimonious, and having his whiskey and little store on the side. Now all that was not quite enough. Other farms began to lose their tenants and sharecroppers.

When he was drinking in front of the fireplace in the living room or on the porch, chain-smoking, Jane would come sit with him, making his cigarettes with the little red tin rolling machine, but he was so distracted it was hard to keep the fact of her presence in mind if he wasn't taking one from her little hand. Whenever he had smoked one down, she would build another, and by the time he had tossed the butt of the one into the fireplace or the dry dust of the front yard, she would hand him the next. If they were by the fire he would light it with the end of a stick he kept by his chair, which he would lay into the fire for a moment until it caught, and then bring it up to his cigarette and smoke. If they were on the porch she would strike a kitchen match and hold it up for him, then let the match burn down in her fingers before blowing it out.

He talked to himself even when she was there beside him, forgetting he wasn't alone there with the people who lived in his mind. "Is that what you think, then? I'll tell you what I think about it, and you can have your damned opinion on the matter. But I'll not abide such as that, by God."

Or, quietly, "I have done my best, God knows. I have done my very best. A man can't do better than that."

One time his daughter's small voice intruded on him while he was lost in such conversation, waking him to her presence, and asked him who he was talking to. He was startled out of his distraction and for a moment didn't even recognize her, and it gave him such a fright he felt his heart might stop, and then a different kind of fear when he realized who she was, a fear that flooded through his body into his mind like the shock of sudden freezing cold. He began to tremble so badly that he had to get up and go walk it off, leaving the girl there looking as if she'd seen a ghost.

On the days when he would hitch mules to the buckboard

and take what stock he could trade into town, he would not eat nor drink during the long ride down except for a little jerky and water, stopping at a creek beside the road to let the mules and cattle drink and graze a bit. He would deliver his cows to the market, make his meager deals, have a simple supper at the café next to the stockyard or just a hunk of cheese and a few crackers, and then begin the long ride home, which he would not complete until after dark. And invariably on the long quiet ride, no cattle tethered to the rig and making their sounds of adjustment and discomfort, just the creaking of rigging and suspension springs, the grunting groans of the mules, and the sound of many dissatisfactions and regrets inside his head, voiced aloud to the dark looming trees and shadows along the road, he would begin to drink. If he had made decent money on the sale he might have given in to temptation and bought a bottle of good bootleg rye whiskey from a man who kept it in the trunk of an automobile parked near the stockyard. A nice change of pace from the pure corn. If he had not traded well he would nip from a jug of his own distillation, as he always brought one along just in case he couldn't stand being with himself without it.

On this clear night when the full moon rose into a sky still blue but darkening, he began to sip from the jug he'd brought along, at first corking it between sips and then just squeezing it between his boots on the buckboard planks and sipping more often. On his mind was a man at the stockyard who'd called him a swindler because he'd simply done what he did best: bought a cow that seemed worthless for next to nothing and nursed it back to health and sold it for a decent profit. It was the man he'd bought it from the year before who'd confronted him: "You knew it wasn't sick and could have told me, but you taken advantage and now you're making money off my misfortune."

"It *was* sick and could have gone either way," he said to the man then, and again to himself now, aloud. He hadn't said to the man what he should have, which was, *Ignorance don't come cheap. Neither does foolishness.* He said aloud again now what he *had* said then: "If you don't know enough about your own animal to know it's got promise, don't know enough to keep it healthy on your own, then you get what you deserve, which is to lose the cow and lose money on it. I took my own risk, taking it on." Then the man had said, *You could have said it was a good cow and give me a little neighborly advice on how to bring it on back to health.*

"Horseshit," Chisolm said aloud again now, playing it out in his head and hearing his own words in the quiet night, angry again, but the sound of his words giving him some salve, knowing he'd defended himself with good reason. "I could have been wrong, too. I took a risk. And you think you would have taken my advice? You'd a sold that cow to someone else for more than I paid if you could've, but I gave you more than it was worth because I was willing to take on the risk, and that's because I've taken a risk before, and made it work. You see all these others, you don't see *them* taking risks with a poorly cow. I know you. I been knowing you many years and I know what you would've done and what you would not've. Call me a cheat? Then don't ever look to me for help when you need it. Even when you deserve it.'"

He hit the jug again, stobbered it, and set it between his shoes.

When he got to the creek bridge just below his place, he stopped the rig and assayed the situation, still a bit lost in rumination. But he was just sober enough to dismount from the wagon and lead his team across the narrow wooden structure, then remount and cluck his mules to pull up the hill and turn onto the two-track driveway. Daughter Jane had heard him coming and was waiting to unhitch the mules and lead them to the barn. He saw her glance at the jug hanging from his crooked finger for a second before looking away and saying, "Yes, sir," to his instructions concerning the mules.

Chisolm stood in the yard in the moonlight and took one more long draft from the jug before corking it and walking over to the shed and placing it behind a nail barrel there. Then he went into the house.

His wife was at the fireplace repairing a torn quilt and did not look up at him when he entered. He stopped and stared at her, angry, and only by a hair did he keep himself from taking it out on her, sitting there in her false, infuriating placidity. As if *he* were the problem, whereas if it wasn't for him they'd be eating clay for sustenance. He said nothing but took the few bills and coins from his sale and dropped them into the jar in the cupboard. He went back onto the veranda and out into the yard, made a cigarette, and smoked it, watching the shadows from the coal-oil lamp of Jane and the mules in the barn as she brushed them down and forked some hay into their stalls, then gave them just a bit of field corn, not too much. *Girl's not a bad hand*, he thought.

As the moon had risen high above the farm now, illuminating the plow and disc, harrow, baler, and the high sharp peak of the barn's roof and the shed and outhouse off to the south of the yard and the shadowed chairs on the rough-hewn floor of the veranda, he walked over to the shed and retrieved the jug he'd set there earlier and brought it back to the veranda, where he drank from it and rolled cigarettes until the moon was down at the tips of the pines in its descent. He calmed a bit, but it wasn't long before he resumed his low and angry conversation with demons real and imaginary in his mind. He hardly noticed when his wife came out and fetched the girl, hadn't noticed she'd been over by the door, sitting in the shadows. Hardly heard their sibilant voices just inside the house, listening instead as he was to the louder voices inside his head.

IN THE KITCHEN her mother whispered, "You take care you do not get his ire up." And she looked at Jane with a hard expression until Jane turned and left to go back to bed. Jane could still hear her father talking to himself and his people, a low murmuring that became the murmurings of small crowds of faceless people who had lost their way to wherever they were going and occupied the evening's crepuscular landscape, not understanding they had passed from one kind of living into another, unrecognizable one.

Essentially Normal

Despite Jane's isolation, she began to be interested in boys. It was a slow, gradual accretion, this new awareness. Of boys as *boys*, that is, strange creatures, like another species retaining the general physical qualities of her own but with hidden secrets, secret differences. Significant perhaps in some way to her in particular. She saw them when they passed by in buckboard wagons on the road sometimes, or at the occasional sermon she deigned to attend, and sometimes they would come with their fathers to shop at the store. She wondered, feeling foolish as she did, if they had heard that she often tended the store and had come along so as to see her. She had begun to notice them in a different way. Almost in the way a forest animal or bird, at rest and hidden safely away, may take notice of a new animal walking through its woods, walking upright, carrying with it some strong, exotic scent.

She did have a sense that she herself must be some kind of mysterious creature. People must gossip, for her mother gossiped about other people at times. Grace never had, of course. Grace had despised most of them to the point of disinterest, as far as Jane could tell. Jane could imagine coming upon some boy, somewhere, alone, maybe like in the clearing where she'd seen Grace meet and do it with the Barnett boy. They would both stop in their tracks, surprised. He would come closer to her. But then unlike the dumb Barnett boy he would be like Lon Temple with Lacey, tender, and would ask if he could touch her, but in innocent ways, on the cheek or her arm or hand.

This was all soon accompanied by a kind of discomfort, a swelling or tightness in her lower belly, like things being squeezed up in there, and when she mentioned it, her mother stopped what she was doing and looked at her with eyebrows raised, and it seemed to Jane that she was looking at her in a way she hadn't before. When a few days later she noticed what looked like blood in her diaper, she was frightened. Her mother said she needn't worry, but seemed not to know how to talk to her about it and looked worried enough about it herself.

Soon followed a visit by Dr. Thompson, who sat her down and asked her some questions, examined her bloody diaper, and probed at her belly with his long, knuckly fingers.

"Well," he said, "you are becoming a woman, after all."

"What do you mean, 'after all'? Besides, I'm only fourteen years old."

"Comes to lots of girls even younger, and some closer to your age. A few even later, though rarely. Depends on the individual. Anyway," he said, and sat to look her in the eye, "it is a good thing. In your case, see, even though we believed you wouldn't have trouble with it, we couldn't be entirely sure. Reasonably sure but not absolutely."

"What kind of trouble?"

"I was concerned about the possibility of a blockage. Of the blood not being able to come out."

"That doesn't sound good."

"It could have been a serious problem. But now I don't believe we have to worry about that anymore." He pulled his pocket watch from his vest pocket, checked it, then settled himself in his seat, looked squarely at her again, and explained to her as best he could about menstruation. Though he didn't talk beyond the bodily mechanics of it.

"And it happens for the rest of your life?" she said.

"No, at some point in a woman's life, later on, it stops. And then she can no longer have children. It's a natural thing because then she's too old to have children without endangering her life or the child's."

She sat looking back at him, wondering whether to tell her secret. His kind, familiar, and calm gray eyes then set it free, and she said, "I know how people make babies."

"Well, I did give you that pamphlet drawing, but of course there's more to it than that."

"I know that, too."

He said nothing, his own bushy eyebrows gone up.

"I have to wonder how you know it."

She told him, after making him promise he wouldn't tell, about Grace and the Barnett boy. She didn't tell him just then about Lon and Lacey Temple.

"I see," he said.

"How come Grace didn't have a baby, then, from that?"

"It does not always result in a child. Sometimes it just doesn't take."

"I know it won't ever happen to me."

Again he was gazing at her in that way he had of making her feel she could trust him with just about anything. Then he sat back and cleared his throat, and looked down at his hands as if to see that he held something curious there.

"Well. I believe that you have everything you're supposed to have, inside. But whether or not you will ever have children—" He stopped and just looked at her for a long moment, which made her scalp prickle. "I guess I should speak plainly. It would be hard for a man to deal with the way you're different. And even though you have everything inside of you that you need, I don't know that the act of intercourse—that is what happened between your sister and that boy—would actually be possible, or at least not in a way that would result in your conceiving a child. Or if you did, I'm not sure you'd be able to carry it through gestation—the time it takes to grow inside you before coming out into the world."

"I know that, too."

"Do you, Janie?"

She didn't answer, thinking. It was coming on late afternoon, and for a moment it was like she was in a dream she sometimes had, where it's the gloaming coming on and the trees are a beautifully darkened green and the sounds in their shadowed crowns begin to rise like some kind of otherworldly singing inside of herself.

Yet outside the window now the trees were nearly bare in their early December secret trembling.

He put a hand on her shoulder.

"You're essentially a normal child, Jane, as I've said. Complicated, but essentially normal." He looked at her. "I'll bring you something more to read about all this, what we've talked about. With more pictures. It'll help you understand."

He told her not to lose hope. That one day there would be a way to fix her. He just couldn't say when.

"I believe it," he said. "Maybe it's wrong for me to say so, because I can't say when. But I believe there will one day be a way."

"I don't deserve it," she said. Then she couldn't speak.

"Don't say that. Here, now." He gave her a clean handkerchief. "Why would you say a thing like that?"

She told him about spying on Lon and Lacey Temple and how she was afraid she had somehow tainted their union by doing it, and how Lacey had wept, as if she knew they had been tainted.

Dr. Thompson sat quietly, waiting her out. When her eyes cleared, he was gazing at her, a look a bit sad but simply calm, too.

"How could you not be curious?" he said then. "Natural curiosity. There was no harm in it. Not for you, anyway. For a grown-up, yes. But you are a special person. Just as the way you are denies you some things, it also gives you license that others may not have. In my opinion you live on a higher moral ground. I mean to say you are a good person. You were not being bad, doing that. You were trying to learn about things. And about yourself."

"But how come they never had children, then? They'd been married long enough."

After a pause, the doctor said, "Have you ever wondered why Lett and I never had children? We were certainly married long enough."

She looked at him, not knowing what to say. Why had she never wondered about that?

"I am not able to have a child, Janie," he said. "We tried. We did what you do, as you said, to make babies. But to use the phrase I used about Grace, it 'did not take.' And it's because I am infertile. Like one of your pecan trees that won't produce pecans sometimes. Or an ornamental fruit tree, a pear or peach, looks like any other pear or peach tree but no pears or peaches." He smiled. "I hope that doesn't embarrass you. But know this: You had nothing to do with those two young folks not having a baby. And like as not young Lacey knew why they couldn't get pregnant. It had nothing to do with you, but with one of them. And that's why she was crying, hon. Not because of some spell. Life is not fair in that way or any other way. We are who and what we are. It's just what it is."

FOR SOME TIME after that she was lost in a kind of distraction, focused on this most strange business of menstruation. The idea that she was becoming a woman in that way, but in another way could never be. She noticed *others*. The peculiarity of their different shapes. For the first time since she'd been weaned of nursing, she thought again about breasts. The doctor had said that hers would begin to change. There was a lumpish thickness beneath her nipples, hardly noticeable in the mirror but evident to the touch. It occurred to her that, compared to her mother, her sister was quite buxom. She remembered the Barnett boy placing his hands there, which she had thought odd, but Grace had moaned in a way that sounded like pleasure, and lain down and made him hurry up and do what he was going to do.

The next summer she looked for and found another of the infamous stinkhorn mushrooms. The cap on this one was black and did indeed stink. She broke it off at the base and looked until she found a mushroom that looked vaguely, very vaguely, like the drawings Dr. Thompson had shown her of the female parts. She looked around to make sure no one had followed her, then carefully pressed the stinkhorn into the other mushroom, pushed it inside there as far as it would go, and then sat for a while, pondering. Moved it back and forth a little bit, then felt silly. Before she left the spot, she tossed the stinkhorn into some bushes where no one would see it.

Somehow all of this made her feel more alone in the world than she had up to that point. Her dog Top had gotten old, and in her distractions she'd hardly noticed it happening. But then she did, and he was obviously old. Gray-bearded, creaky. She couldn't understand it.

"Dog ages a lot faster than a man," her father said. "You knew that."

"I guess I forgot," she said.

And it wasn't much longer before Top went away. She called to him for an hour that afternoon, all around the place and down into the woods, but he didn't come. Nor the next morning. Her father said dogs sometimes did that, just went off to die.

"Papa. You didn't take him off, like you did with Hound, did you?"

He looked astonished.

"Lord, no, girl. He was your dog, not mine. I wouldn't have done that." He looked perturbed, bothered by the question, like it was an accusation. "Unless you'd asked me to," he added.

"I'm sorry," she said. "I didn't mean to say I thought you'd done that."

She waited several days, hoping Top had just gone off on some kind of odd dog journey and would come back around. But he didn't. Spring arrived in its first stealth, then its open leafing and blooming. She felt something change inside her, felt her old companion's absence like a weight in her heart. She mourned him.

DURING ONE OF his periodic examinations that summer, Dr. Thompson palpated her abdomen. "Any discomfort there?" he said. No. "There?" No. Then, after pausing his hands a moment, he began palpating a little lower down. "Any discomfort here, Jane?" She said nothing, then placed her hand over the doctor's and said, "Wait." The doctor gently took his hand from beneath hers and stood back, removed the stethoscope tips from his ears and hung them around his neck, and looked at her for a long moment before nodding to himself and gathering his bag to leave.

"It would do you no harm should you decide to examine yourself, in privacy, of course," he said as he was walking toward the doorway. "No harm in becoming more familiar with your own body as you grow on." And then, without turning around, he took his leave.

After that, sometimes, during her walks in the woods, she would lie back on a bed of fallen leaves (after checking for poison ivy growing among them) and palpate herself in that place until the strange and pleasant sensation returned and a shivering rush of blood ran through her entire body and it was as if she blacked out for a long moment, and when she came to, the world was almost a surprise there all around her, and she lay tingling and warm in a way that she never had before she had this thing she could do to herself.

She didn't do it very often. The fear that her father or mother or even a stranger might come upon her while she was blacked out like that was too alarming. It would be too embarrassing to ever recover from. And she couldn't help but feel it must be shameful despite the doctor's words, because it felt too good, and *down there*, and the lingering pleasure was always interrupted by the fear of discovery that brought her back to her senses and hurrying back to the house.

IN A LETTER to Ellis Adams in Baltimore, the doctor described the examination and again reminded him to keep his ears open and to let him know if there were any new developments that might be used to help Miss Jane Chisolm, developments that would change the current prognosis. To let him know if anyone figured out a way to work with or around the problems posed by her particular condition.

It would seem the strangest thing to me, he wrote, *to have everything a normal person is supposed to have in that regard yet know it is trapped inside my own skin and all but inaccessible to anyone or even anything beyond my own blood, other bodily fluids, the microscopic eyes we might imagine to exist in the very cells that make up what and who we are.*

Do You Like What You See,
Who You Are?

〰️

The farm next to theirs on the west side was owned by a family named Key. One of them was a boy about her age, maybe a bit older, slim, with fair skin, sandy hair, and oddly beautiful pale blue eyes, not the deep dark blue of her own. And though she remembered him from her brief time in school as just another boy, not someone who'd made any more impression then than anyone else, now he set off a blushing, tingling feeling in her when they looked at one another in the store, the boy silent as his father gathered their few supplies and she totted them up. He looked back at her when they left and gave her a little wave that, when he'd shut the door, she thought might send her heart into a flutter-flump.

On her wandering one day she came up next to the boundary between their two farms, and saw one of the family hoeing weeds in the cornfield there. She thought it was him, that boy. He wore a broad straw hat, so she couldn't quite see his sandy blond hair. She knew he had brothers. But when he got closer she could make out his features, and she stepped from the undergrowth and up to the

barbed-wire fence at the edge of the field. In a minute he seemed
to see her, stood up straight, turned away for a moment, then
turned back and waved. She waved back. He set down his hoe
and made his way through the dozen or so rows between them
over to her, walking carefully. He wore a loose white work blouse,
worn denim overalls, and a pair of old ankle boots that he stopped
to shuck off before he reached her. He wiggled his bare white toes
and looked over at her as if he may have embarrassed her, doing
that, for some reason. And the look gave her that flushed feeling
so suddenly that she felt herself having an accident, and so the
feeling turned to shock, her face burning, and she called out, "I'll
come back here tomorrow sorry I have to run I forgot something
important," and she dashed back into the woods and ran all the
way home, nearly in tears from embarrassment.

She didn't stop at the house but went straight to the creek in
the woods down the hill behind it. She was so overfull with emotion she couldn't sort out, didn't sort out in the course of her
running so hard she could hardly breathe. When she got to the
creek she immediately pulled up her dress, unpinned her diaper,
wiped herself with a clean part of it, and plunged it into the creek.
The bottom was sand, so she scrubbed it against the grit, then
took wet handfuls of it and scrubbed straight into the soiled cloth
until there was nothing but a dim stain that would take strong
soap and baking soda to get out. She wrung it as dry as she could,
fastened the pins into a part of it, sniffed her hands, took off her
shoes, lifted her dress again, and lowered her bottom into the
creek for a minute, the cool water running over her skin, a shock
and then a pleasure. She stood up, calmer now, and walked back
up the hill to the house.

She got soap and baking soda from the basin on the back porch,
made a paste of the soda and water, but then she thought, *What*

if he is still there? Then, *What if he isn't there tomorrow?* She hast-
ily washed her hands and, not even bothering to dry herself,
began running down the drive and then through the pasture,
still barefoot, dodging sharp sticks and fallen pine cones, one eye
out for snakes, toward the narrow ridge of woods between their
properties.

She came out of the brush and stopped, out of breath. He was
not in the field. She could not see the hoe where he must have
laid it down. She felt tears coming up again, this time from anger,
then heard his voice call out to her. She looked to her right and he
was sitting beneath an oak tree not a stone's throw away, his feet
still bare, a jar of what looked like tea beside him, and eating a
sandwich. Probably ham or bacon with fresh tomato slices or just
the tomatoes. And then she was impressed that he was eating a
light bread sandwich in the middle of the week. Her family ever
only had light bread on the weekends, on Sundays, and would
finish it easily by the evening meal. She called out to him, and
waved, feeling awkward.

"Come on over," he called back. "You hungry?"

She walked toward him, staying on her side of the fence. And,
nearing him, was suddenly mortified realizing she hadn't put on a
fresh undergarment and was naked beneath her dress. She stopped
still, feeling the blood rush to her face, but luckily it caused no
accident, and when he looked at her curiously, grinning in a ques-
tioning way, she tried to put the thought of her near-nakedness
out of her mind and went on toward him. She was just a girl, after
all, with no big hips to poke a dress out, no big bush of hair down
there to pooch obscenely against the dress like she'd seen it do on
Grace when Grace sat on the porch after a bath wearing nothing
but a summer skirt herself, to cool down, the wet spot on the
front of her dress gradually drying in the heat. Until her mother

came and saw that and sent her inside with harsh words about the nature of her character. Grace said, "Well, who in Hades is going to be watching me sitting on a porch here in the middle of nowhere, I might ask?"

"God sees you," her mother had said once, in as cool a tone as Jane had ever heard her use with anyone. Like you couldn't be sure if she really believed God cared about such a thing or not but it was something she could use on you if she wanted.

Grace had said back, just as cool, "Does he like what he sees?"

And her mother had slapped Grace, not hard, but in a way that ended their exchange. Grace went inside and put on some underpants and a bra and shoes and took herself out to the barn, her brooding place.

NOW JANE WAS STANDING just a few feet away from the Key boy, though still on her side of the barbed wire, and he stood up. Remembering Grace, she glanced down in fear of seeing her own dress wet from dipping herself in the creek but somehow it was not. She looked up again. Except for his hair being smashed down on his head from sweating in his hat, and the fading flush of his skin from the heat as he sat now in the shade of the oak tree, he was the same boy she saw in the store.

"You're Jane Chisolm."

"I don't know your name, except your last name," she said.

"Elijah Key." He stepped over with his hand held out as if to shake, like with a man. She took it and returned his grip.

"Nice grip, for a girl. Most girls just kind of, you know," and he made a pansy-like motion with his hand.

"I don't really hang out with any girls," she said.

"I know," he said, letting the words out slowly like the release of a breath. Looking at her with his head cocked just a bit back on his neck. But not unsmiling.

"I guess people must talk about me."

He shrugged, glanced at the corn he'd have to be hoeing again in a few minutes.

"I don't listen to rumors."

"What kind of rumors do you not listen to?"

He looked down, suppressed a grin, and shook his head.

"I don't know," he said. "Nothing true, I imagine, you think about who all it comes from, that sort of thing. I don't put any mind to it. It's girls that talk the most, and I don't have much to do with the girls at school."

"You don't seem to like girls too much."

"No, it's just some girls. Mostly the popular girls."

"What's the matter with them?"

"Nothing. They're just . . . kind of mean-spirited sometimes," and he waggled his head, shrugged. "I don't know. Knuckleheads."

"I thought only boys got called knuckleheads."

"Huh," he said. "Maybe so."

Then he said, "So how come you decided not to go to the school?"

Now she wished she hadn't approached him. She said, "I'd have figured those rumors would cover that."

"It's been a long time," he said then. "I don't even remember them, really. I'm sorry for bringing it up."

She didn't say anything, wanting to walk away now but unable to make herself do it.

"I used to hate it—school, I mean," he said. "That's one thing I thought about you before. That you were lucky they let you quit. Whyever they did."

"You like it better now?"

"It's getting a little better," he said. "So don't you know how to read and write?"

"Yes, I do."

"So you learned that without even a whole year of school. Yeah, I remember you coming just that one fall, but you were just first grade and I was already in fourth. I've seen you at church every now and then. You must not like it much, either, no more than you go."

She shrugged. "It's all right."

"What about numbers?"

"What about them?"

He laughed. "How'd you learn numbers without school?"

"Tending my papa's store."

"That's what I thought."

He looked at her for a moment with that curious smile again.

"You've just about grown up. You don't have a secret boyfriend, do you?"

"I don't have any friends at all."

He looked almost alarmed at that. Then as if he were thinking. Then as if he couldn't decipher his own thoughts into a reply. Then, "I guess it's hard to have any friends out in the country, if you don't go to school. I guess it was that way for everybody, back when they didn't even have schools up here, and folks had big families. They just got along knowing each other."

"That's the way it is with me, I guess."

"I guess they'd know some people from going to church, though."

"I guess so."

"But you don't have to do that very often, either. I'm feeling a little jealous of your freedom."

"Huh," she said, then shut her mouth.

"Are you an atheist?" he said then.

"What's that?"

"I thought you were smart."

"I just never heard of it."

"It's somebody doesn't believe in God."

"No, then. Though I really haven't thought about it. I just thought everybody believed in God."

"Well, everybody I know *says* they do."

Then they were silent and awkward for a minute. She realized she was staring at him. He squinted at her.

"Don't do that," she said, teasing. "I can't see your pretty blue eyes." Then she couldn't believe she'd said that.

He blushed and looked down, then reached into his bib pocket and pulled out a pair of thick-lensed wire-rimmed eyeglasses, hooked the earpieces over his ears.

"I hate wearing them," he said, with a kind of gloomy grin. "I was hiding them, didn't want you to see."

"I saw you take them off one time before y'all came into the store."

"Oh. Well." He looked at her again. "My pretty blue eyes are blind as a bat."

"They just got bigger and bluer," she said, and they laughed.

"I'm glad I put them on, now, so I can see yours. They look like—I've never seen blue eyes like yours. They almost don't seem real."

"Well, they are. My papa and Dr. Thompson told me they haven't changed a bit since I was born. I guess that's a little unusual." And thought, *Like everything else about me.*

"Do you know about the dances?" he said.

"What dances?"

"The ones at the community center. Damascus."

"Oh. Right. Grace told me." They were at a loss for a brief while, like social animals, after a greeting, gone into other distractions.

Then he said, "Are you happy with it?" Kind of soft-voiced, like he didn't know how she'd respond.

"With what?" she said, her own voice quieter, too.

He hesitated, then shrugged again, glanced back at the corn, said, "Everything, I guess. Your life."

She didn't know what to say. She'd never put a word to the sadness she could sometimes feel, especially in the last couple of years, that would linger at the edge of her thoughts like the invisible ghost of someone she thought she recognized but didn't know who it was, some kind of familiar she couldn't quite grasp.

SHE COULD TELL he liked her. She would see him, in the store, or passing with his family on the road near their house, and other times like the first time they talked, when she would bring a little bite to eat and think of it secretly as their picnic. In her mind their encounters were episodes in a casual courtship. Yet it occurred to her that he probably didn't think of them that way at all. And she was embarrassed and felt foolish, and worried that he may have told others—boys, if not girls—about his occasional odd visits with the mysterious girl Jane Chisolm.

She didn't want him to think that way about her.

And so, during the autumn she turned sixteen, she began going to the community dances. Elijah Key had told her about them and, slowly, a desire to take part had grown stronger in her until it became a resolve to do so. She was tired of being alone. She realized that, aside from her occasional, innocent encounters with Elijah Key, she'd been bored for some time. Maybe the encounters weren't so innocent, if she looked forward to them so much. And sometimes planned them, truth be told. Well, she always did. She would not eat or drink anything on the morning of a day she thought she might run into him. So she could linger with him for a while without worry.

She had been a spritely young girl, slim and a bit lank-haired but with a sweet face and good humor, but by now had grown taller and begun to take on a gaunt, dark-eyed beauty, and moved with a kind of natural grace, as a leaf will fall gracefully from a tree in barely a breeze.

When she made up her mind to attend the dances, her parents were surprised, but she seemed to want it so much they gave reluctant permission. "It's only going to be a heartbreak one day," her mother said.

"It's just dances."

"What about when you get older than the others and have to stop going or look foolish?" her mother said. "And I don't know how you're going to manage it, anyway, you know."

"It's just working against the loneliness," her father said, "like any child living on a farm." His wife said nothing and returned to her work.

She and her father stood there on the porch, silent, looking out at nothing. He seemed slack-jawed, not so much silent as mute. His eyes empty.

"Are you all right, Papa?"

He took his hat off and ran a hand through his hair, made a grimace, put the hat back on.

"Nothing to worry about, daughter," he said. "You go on to those dances, try to have yourself a good time. Of course, I'll be keeping an eye on you, if you don't mind."

He went on down the steps, as if there were really nothing

more to say. Or nothing more he knew how to. She watched him disappear into the shadows of the work shed, head down, maybe mumbling to himself.

For an entire two days before the evening of a dance, she fasted. First thing on the first morning, she dosed herself with castor oil followed by a little buttermilk, just to have something on her stomach, and stayed in the privy until she felt herself emptied out. She spent the entire next day beneath a tree in the middle of the pecan grove, or beside the fishing pond, or lying in the middle of her favorite little clearing in the woods. She would take along a piece of bread and maybe bacon, but scattered the bread for the birds, tossed the bacon to the fish or along a trail for some fox or stray dog to surprise upon.

Not thinking. Just being, or simply being, Jane. As when she was younger. On the first day she would allow herself to sip a little water from time to time.

At some point in the second day there would be an almost hal- lucinatory clarity in her vision, in the presence of things around her, in the sounds, of birds and farm work and dogs barking, the sounds of the livestock, and of people talking.

Even the breezes gently rustling leaves in the trees made a sound that seemed to fill her mind in an intoxicating way, as if the very tips of the leaves were tickling her awareness, a temptation of the senses that she allowed to wash through her, to flush her with calm anticipation.

This had not just a little to do with her strange, alluring grace in those days.

She walked about in such a dreamy, distracted state that her mother let her know that she'd checked her laudanum bottle to make sure the girl had not got into it.

The afternoon before her first dance her mother said to her, "You can't get too friendly with these boys, Jane."

Jane said nothing, just listening, oddly calm in a way her mother seemed to find unsettling.

So she went on, "Do you understand? You've long known it."

When Jane only smiled, her mother stood up in mild exasperation to walk away. As she did she said, "You have to be careful. It might not only be you that gets hurt."

"Dr. Thompson said he believes they'll be able to fix me one day. I could have a regular life with a man someday." Though he hadn't said exactly that.

Her mother stopped and looked at her long and silently.

"Believing is a matter of faith," she said. "Not certainty."

Jane had never seen the look in her eyes she saw then. She almost looked empty. And for the first time Jane could remember, she saw her mother as a woman whom life had made not just hard but also exhausted and plain. Older-looking than her years.

Then, as if she could read the unspoken words in Jane's eyes, her mother's expression darkened again. Her own eyes glistened, about to shed tears.

"What would you know about 'life with a man'? And what of your little experience in this world would make you think it such a fine thing?"

Jane watched her go out the back door, feeling more sad for her than abashed at being upbraided. Her mother's words weren't able to dispel the deeply calm pleasure she felt in these new days, this new self.

She did not wear a diaper to the dance, only a little padding as if for possible light menstruation, so there were no bulky undergarments to interrupt her slim figure or graceful movements, and she'd made herself a light, more slim-fitting dress and wore a pair of shoes her father had bought for her in town after drawing an outline figure of her foot on a sheet of school paper to show the shoe salesman there. They were hardly more than slippers with a low heel.

She attended two dances before any of the boys got up the courage or got past their bashful curiosity to ask her to dance, but that was good, since it allowed her to study their movements so she could mimic them later. And then, finally, Elijah Key did ask her. She had seen him standing against the wall in the shadows of dim light from the Japanese lanterns the organizers had hung in the hall. He wasn't wearing his glasses and probably had no idea she was there. A little later she saw him again, spectacles on, looking at her. Maybe someone had mentioned her. Seeing her seemed to surprise him into something like shyness. Then, when she let her attention wander that second night, wander as it tended to do in her state of mind, she looked up and there he was, standing in front of her and holding out his hand. After he danced with her, some of the other boys also began asking her onto the floor. She felt something then she'd never felt before. The pleasure of flirtation, though she didn't even know the word. The boys liked her, and she liked them. But if any one of them seemed about to like her too much, she had her way of withdrawing just enough. Like a scrap of paper the wind keeps breezing just out of reach. Her oddly calm, distracted state seemed to fascinate them into stupid muteness, and when she would fix her gaze upon her partner that boy looked dumbstruck, as if thinking he might be falling in love. But she was so obviously democratic in the dispensation of her new, strange charm that none of them was moved to any sort of foolish words.

She could see Elijah watching her when she danced with other boys, her light thin figure in her homemade dress, her straight dark hair long and loose, her darkling blue eyes. She could see the stick-thin figure of her father, too, hat held in both hands, in the moonlit doorway.

She kept a few sprigs of mint leaves in the pocket of her dress, chewed them gently, then stored them in her cheek, as a man might a small bit of chewing tobacco. The mint kept her dehydration from giving her bad breath, and drew what moisture there was in her body to her mouth and her lips, allowing some minimal conversation. She smiled and laughed with the boys who danced with her, and seemed happy. In the pale quivering candlelight their faces seemed luminous, their voices melodic, just a bit out of sync with the modest movements of their lips in speech.

She was hardly even conscious of how the other girls were now jealous, and certainly couldn't be bothered to care. It flickered in and out of her awareness, a coruscation of whispers and glares.

When she danced with Elijah Key, she was happiest. He would speak to her softly, leaning close to her ear: "How did you decide to start coming out like this? You're so pretty. But you seem a little strange."

"I am strange," she said.

So she delighted, allowed herself to be delighted, in this attention, in the public intimacy with Elijah Key, in her flirtation with other boys, in the flaunting of herself before the other girls. Even though she knew this was something with no long life ahead of it, she was able to press into the moments of pleasure in the movements of her own body. She understood somehow that she was lucky in her special way to love these events without the complicated, pressing question of physical love, to absorb life from the center and its periphery at once, so she could for a while take it all in with the sweet fullness of the entirely human and the utterly strange, without apprehension or fear.

Some Other Ghost

Chisolm stood in the open double doorway and watched as the young folks made their awkward ways together. He was glad to see that the boys still acted like gentlemen with the girls, the way it had been when he was young. He pulled his hat down low on his brow so he wouldn't seem to be staring, but he kept his eyes on his daughter, sitting there in a chair off to herself a bit, and even that made his heart heavy in his bony chest. It was hard for him not to feel he was somehow responsible for the child's condition. He was ten years older than his wife and she'd been too old to have another, yet he'd had his way with her. Drunk. Too tight-fisted to buy a fling with a two-dollar whore. And the curse of it all coming down not on him, not on the wife, no matter how they both felt that at times. It came down on this girl here. Innocent. Pretty. And pretty much doomed to a disappointing life lived alone. But here she was, game, willing to risk her pride just to be like everyone else for a while. To be a regular girl going to a dance, dancing with boys.

The community center had been a large old barn, and everyone had pulled together to shore it up between his youth and Jane's. Gone was the old hayloft where couples would sometimes sneak away for a little sparking. Now it was entirely open to the high ceiling, like a rustic cathedral, and there were polished wooden floors instead of hard-packed earth still smelling faintly of cattle and horse manure. When he'd met Ida at one of these dances almost forty years earlier he'd been about as full of himself as a twenty-seven-year-old farmer and aspiring cattleman could be, living as a single man working land his father had sold him without interest, on time. He knew he would do well. And feeling that way made others think the same about him. If he'd been the man he was now, mentally anyway, he never would've got her attention, and maybe that would have been a good thing, except that who knows what worse may come down the pipe at any time?

The old loft doors were thrown open to let out the heat, draft a breeze. The light came from crude Japanese lanterns and candles inside flues on stands affixed to the walls. So the light was adequate but romantically soft. The same as when he'd been young. Some of the ladies involved in the restoration had argued for keeping it that way. The men pretended not to be sentimental and argued for gas lamps but they'd given way easy enough. Who wasn't sentimental about his romantic youth? And now his daughter was making sure she had it, even though it would no doubt be brief, and end with a swift finality that would indeed be hard to endure.

After his daughter's first time there, when no one had ventured to ask her onto the floor, they rode home in silence. He thought she was trying not to cry, doing a damn good job of it. Just knowing that made it hard for him to control his own emotions.

And so he was relieved, his heart felt lifted, lighter, when at the second dance he saw the Key boy go over and speak to her, hold out his hand, lead her onto the floor. He was worried about that boy, but in the moment grateful, too. Then he remembered the first time—maybe it was the first time, hard to know for sure after all the years—laying eyes on young Ida McClure, only to see she was standing still and flagrantly staring at him and didn't bother to avert her eyes when he caught her at it. Gave him such an instant rise he'd had to step out and subside before going back in, his will set against an obvious passion, to ask her to dance. Yet when they'd got on the floor it happened again and she brushed against him, he'd thought by accident but later realized it probably wasn't, and locked her eyes on his in a way that just about took him over the edge.

Now he wanted to rush onto the floor and grab his daughter by the hand and pull her out of there, but summoned the restraint to stay where he was, peering at them to detect anything improper. It didn't seem so. She looked flat-out blissful, and the boy seemed happy and bashful.

Well, of course he didn't have a flagrant seductress by the hands out there, like he, Sylvester Chisolm, had nearly forty years ago. You could look back on a love and recall so clearly when it was good, joyful, wild. And also in some gray area you retained the images and moments marking decline. How could a man keep a woman from hating him for the very thing she wanted from him in the first place? Especially if both were disposed to darkness of spirit? How had he not known it, when they were young? Or maybe the question was, how had he managed to ignore the truth? Well, when you're young you want what you want, right then, and that would be the simple truth of it.

It was over, then, the members of the little band putting away their instruments, people bustling to wagons, a few trucks and cars. He let Jane and the Key boy talk for a bit, not minding as long as he was looking on nearby, not minding that the others were clearing out, as he disliked a crowding of vehicles as much as if not more than a crowding of pedestrians all trying to get somewhere or away. And on the way home she still seemed as she'd seemed on the dance floor, just full of bliss, and not talky except to say, "Thank you, Papa, I had such a good time."

"You enjoy the dancing, then."

"Oh, I do," she said. "So much. I've never had so much fun."

"Not even as a little girl, when you had no cares?"

"Not even," she said. "But even a little child has worries."

"I guess I'd forgotten that, if it's so. I guess most grown-ups do forget, at some point." After a bit he said, "And you have no worries now, about how all this might turn out?"

She didn't answer, and looked away, so he let her be. They were quiet the rest of the brief ride home then, his thoughts drifting away as they tended to do more and more often. He sat alone on the front porch, smoking and sipping a bit. Jane came out to sit with him for a little while, unable to go straight to sleep. Then she kissed him on the cheek and went in. His wife came out momentarily. He looked up at her standing there.

"She had a good time," he said finally, after she'd said nothing. Her expression didn't change. She went back in. He took a long drink, coughed, rolled another smoke. He heard a dog barking off somewhere, maybe at the Key place, and thought about old Hound. How had Jane known he'd put the dog down, back then? He hadn't spoken of it at all. He'd noticed the dog losing weight, walking like a cripple, eyes looking in pain, though he wagged his tail when Chisolm took up his rifle. Said he was going deer hunting and walked far down into the woods with the dog hobbling along, grabbed a shovel from his still shed along the way. They walked through the woods and out into the far pasture there and over to the very far edge of that. When he stopped walking, the dog plopped down, exhausted. He knelt next to him, stroked his forehead with a thumb. The dog looked up at him without raising his head.

"You got a broad forehead here," he'd said to the dog, whose long ears lifted just the slightest at the words, then fell. "So you been around people a long time, you and those you came down from. What they say. People like a dog they can pet. Partial to the ones with your wide-set eyes." The dog looked up at him again, but only a moment, too tired to even move his eyes anymore.

So then he'd done what he had to do. Out of kindness, he liked to think.

And when he'd gone back to the house with no deer and no dog, no one had said anything to him about it. Nor he to them.

ELIJAH TOOK TO riding over on Sunday afternoons on his bicycle to see her, and walked with her down to the pond and along the fences of the grazing pastures. The first time, they walked down to the edge of the woods bordering the lower pasture. Jane could hear her mother calling and could see her small figure up on the hill at the edge of their yard. They laughed and crossed the pasture back up toward the barn, behind the house, and into the leafed-out and budded pecan grove, the arrowhead-leafed shadows darting on the grass and on their faces as they passed through. They started for the barn but heard her mother calling out, closer now, *Jane?* and knew if they went in there she would come hustling up to scold and chaperone or herd them back to the house. So they sat down beneath one of the trees and took in the late spring air and let the breezes slide over them, breezes that felt to Jane like silken water, as if she were in the world but underwater. They looked down over the cattle pond and the stand of pines and small oaks beyond. Jane stole looks at him when she could, as he did at her, and when their eyes met they grinned and Jane felt that feeling run through her that thrilled her and kind of frightened her and, in some way she didn't let herself hold on to, saddened her at the same time. How could a person's face, his whole self, what was after all just an ordinary body, well shaped and good-looking but certainly another mortal walking around, come to seem so beautiful and take over a heart and a mind in that way? He wasn't the only good-looking boy around, nor the only nice or even sweethearted one. But maybe he was. He seemed so, really, to her.

He was a little bashful. He was quiet. He wasn't shy around people in general, it wasn't that. She'd seen him banter and rough-house with the others after church or lately along the wall of those waiting to dance again. But she could tell there was a softer kind-ness in him than most, if not all. So it seemed to Jane. She loved his sandy-colored hair, the smooth skin on his face, his clear blue eyes. He had dimples when he smiled that she imagined he didn't like so much. It would embarrass a boy like him if she were to comment on them, so she held back on that, much as she would have liked to tell him how cute they were. But she was smart enough to know that boys didn't like to be called cute.

She felt a little drunk. She'd had only a sip of buttermilk and a bite of bacon that morning, the only food in three days and the only thing besides a little water in two. She knew that was overly careful, and a longer stretch than usual, but the fasting had become a habit, one she enjoyed. In this state, an elevated sense of physical lightness and mental clarity, the Elijah Key sitting next to her seemed to be almost as much like something in a dream as in real life.

He looked at her, just a slight grin on his lips, head cocked back a bit the way he did.

"Are you all right?" he said.

She nodded her head. She wasn't saying much of anything, to tell the truth. She nibbled the end of a stalk of Johnson grass she'd plucked on the way to the grove. The taste was sour and sweet at the same time.

He continued to look at her. The grin widened.

"What?" she said.

"Sometimes you seem like you've been hypnotized or something."

"What's that like?"

He'd seen one in town once, he said. A hypnotist. But it didn't seem real. It seemed phony in an odd way. The hypnotist would do something like ask a person to close his eyes and he would talk to them in this lullaby way, not singing, just talking real quietly, or calm, or he might do that thing where he swung a pocket watch on its chain back and forth while he was talking and made the person go into a trance, and they would do anything he said to do.

"What kind of things?"

"Silly things, mostly. Like go over and drink a glass of water that's not really there. I don't know. I got bored at some point. But I thought it was funny the way the people would kind of go out of it, like they weren't all there."

"I'm all here."

"I didn't mean that. Anyway, when the hypnotist wanted to bring the man or woman out of the *trance*, he would snap his fingers in front of their face, like this," and he snapped his fingers in front of Jane's face. She laughed.

He got up and walked in a kind of slow circle in front of where she sat, hands in pockets, toeing at a fallen nut or twig here and there. He wore a pair of old Keds without socks and he kicked out of them and spread his toes in the grass.

"I could go barefoot all the time," he said. "One thing I don't like about working or going to school is wearing shoes."

"I bet they'd let you dance at the dances without shoes."

"I bet I'd get my toes stepped on all the time, 'cause that happens with shoes on, anyway."

"I've never stepped on your toes."

"No, you're the best dancer, you really are."

She looked away, embarrassed.

"I mean it. You're a natural."

"Do you like me?"

After a moment—"Yes."

"Is that why you like me, 'cause I'm a good dancer?"

"That's one thing I like *about* you."

"What else do you like about me?"

He grinned and laughed, worked his shoes back onto his feet without using his hands, buying time or thinking.

"What?"

He hesitated, then reached up to take off his glasses and put them into his pocket. As if he was embarrassed to see her with the full clarity of vision they gave him.

"All right. Well. You're pretty. And you're nice. You're not stuck up like other pretty girls, or most of them anyway. You don't talk a lot of junk."

"Maybe I don't have much to say."

"I'd bet you do. You just don't talk just for the sake of jabbering on. Sometimes I think most girls jabber on so much because they're afraid of not talking, or being with somebody and just being quiet. But that's when you can really see somebody, when they're quiet."

He stopped and looked at her.

"Do you ever do that with animals, just sit and watch them, not saying anything, and just let everything get quiet until you can kind of hear everything, everything you couldn't hear when your mind wasn't calmed down, and you can see the animals calm down? Especially with horses, it's like that."

"That's about the only way I can be around horses," Jane said.

"You don't like horses?"

"It's not that I don't like them. I guess I just don't trust them."

"Well, that's probably smart. Any one with any spirit is going to be a little wild. Anyway, that's something I like about you. What I was talking about before."

There, he seemed to say, *that ought to be good enough for you.*

"But I'm strange," she said then.

He looked at her seriously.

"I kind of like that," he said.

She felt like asking, *What about how else I'm strange, not the way you're talking about? About how everybody knows there's something wrong with me?*

But if it didn't seem to be something that was on his mind, that was good enough for her, too.

And after he'd gone, and she'd sat awhile in the grove by herself, and after she had walked back and was almost to the house, she stopped. She felt something building up inside her that she didn't recognize. She wasn't sure if it was love, or some kind of terrible fear that she didn't recognize at all. Or both. And the voice of her mother was in her head saying, *Just what do you think you're doing, daughter? What do you think all that's all about?*

MRS. IDA CHISOLM knew it was most likely the devil's work, but it seemed like the only person she could go to who might—black magic or not—give her some kind of words to think on, to lean on, and no one would know, if she was careful. She took money she'd hidden away from sewing work she occasionally did so she could pay the woman well enough to keep her mouth shut. On the other hand, the more she thought about it, the less she really cared what anyone would think about her going to a fortune-teller lady who read palms and had visions. It was the latter part that was a little frightening, though. It was said that before Eugenia Savell's husband died they would dress up and go into their parlor and she would play the piano, old-timey songs, and the ghosts of dead soldiers from the old war would drift down from the high ceilings and dance. Some kind of ghostly minuet. Well, if that wasn't the devil's presence it would be hard to say just what it was.

She rode into town with Mr. Chisolm next time he went in for the stockyard and store supplies. Went with him into Tom Lyle's big grocery and wholesale, where he made his order to pick up on the way home. When that was done she told him she would stay in town and do a little window-shopping on her own. Maybe get some fabric from Klein's.

"All right, then. I'll be done in a couple of hours."

"I'll be at the corner there."

He stood there looking at her.

"What?" she said.

"Don't get yourself run over by a train or something."

"Ought to hope I don't hitch a ride on one."

"To where?"

"Away."

As soon as he'd rounded the corner in the truck, the two cows shuffling for footing, making the occasional forlorn moo, she caught the streetcar toward the west side and got off in a neighborhood of what was once grand homes, now all looking a bit spooky with their mostly Victorian styles, most built just after the war when Sherman had burned almost everything down. Mrs. Eugenia Savell's house was one of the few exceptions, having served as a hospital for both Union and Confederate troops during the battle. Which was part of what made the story of dancing ghost soldiers even spookier: It was said the ghost ladies were dancing with soldiers blue and gray, infinitely polite to one another in death, all sanctioned murderous allegiance no longer lingering in the spirit world.

The Savell mansion sat on a hill on a large lot, surrounded by an ancient-looking fence that looked to have been made of iron spears. The gate stood open. The house itself was not in the Victorian style, but some kind of Greek Revival. It loomed there, columns crumbling, the oddly pink plaster faded, cracked, chunks fallen off here and there and lying in pieces in the weedy grass around the house. She made her way up the brick walkway, peavine weed growing up through it. A monstrous live oak stood to one side of the house and, ironically enough, a woman's-tongue tree just out from the gallery, its dried pods clattering in a bit of breeze. Ivy was taking over the house, climbing the peeling columns and ruined plaster, curling into closed windows beneath what looked like rotted sash. She realized she didn't even know if this woman was still alive, much less still plying her trade, if you could call it that. She only knew of it because her own mother had pointed out the house one time when she was smallish, told her the stories, scaring her. She never forgot it. Still, she was amazed she knew how to find the place, walked right to it as if she had a map in her mind. She lifted an old boar's-head knocker and clanked it against the door a couple of times, and waited. She heard footsteps, not heavy but light. Then the doorknob rattled, turned, and the big door opened just an inch or so. She could see wiry white hair and a red-veined eyeball there. After it looked at her for a good long bit, the door opened and what had to be Mrs. Eugenia Savell stood there in a ratty nightgown and an oversized pair of worn men's house slippers, ankles and shins a crazy map of blue vein lines and bursts. Her liver-spotted hand on the door was long, blunt ends on fingers with yellowed uneven nails. She stared at Ida Chisolm in a long silence, in the face, then up and down. Her face lined and wrinkled as old cottonwood bark. Her eyes, though red-veined and cupped in softer, bruised depressions, alert and intelligent.

"You've come to me about someone else," she said.

"I have."

"Come in, then. Follow me."

The old house was heavily cluttered with something between junk and odd collectibles, so numerous they had to follow a path through it all, and through a big open kitchen filled with potted plants, some taller than a man, and into a sunroom in the back, filled with other, more exotic plants like elephant leaf and bamboo, and a ficus big enough to shade a picnic were it out in the yard.

"Sit," the woman said, pointing to a sofa she'd hardly noticed for all the foliage. Mrs. Eugenia sat herself down in an old wooden wheelchair. When she saw the expression on Ida Chisolm's face she cackled and said, "You know I'll need it one day. Right now, it's just kind of fun." Then she said, straight-faced, as if she'd been asked a question, "It was my husband's." She leaned close, grinning, the wrinkles closing up around her cheeks and eyes. "I did covet it, while he was still alive." Then went serious and said, "Is this about your husband?"

"No, ma'am."

"Child?"

"Yes. Daughter."

"How old is she?"

"Sixteen."

"Don't tell me any more. Let me have your hand."

She took her visitor's hand in her larger, almost leathery one, closed her eyes, and went silent. Ida could see her eyeballs moving back and forth behind the papery lids.

"Something is wrong with her?"

A lump came into her throat and she couldn't speak. Tears came to her eyes and so she closed them. When she opened them again and wiped tears with the back of her free hand, she saw Mrs. Eugenia looking straight into them, saying, "She's not sick."

"No."

"But she is afflicted."

Nodded. Said, "I want to know if she will ever be better. Normal, like other girls. Women."

She thought Mrs. Eugenia would close her eyes again but instead she continued to look deeply into hers. Then she dropped Ida's hand and rolled her chair backwards, stopped, looked at her again, then out the window. Ida followed her eyes and saw that, oddly, the back yard was a beautiful garden, as immaculately tended for its flowers and hedgerows as the front was ignored. They sat there like that for what seemed minutes, silent. Until Mrs. Eugenia finally turned her chair by pushing on one wheel to face her again. The look of resignation in her face said everything.

"I don't see a change," she said then.

"Will she die?"

"Not young."

Ida nodded again.

"She is strong. Even stronger than you," Mrs. Eugenia said then. "She may even be relatively happy in life. Unlike you."

Ida then laughed a curt laugh of her own.

"Nothing to be done about that, I suppose."

"We are who we are," Mrs. Eugenia said.

"Yes." The bitterness now settling back deep in her heart, having lifted a bit in some silly, futile hope that a crazy old woman would tell her that her daughter would undergo a miracle and become whole. She reached into her purse.

"What can I give you, Mrs. Savell?"

"Call me Mama Jean," Mrs. Eugenia said. "It's my common name."

"All right."

"If you have a dollar, it would help me with my groceries, and some fertilizer."

Then again, it was all strange enough to be true. She found a silver dollar in her change purse and laid it carefully into the surprisingly smooth palm held out to her, and the long, thick fingers closed over the coin, opened again with Mrs. Eugenia looking at it as if she'd made it appear there by sleight of hand.

"Mama Jean," Ida said, "I wonder. There's a story that the

ghosts of old soldiers would visit you and your husband, and the ghosts of ladies in the town, and would dance here in your parlor."

Mama Jean looked blankly at her as she posed the question, then blinked and looked at a spot in the other room.

"Not since I sold the piano to pay for my husband's funeral," she said.

Ida showed herself out. She could see a storm coming over Sand Mountain to the south. Sky full of hazy blue light above, a strange deep blue almost black in the hills, and silent, as if it meant business. They would have to hurry to get home before it hit. The creek would be up in such a rain, if it didn't dump all of itself into the valley where the people of this town sat awaiting it, powerless like all of God's children on this earth, who needed such reminding now and then that they were mortal. Ida Chisolm didn't.

The Boy with the Camera

Elijah came over with a Brownie camera one day and took some pictures of her on their walk. He mailed the film to town to have them developed and printed. One, his favorite, was of Jane looking over her shoulder at him in a flirtatious way, and she made him give her the print of that one, she thought it was so funny. "But it's my favorite one," he said. "Well, you just get yourself another one made up," she said.

Her mother and father, demure in their greetings but not impolite, watched them from the front porch as they would pause and turn to one another, as the Key boy would sometimes take her hand when he spoke to her.

After having seen the photograph and thinking about it as he sat before the fireplace late into an evening, her father had an idea to send Jane into town to live with her sister Grace, who was now proprietor of the dry-cleaning operation she'd started out with as a seamstress. Chisolm worried that living in town might afford Jane less freedom to get out and about—at least here she had roam of the property without socializing if it wasn't convenient—but thought it might be a good thing to separate her from the Key boy, for the good of them both.

"Better to have her upset with me than have her heart broken by that boy one day," he said to himself.

"Of course," his wife said, surprising him. He hadn't known she was in the room. He looked at her, a bit irritated by her sneakiness and her sarcastic tone.

Things were getting no better moneywise, either. He would worry less, maybe, if she wasn't around, if she was in town learning how to live off the farm, moving toward learning how to be on her own in the world. Once he'd really thought about it, he couldn't imagine she'd want to live on this farm by herself when he and the wife were dead and gone.

And to himself he admitted he was drinking more. Craving it more. Slipping off to his makings shed more often. But after a few drinks he would forget or not care about discretion and bring the jug or jar back up to the house. He worried about her seeing that.

His wife suggested that Jane could take in some sewing, maybe from some of Grace's customers, to help out with expenses. She might build up a little business of her own that way.

They presented Jane with the idea the next afternoon before supper. She looked at them, sitting there at the kitchen table beside which she stood, listening. Her face had taken on the kind of look she'd put on as a child, when something upset her.

"I'd rather just stay here," she said. "I can earn my keep."

"Well," her mother said, deliberately not looking at her. "We think it's the best thing for now."

Jane went into her room and sat on the bed, hearing her father go out again and her mother get to work on the meal. In a while, she got up and went back into the kitchen to help. Her mother stopped to look at her, then went back to what she'd been doing.

"You could take in some sewing work, like I said, just to help Grace out a little," she said. "She practically raised you, anyway."

"Yes, ma'am," Jane said. "But don't make me leave right now. Please. Not just yet."

Her mother looked at her long enough for Jane to feel the room begin to close in on them, the outside world to disappear from her senses. "And why do you want to stay here, with just us? Why do you want that so much just now?"

"I'm not like Grace. I've never wanted to get away, restless. Let me stay at least through the spring. For the dances, then. I had such a good time."

"Maybe you are restless," her mother said. And they stared at one another until her mother stood up to leave the room.

"If you would watch those peas on the stove," she said as she left, "I'd appreciate it. Don't let them boil over. I need to get out of this house for a bit."

"All right." Although she said it softly and her mother didn't appear to be listening, reaching for her tin of snuff up on the mantel before going out onto the porch to sit by herself for a while.

THERE WERE LIGHT breezes passing through the hay stalks, cotton bolls beginning to bloom, the corn leafed out deep green. Jane walked with the doctor down into the woods and around the fishing pond and he talked about his love for fried fish and potatoes and patted his growing belly. Occasionally he pulled his briar pipe from his vest pocket and loaded it with tobacco and stopped to smoke leisurely while she waited. He was getting on in years, not really old but seemed so to Jane, and he stopped often to catch his breath and sigh out about how he knew he *wasn't* really getting old, but he sure wasn't young anymore. When they came out of the woods and walked down to the pasture below the house, he paused in his gait, knocked ashes from his pipe, and said, "Well, I have put off showing you this, or giving you the information that I promised I would, but from what your parents say, you and the Key boy seem to be courting in earnest, and so I thought I should not put it off any longer."

She listened, her ears burning with what she half knew and feared he was going to say.

"You showed me," she said.

"I showed you the simple stuff," he said. "And gave you a general explanation. What I have to show you now is more detailed and specific."

"Okay."

"I know you're both still very young and I doubt seriously either of you has thought ahead to anything more serious between yourselves. But still."

He pulled from the side pocket of his jacket a printed pamphlet, with illustrations, and gave it to her.

"My friend in Baltimore sent me this pamphlet. It's part of their stock-in-trade, see. It explains—graphically and in detail—how it is that a man and a woman come to be with child," he said. "I know you've seen things," he murmured, almost to himself. "But. In any case, if you'll pay particular attention to page three, the inside-view illustration there of the usual female anatomy. As I said before, while you were growing inside your mother, becoming who you are, something happened to alter or change the normal process of this development. Or more likely stopped the development before you were fully formed. But now, after you have read this and seen the illustration he's made and put in here—after talking to me and to that Dr. Davis in Memphis—you will understand what I mean when I say that, in your case, conceiving a child and carrying it to term would be extremely unlikely without major surgical repair or alterations, and as I said, I believe that will be possible one day but there is just no way to say when. And if you, as you are now, were able to engage in intercourse or sexual relations—do what you've seen your sister and, ah, the others do—it wouldn't be the same as it is with people who have what's considered the 'normal' anatomical makeup. I've said that you are a normal girl, and you are. But inside you down there, because you stopped developing before everything was finished, and maybe some wires got crossed in the process—that is where you're not 'normal.' I'm afraid that if the Key boy were to marry you, on your wedding night—I'm afraid he might feel confused and unsettled. He might even believe he had been betrayed. There is nothing in this world that saddens me more than to have to tell you this straight-out. But it simply is not right to get into a serious relationship with someone without everyone knowing the facts. Or at least enough of them."

The doctor paused.

"You see the slip of paper there in the back of the pamphlet."

"Yes."

"You can look at that and compare it to the illustration in the pamphlet, which is a drawing of the interior female anatomy without any sort of complications."

In the margin of the pamphlet on that page he had drawn an arrow and written, *This is where one has access to the part inside that allows a child to be conceived.* And there was another arrow pointing to the drawing of the male parts, without additional words, as if to say, *This is self-evident, no?*

"You can see the obvious and extensive difference if you look here"—and he pointed to the pamphlet graphic—"and then here"—and he pointed to the handmade drawing. It looked to have been traced from some professional document. Looking from the one to the other, the printed drawing in the pamphlet and the drawing on the slip of paper, she felt a cold heaviness flood into her heart. It wasn't as if she hadn't known it anyway, on some level. But she had never really been able to imagine the details. Seeing it there, laid out so plainly, was a form or level of confrontation with the reality of her self that she had essentially avoided—just by being herself, she supposed. She dropped her hand holding the drawing and pamphlet to her side, fought back useless tears. There was no sense in being upset over what just couldn't be. Or at least no sense in making a scene over it in front of anyone else.

He held out his long, big-knuckled hand and took hold of hers. She tried to withdraw it but he held on.

"I may have overstepped my rights," he said.

"Did you tell *him* all this?" she said, butting in. "Did you show him *this*?"

"Heavens, no, child. No. I did talk to him. I kept it private, just him and me. I said nothing more than that it was not likely you could ever conceive a child. And that for the sake of both of you, you ought to take that into consideration. I beg your forgiveness if I have gone too far. But I thought it might be easier on you for me to tell him that. And only that."

She held his gaze and said, deliberately, "What if *I* just told him right-out, told him everything, and see what he says?"

"Do you think he would be able to understand, Janie?"

She couldn't answer that, and fought to control her emotions. She knew the answer to the question.

"What they call your condition is printed there, you see. There are variables—not every case is exactly the same, so this is what I guess you might call a generalization. But the variations are generally not great. And from what Dr. Davis saw during his examination in Memphis, and from what I can tell, myself, I think it's pretty accurate."

She said nothing, trying to control her emotions.

"You are starving yourself," he said. "And dehydrated. I've heard of young women dying of such measures, for whatever their reasons."

"Well," she said. "That won't happen. I'm fine."

Then, when he still stood there, she said, "I understand, Dr. Thompson."

He left her there and walked back to their house. She saw him reach the porch and speak for a little while to her parents, who said nothing. She saw her father nod and say something. Then the doctor got into his car and drove off.

When Jane approached the gallery her father got up and walked past her without saying anything. Her mother, when Jane met her gaze, gave a small, grim-faced nod of approval. Jane went past her and on into her room. She sat on her bed, set down the pamphlet, looked again at the drawing. Read the words she'd never seen or heard before printed there, defining her: *Urogenital sinus anomaly. Persistent cloaca.* They made no sense.

He should have let me tell him, she thought, anger welling up. Then she realized the truth of the matter. She wouldn't have known how to do it. She would have had to just turn her back on him. And she didn't know how she could have done that.

Dear Ellis,
Thank you for sending me those materials, although it was pain-ful to use them. She took it hard. Maybe harder than I'd even expected. I'd fooled myself into thinking she had not indulged in some illogical youthful optimism.

It was impossible to tell just what went through the parents' minds as I was telling them what I told the girl. Essentially. Seriously if I were a card player I would want Chisolm's deadpan visage. Not as if he doesn't wear his hardships in that expression that is somehow not hard but enduring. Like the surface of some hard-traveled rutted clay road. As if made for that. The wife shows more, albeit not without some amount of the inscrutable.

Not as if the whole thing isn't something these folks hardly ever talk about. Not comfortably, anyway. Country folks being the kind who kindly turn away, out of discretion and courtesy as much as helplessness.

If any consolation's to be had from this it is possibly that young Jane will stop starving herself to death, and suffering dehydration, in some kind of last-century version of lovesickness. She looks almost like those consumptive maidens my father would talk about sometimes, wooing young gentlemen with their darkened eyes full of death. Visibly becoming ghosts of themselves until the ghost is given up.

I wished I'd thought to hint at the possibility of a fresh bit of corn whiskey from the man before leaving. Would have felt awkward, though. Barely had the heart to look them in the eye after I said what I had to say. Nor did he have the heart to look at me. Mrs. did. Like some bitter, deposed old queen thinking to kill the messenger.

Ed

ONE DAY SOON after that, Jane took her solitary walk in the woods and went down to sit in her favorite little meadow, shaded on one side. It was her private place. The shaded grass was cool on the soles of her bare feet. She heard something and looked up to see Elijah Key standing only a few yards away, seeming a little abashed at having followed her there. She thought he must have been watching the house. She was startled, but when she saw it was him, she breathed again. Then another moment of alarm until she realized she was clean, not having thought about it on her way out. Then she burned with the knowledge of why he was there. He moved closer, hands shoved into the pockets of his overalls.

"I hear you're up and moving to town," he said in his quiet voice.

"I guess so," she said. "My sister needs help at her dry cleaner's, I guess."

They walked together back up the path toward her place.

"What about you and me?" he said.

She looked down at her feet in the soft earth of the trail she walked. It was into June now, and heating up every day, and the birds were most alive in the cooler shade trees deeper in the woods, their leaves still the deep green of late spring, and the sunbeams the trees allowed down through their limbs were slanted and cleaved through the general light, canted columns of yellow-gold with no substance beyond phenomenal beauty and perfect stillness.

"It's complicated," she said. "I guess it's just not to be."

He stopped her and gently turned her shoulders so she could face him.

"But why not? You can tell me."

She felt the color rise in her throat and face and she thrust her tingling hands into the pockets of her skirt and said nothing.

"Is it something about me?"

Still she said nothing, and tried to calm herself into an attitude and expression that said nothing, gave nothing. She looked away.

"You know it's not," she said.

"Dr. Thompson told me you can't have children. I don't care about that."

"You might, one day, Elijah. I don't doubt you would."

She shook her head and stepped away.

"I'm sorry," she said. "It's more than that, anyway. I can't talk about it."

"I'll come see you in town."

She shook her head. This was becoming too hard.

"No. Don't."

Neither said anything. And then he spoke.

"Won't you give me a kiss before you go?"

She felt herself blushing again and was frightened. Then she nodded and stood still. Elijah Key walked over—he was barefoot, too, his feet grayish red with dust from the road and the trail through the woods. She thought he had nice feet. He moved closer, removed his eyeglasses, revealing undistorted his beautiful blue eyes. She thought he might kiss her on the lips and with tears forming in the corners of her eyes quickly gave him her left cheek, and he very gently put his lips there, and gave her a soft kiss in the hollow between her cheekbone and her mouth, lingering. She felt the warm breath from his nostrils as he kissed her cheek. He smelled sweetly of horses and clod dirt and hay. And then he said softly, "Good-bye, sweetheart." He put his glasses back on and ran off down the trail at a trot. She hadn't even noticed that he wasn't wearing a shirt below his overalls' suspenders.

Jane would ever be sorry she didn't have a photograph of Elijah Key, and berated herself for not thinking to ask him if she could take his picture that day after he'd taken hers.

She thought there had been a catch in his voice, there in the leaf-dappled light on the trail. She thought she might weep, herself. But only for a moment. She swallowed it down thickly in her throat and walked slowly back to the house, seeing nothing until she arrived in the yard, which was empty but for the chickens let loose from their pen—her mother's doing, no doubt—dawdling and pumping their heads walking around. The light in the yard so bright on them that at first they seemed like something else, otherworldly birds alighted there in a migration she might have been the first to see. Then she blinked in the hard light, held a hand over her brow to shade her eyes, and they were just chickens.

After Her Kind

So in the fall of 1932, when she was sixteen going on seventeen, she went to live with Grace in town. Grace's personality hadn't changed much, but it did seem that she took things easier here, on her own. She'd married the owner of the dry-cleaning business, a man with the unlikely name of Noble Sidebottom. Then Mr. Sidebottom—who must have truly had quite enough of Grace—ran off with an even younger woman, leaving Grace the business, house, and automobile but not a word of good-bye. Took what cash they had, too. Grace said she figured they hauled off to Mexico, where life was cheap. Some afternoons she drank beer or gin and smoked cigarettes, right out on the front porch where anybody walking by on the sidewalk could see.

Weekdays, Jane worked as a seamstress in Grace's shop, mending and hemming men's britches and shirtsleeves, repairing the stitching in winter coats, vests. She had learned while living with her mother to make dresses, skirts, shirts from whole cloth. She sat at her machine and pumped the treadle with her foot, humming tunes of her own making as she worked. She kept the big washing machine going for the laundry customers, and hung clothes on the lines out back, and helped Grace iron when she could. It was hard work.

She had ended her habit of fasting, as she had to keep her wits to get everything done. She had little contact with others, anyway, outside her very controlled environment. She'd taken to wearing several slips beneath her dress, as many as five or six, hoping that would muffle odors, and a protective rubber garment. And perfume, a slight distraction. And it was Grace who gave the customers their items and took their money. Jane stayed in the back, working. Clients came to the shop to drop off or pick up items they'd had repaired or sewn, but she rarely saw them.

Their house, just a couple of blocks north of the new hospital, was one of those plain Victorian homes of plank siding painted white, with tall windows and a second, attic floor with dormers, where Jane made her rooms.

The streets were paved to just north of Fourteenth Street, so in all seasons Jane and Grace could hear the clopping of horses' hooves when wagons and buggies passed, going to the hospital or down the hill to town, and also the chustling of old vehicles and the whining acceleration of the newer motorcars owned mostly by townspeople who lived in the outlying areas. At all hours of the day and night came the plaintive steam whistles of freights and passenger trains plying the tracks along Front Street, south to Hattiesburg and the coast, north to Columbus and Tupelo, east to Birmingham, west to Jackson. To Jane, who'd never heard trains so close with such regularity, the wailing whistles and the banging of cars together in the rail yard, rumbling out of the valley in all directions, was comforting. Up in the attic apartment, her windows open spring, summer, and fall for breeze, she heard these sounds, along with the sloppy hard-edged language of men walking home from the saloons in late evening, and she felt most times as if she had little real privacy, so accustomed she was to the quiet farm with its occasional cow or bull sounding off, bellowing at the moon or calling a calf or hailing a harem of heifers, a horse blowing a big flappity sigh, restless in its stall, a dog barking, an owl hooting now and then, and the startled songbirds' calls in its wake, or their silence. Coyotes. Crickets. Cicadas. Tree frogs, and bullfrogs down by the cattle pond. And during quiet moments in the summertime, the breezes rustling the full-leafed stalks in the cornfield.

If she was to stay there and live in Grace's attic, then she was to be the primary cook, washwoman, and cleaning woman, in spite of the fact that she put in a full day six days a week at Grace's shop for meager wages, as well. Grace was hard in her determination not to be soft in a world where men expected that of women so they could have their way.

In one of her more callous moments, she said to Jane, "You don't know how good you have it, not even having to think about dealing with a man pawing at you all the time, bossing you around."

They were in the kitchen, Jane having cracked several eggs into a bowl to scramble them. Grace leaned over to look into the bowl.

"You didn't take out the little squiggly things."

"Why should I?"

"It's the rooster jism," Grace said. "Sperm."

"It is not," Jane said, looking again at the eggs in the bowl with revulsion.

"Well, what would you know about it? You've never seen it."

"That is just not possible," Jane said.

"Sure looks like it," Grace said.

WHENEVER HER FATHER would come to town to sell a cow at the stockyard, which wasn't so often anymore, he would stop and pick up Jane and let her go along. It was always a Saturday, and he would always just pull up to the curb in front of the house and sit in his big cattle truck smoking cigarettes, until one of them would hear the cows in back complaining of being cooped up and go out to speak to him. If it was Grace, he'd nod and just say, "Tell sister to come on with me to the stockyard."

"He must think I have an eye for cattle," Jane said.

"What I figure is he knows he won't drink till after the trading if you're along," Grace said.

Jane would try to talk to him but he had become a man of even fewer words. His lean and chiseled features now more lined, the jawline softer. Eyes seeming to go gray behind spectacles that gleamed in sun or streetlamp light like glass coins in filament frames. Just after the auction—and the loading of a cow if he'd bought as well as sold—he would go off by himself, come back, and begin to take furtive swallows from a pint bottle of liquor he'd acquired from some local purveyor or another hanging about the lot like a regular truck farmer. One evening they were driving back to Grace's when a policeman pulled them over, ringing away at the bell on the roof of his car. Her father looked annoyed and puzzled. The policeman came up to the truck window and spoke to her father. Evidently he knew who he was. He looked around her father and tipped his hat to her.

"Ma'am," he said, touching the bill of his policeman's cap. Then, "Mr. Chisolm, did you realize you were exceeding the speed limit?"

Her father looked at the young man for a good long moment and said, "It's getting late and I'm in a hurry to get home."

"Yes, sir, I understand that. Have you been drinking, Mr. Chisolm?"

Her father just looked at him as if he hadn't said anything at all. Jane took a furtive glance at the pint bottle lying beside her father's leg on the seat.

"I need to get on," her father said then. "I have to drop my daughter off at her sister's house and then drive clear out to my place, a good five-six mile from here, and I like to get to bed early, you understand."

"Yes, sir, I understand. If you could wait for just a minute, though, I'm afraid I'm going to have to write you a citation."

"A what?"

"A ticket. For the speeding. I'll let the drinking go, as you seem capable of driving, if you'll keep the speed down."

"All right, but I need to get on," he said again then.

"Yes, sir, it will only take a minute."

But when the officer went back to his patrol car to get his ticket book, her father simply put the truck into gear and drove on.

"*Papa*," she said. She looked through the rear window at the policeman, who was standing there beside his vehicle looking after them as if someone had just asked him a question he had no idea how to answer.

Her father said nothing. Dropped her off. She kissed him on the cheek and said good night. He looked over at her then. His features had drawn themselves down into what looked like a permanent sadness, as if he no longer had the will or strength to pull them up into any expression but the forlorn. She wanted to say, *Papa, how bad could it be? You still have the farm, the land. Others have it worse, for sure.* But she knew what pride he took in having made something out of nothing, only to see it threatened by hard times. She supposed she could apply that thinking to not just the farm but his whole life. There now living alone with a woman who must seem a hostile stranger to him, and him a hollow one to her.

"Night, daughter," he said, and drove on.

She watched his truck slowly gearing up the hill and away. Right in the middle of the road, but steady. The shadowed shape of his hat and head there in the truck's cab, visible in the gaps between the oak boards of the cattle guard. She felt the ghost of an apprehension. He still looked strong but in many ways ten years older than he was. She had a sudden irrational fear that this would be the last time she ever saw him. But she fought that down, knew it was foolish, superstitious in some way.

Later, Grace would tell her that the story of the foiled traffic ticket had got around town. Apparently their father was quite the local character, and the young policeman suffered much derisive joking for having tried to give a ticket to Mr. Sylvester Chisolm.

THAT WAS HER LIFE there, in town. She stayed so busy and tired that it seemed like time didn't matter anymore. Didn't so much pass as disappear, like memories neglected and forgotten. Years can slip away in such manner, in such a life.

Somehow, even as the thirties wore on and things worsened, Grace held on to her business by cutting costs, undercutting competitors' prices, shamelessly complimenting the women who came in, whether they were beautiful, plain, or just plain ugly, flirting furtively with the men (and sometimes more than flirting, Jane strongly suspected—from long lunch hours when Grace made her tend the counter, or sent her off to lunch at the house and when Jane came back she would see Grace turning the door sign to Open again).

Jane had wanted to put in a vegetable garden, and after first saying no, Grace changed her mind and practically ordered her to do it. At least she helped a bit with the canning. They pretty much gave up meat aside from a small cut of pot roast on Sundays. That was fine with Jane, who'd never eaten much meat, anyway. It made certain odors stronger.

She learned how to get along with Grace by holding her own in an argument and by getting out every now and then on a Saturday, for the whole day, wandering town, window-shopping, and having a modest meal such as a Chik Steak at the Triangle, only a nickel in those days—they used breaded pork loin but it tasted so good she couldn't resist—and then going home. She would practice the fasting and dehydrating before an outing, as she had when she was a girl, so generally she was back home at Grace's before the possibility of an accident, and well before the possibility of a "serious" one. She wrote home every week, and received in return the occasional postcard from her mother: the blank manila ones with nothing printed on them, not even a vertical line on the side where you wrote the address, the back side filled with her mother's scrawl that read like a diary she might have written for herself or posterity: *There's no ice because the iceman's truck broke down. One of the breeding cows died and your father does not yet know why it happened. Had rain most of last week, couldn't dry a stitch of clothing on the line. Mister Chisolm* (as she had always formally called her husband) *had to shoot a fox that was getting into the henhouse, gave it to the Harrises for the skin although for all I know they ate it too. Your father is not up to hog killing anymore and had to hire Harris and his boys to do it, he knew it needed done but he didn't really care one way or other, gave them half the hog for the job, a sunny winter day, thank the Lord. He is not exactly behaving himself,* she would occasionally say, which Jane took to mean he was drinking too much more often.

They were just hanging on through these times, she wrote.

One ended with the odd mentioning, *Crows flocking into the pines at dusk. I find it frightening, hard to sleep.*

At least once a month, when the weather was good, she badgered Grace into driving them up to their parents' place for Sunday dinner. When Grace tired enough of that, she taught Jane to drive her automobile in a flat field on the south side of town and after that Jane would visit her mother and father by herself when she could. Sometimes she went up early enough to stop for coffee with Dr. Thompson before going on to the home place. She always drove back to town before dark. Her father seemed to be in decline. She would come upon him standing at the edge of the pasture, looking at his cows as if he hardly knew what they were. Or he would sit on the front porch by himself, smoking. He drank before breakfast, and then periodically throughout the day.

"Papa?" she'd say.

"Yes."

And sometimes they would say no more than that, as if that were enough, or all there was, a generic reply to her all-but-unspoken query into his condition. She sat and looked at his lean, hard profile, now bearing the wire-rimmed spectacles, and wondered what he was seeing as he stared straight ahead into the yard beyond the porch, seeming deep in thought but saying nothing.

Suitors

Sometimes when one of Grace's gentleman friends came over Jane crept out and walked the mostly empty evening sidewalks downtown. She liked the evening air, the slow and scarce traffic that rolled or clopped through town at that hour. The smells of the bakery baking on the night shift. The coal smoke from the trains. But she was lonelier than ever, and many a night such as this she longed just to be back on the farm, alone in that way. It seemed to her to be the place she belonged.

Occasionally one of the "friends" came over for supper, and sometimes he stayed later, when Jane had already gone up to her room, and she could hear him and Grace partly from the stairwell, their murmuring talk, and partly from the outside, where their voices drifted from the windows and into the air and back into Jane's windows above them. On some of those nights, though they kept the radio on to cover their sounds, she heard the faint whine of the bad hinge on Grace's bedroom door, the light metallic click of the door closing. And she might drift over to that side of the house, to the little sitting room she had arranged across from her bedroom, and sit beside the open window looking out over downtown below and listen to the sounds of their lovemaking, so carefully quietened they were, like the whispers of a lover in Jane's own ears, burning with the shame of her eavesdropping.

One of Grace's suitors was a man named Louis Fontleroy. He was a shoe salesman for one of the two ladies' shoe stores downtown. He dressed as if he were more than that, and was handsome, although somewhat in the way of a handsome house-cat, and younger than Grace. He wore engraved tie clasps on his silk ties, and ankle boots that to Jane seemed oddly effeminate, and smoked cigarettes he kept in a silver case. He was infinitely polite to Jane, even bending to kiss the top of her hand some-times when she entered the room. Jane felt he was patronizing, yet she was polite in return. When they dined, he would make pleasant small talk, making sure to address questions to Jane as well as Grace. Once, when Grace had left the room for a moment, Jane was fairly certain that after remarking what a good cook she was, how excellent was the pot roast, he had winked at her. She blushed but when she looked back at Mr. Fontleroy he seemed to be examining his manicured fingernails as if to search for some flaw he might attend to when he returned home. She thought him a dandy.

One evening when Grace had said Mr. Fontleroy was coming for dinner and asked Jane to join them, Jane came downstairs and entered the parlor to find not just Grace and Mr. Fontleroy, but another man as well. She froze in the doorway to the parlor, her heart thumping and anger flashing into her mind, at the same time that both gentlemen stood, setting their coffee cups into their saucers on the coffee table with a little clatter.

"Won't you join us, Miss Jane?" Fontleroy said.

"Come have a seat, Jane," Grace said in a wry voice. "This is Mr. Fontleroy's friend Gabe Satchel."

"Miss Chisolm," Satchel said, nodding, and then he took a step toward her on his long legs and extended his hand. She reached out and shook it, her palm damp, and then sat in the chair next to her sister, her cheeks burning, and rested the damp palm on her skirt to dry it. She hoped she wouldn't have to rush off, embarrassing herself and Grace alike.

This Mr. Satchel was older, looked almost middle-aged, though what looked older in his features was mostly facial, and she sensed that some burden had made them lined in that way. There was also a kind of serenity in the way he listened when someone spoke, looked at them and seemed to absorb what they were saying as if it had kindled his deepest, most intimate interest. It warmed her and made her flush a bit, and she couldn't help but feel drawn to him for this, if not for his looks. But what were looks? How long could anyone stay beautiful, if it came to that?

But then what would he see in her, no doubt still just a country girl, even if she had lived in town with Grace now for a good five years? And why should she even think about such a thing, given the realities of her situation? She'd come a long way toward coming to terms with that.

And yet she sensed in this Gabe Satchel some kind of sadness borne along by a natural kindness. It made her heart leap a bit, and made her feel, at the same time, as miserable as she felt the day she'd said good-bye to Elijah Key.

So now she knew why Grace had insisted that she cook an entire pot roast and more potatoes and carrots than usual, and why Grace herself had put together a salad of lettuce, tomatoes, and onions. And now she had little appetite, and her emotions were building inside her so as to make it impossible even to swallow without difficulty.

As they ate, Jane said little but was courteous. Mr. Satchel was tall, several inches taller than Jane, and slim but not nearly as bone-thin as her father, and as she was becoming. In the brighter light of the dining room (which she hated, preferring a lower light at meals), she realized that for all its almost enchanting kindness, his face was a little bit cockeyed, his ears a bit crooked. Even so, he had good table manners and was not overly loud in conversation. In fact, he was on the quiet side.

"Mr. Satchel was in the Great War," Grace said at one point, to which Mr. Satchel said nothing but smiled faintly at his dinner plate as he cut himself another bite of the roast.

"Did you serve in France, Mr. Satchel?" Jane asked.

"That he did," Mr. Fontleroy said. "He was in battle."

"Well, I'm happy that you came home."

"Mostly, ma'am," Mr. Satchel said then in an odd way. "I was wounded, but thankful I'm alive and in good health. I was never gassed like a lot of fellows I knew."

"Mr. Satchel's family is from up around Tupelo," Grace said, going around and filling everyone's glass with more tea.

"What brought you down here?" Jane said.

"Work," Satchel said. "I've been with the railroad since the war, and they transferred me to here a couple of years ago. I'm hoping what seniority I have holds me through these times."

"Anybody's lucky to be working or running a business in these times," Fontleroy said. "I'm afraid the only way I'm holding on in the shoe business is by wearing the hell out of my own," he said, laughing at his own joke.

"And you are doing well in your business, Miss Grace?" Satchel said.

"Well, if it wasn't for Jane getting so good at repairing worn-out clothing and making it look new, and making new things for such a good price, I'm afraid we'd be in trouble ourselves," Grace said.

"Don't forget the practically-working-for-free part," Jane said.

The evening went that way. Jane had little or no appetite but managed to eat a few bites from her plate. The whole situation was making her feel increasingly uncomfortable, though, as it couldn't be anything other than what it seemed to be, a baffling bit of matchmaking on Grace's part. Her discomfort was slowly turning into anger that Grace would put her in such a spot, and she grew silent. Mr. Satchel asked if she was all right. "I'm fine," she said. Then she felt an accident coming on and started to get up and hurry upstairs but stopped, thought, *Just let it happen. See what the matchmakers think of that.* And after a minute, during which the unmistakable odor of bodily waste began to rise into the air around the table, she could sense the discomfort, see the awkward feeling creep into them, note their averted eyes. All but Grace's, that is. Hers bored into Jane's with unmistakable fury and disbelief.

The men stood to leave, thanking Grace, and Satchel thanking her, shaking her hand, making a valiant effort at normalcy. They'd skipped dessert and coffee. And as soon as she shut the door on their departure Grace spun around and came up to her, face distorted in disgust and anger.

"What the hell, sister?" she said. "What the hell was that all about?"

"Indeed," Jane said right back. "What was it about?"

"I don't doubt even Louis won't come back here, after that little incident."

"Too bad. Such a catch." She thought Grace might slap her,

but instead she banged into the kitchen through the swinging door. Jane followed, banging through herself.

"Seriously, you tell me, *sister*," she said. "Were you really trying to set me up with a man? Never mind how humiliating to me— what about him? He's a nice man, and a kind man, I can tell. What was he supposed to think when I just outright rejected him and couldn't even tell him why?"

Grace started to speak, stopped herself, then kind of slumped in on herself, crossing her arms.

"Don't get so damn mad," she said. "Louis insisted that this man wanted to meet you."

Jane stared at her for a minute.

"And why is that?"

"Says he's lonely and hasn't had a girl since the war, that he was wounded pretty bad. I get the idea, you know, it was something awful."

"He doesn't look wounded. I mean, he's got two arms and two legs, his face is a little cattywampus but it isn't scarred."

Grace just looked at her.

"Maybe it left him like you, in a way. Unable to be intimate with somebody. I'm just guessing."

To Jane it felt as if she could feel the color leave her complexion. If you could feel an almost mortal paling.

"Guessing," she said. "You'd already told this Mr. Fontleroy about me? And I suppose he told Mr. Satchel?"

Grace worked her mouth, twisting a dishrag in her hands. Then she cut her eyes away. "Not everything," she said. "You certainly surprised him on that front."

Jane said, "How could you do that? Grace."

"Well, goddamn!" Grace said, throwing the dishrag onto the

counter. "Damn me if I bother to do anything to help you, sister. Maybe that man would be a good companion to you, what you think about that? Or is it that you just want to be an old maid your whole life?"

"Well, it's what I already am, 'old' or not, isn't it?" Jane said.

"Yes," Grace said, settling just a bit, ears going from pink back to fleshy translucence in the kitchen light.

"So you think because this man cannot have normal relations with a woman he would want to be with me. You tell him I'm 'deformed' or something but I suppose you leave off the part about inability to control my bodily functions. That he would be the companion of a woman around whom he would so often enjoy the stink of the privy. That it would be like living with a grown infant always needing her 'goddamn' diaper changed. I don't suppose you told him that, judging by his reaction at the table, poor man."

"Poor man! Why did you let it happen that way? Why didn't you excuse yourself and go upstairs, the way you've always done?"

After a long moment so quiet the air began to hiss like a tiny steam valve in another room, Jane said, "To make a point, I suppose. To not take part in a lie." Grace said nothing. "I am twenty-two years old, Grace. That was old maid age, in the old days. And pretty much is for me now. If I have to accept it, you might as well, too. I imagine I am boring you to death, after all this time living here like that, like an old maid. So if you want me to leave, find my own place, you just say so."

"I didn't say that and I don't mean that. You're my little sister. I've tried to take care of you."

"And I appreciate that, Grace. But if you want me to leave, want your privacy back, you say so. All right?"

Grace nodded.

"You're not getting any younger, either, Grace," she said, in a softer voice, not unkind. "I don't want to be in your way."

Grace seemed then on the verge of tears.

Jane left the kitchen and went straight up to her room, sat on her bed looking out the window at downtown, not hearing the sounds of it or smelling the smells of it nor even herself. Only seeing the city's nightscape, and some part of her seeming to float out into it, undetectable by others, no more than a little pocket of warm breeze in the shade of a tree during summer, so subtle as to make one wonder at whether it was really there, passed, or was just a moment of one's own disembodied dreaming. That ghost self that now so often seemed to be with her when she was alone.

On Love

Every now and then Dr. Thompson came by to get her on Sunday and took her for a drive in his car. They drove out to the airfield and watched the occasional airplane take off or land. He bought them a box lunch and they would have a picnic at Highland Park and stroll around and toss the ducks pieces of stale bread Jane would bring from Grace's house.

Once, he convinced her to take a ride on the park's carousel. It was a rather tame experience, as he was getting on in years and she did not want to straddle a wooden horse or lion or some other odd animal, so they rode in the sleigh seats. Even so, the whirling of the carousel as it gained speed was a thrill, with the world of the carousel house and the world outside its paned windows in slanting light becoming streaked as if in some kind of drugged dream. And when it slowed and came to a stop she had to clasp his forearm and beg a moment to regain her equilibrium, and then of course hurry to the public pool's bathhouse with her bag in order to change herself, as the ride had made her forget herself entirely for those long moments and when she came out of it she realized that she had that business to take care of before they moved along.

After they had made their way back to his car and got in, he sat for a moment behind the wheel without speaking.

"What are you thinking about?" she said.

"Oh. Just my mind wandering. Got all whirled up on that carousel."

They sat a moment.

"I want to ask you a question," she said.

"Go ahead."

"How come you never got married again?"

He frowned in thought. Then said, "I didn't feel the need. Some people feel like they just have to be married, have a companion. I figured out, after Lett died, that I wasn't one of them. I guess being married to her had helped me see that."

"I'm sorry," she said. "I wasn't thinking. I didn't mean to pry where I shouldn't."

"It's all right. I don't mind. Sometimes people get married because it just seems like a good idea at the time. That such-and-such a person would be a good mate, a good person to share a life with. Have children with. People will get married simply because they judge themselves to be compatible. Just because they figure they will get along."

"Was it that way with you and Mrs. Thompson?" Jane said.

"We got along all right."

She'd been rude again and wanted to kick herself. But she was curious. And still upset about Grace's matchmaking, she supposed, taking it out in a way on Dr. Thompson. Her only real friend.

"I apologize for asking that," she said. "I'd better keep my mouth shut."

"I really don't mind. We did kind of grow apart, there toward the end. I loved her. I think she loved me, too. But she began to have a hard time showing it. I think that toward the end I just wasn't entirely the right man for her. I think she'd have preferred a life in town."

"But your house is almost in town, barely outside it."

He smiled, but just with one side of his mouth.

"I guess I mean she would've preferred a town life. Society." He looked at her. "She was lonely for the kind of life she grew up with. Whereas I never really cared much for it."

"How did you meet?" He'd never told her the story of that.

"Well, now, there you go. I was a biology student at the University of Alabama, intending to apply to Vanderbilt for medical school—although I wasn't decided on that yet.

"In any case, one weekend I went home with my friend Nate McLemore, who was from here in Mercury, and there was a social on the lawn at someone's home, I think it was a family named Meyer, and it was a very hot day. Several of the young ladies had parasols against the sun and heat. But as I was walking past this one girl, who did not have a parasol, she fainted dead away and landed right in my arms. I had her just like you'd bend someone down in a tango dance or something, and I had to hold her close for a moment or drop her, and before I could even lay her down on the grass she woke up, and looked straight into my eyes, obviously startled and shaken, and disoriented, of course. And for some reason, one of those odd things you do on impulse, I said, 'Don't worry, I'm studying to be a doctor.' And do you know what she did then?"

"Tell me."

"She laughed, of course. She must have realized, even in her state, that I was as discombobulated as she was. So that was the start of it."

"She got the chance to look at you close up and intimate. It was by accident but it worked."

He cocked his head at her and let a vague smile come into his expression.

"Maybe."

He heaved a sigh and seemed to laugh at himself. "I don't know, I'm rambling." He turned to her again. "I *have* been thinking about love. And I realize that I don't have the slightest idea what it is. But you felt it for that Key boy, didn't you? You believed you did."

In spite of her blushing, she said, "Yes."

He was quiet for a little while, seeming to study his fingernails.

"Jane. I have to say that I've never been certain that I was right to intervene the way I did, with you and that boy."

"Do you think that's what it was? That you intervened? You said you only told him I couldn't have children."

"That's true. It's all I told him. But I have to ask myself, why? Was I trying to prepare him in some way for—I don't know, for what he would either learn from you being together, or what you might have to tell him yourself someday? I felt like it was my obligation somehow, to say something. But maybe it wasn't. Maybe I should have just let things unfold however they might."

Now she was quiet for a while. Then she said, "I thought about that. Of course. I was angry at first. I thought you should have let me tell him. But you ought to know. I decided that I wasn't at all sure I could even do that. I think maybe I was grateful to you, for at least giving him something."

And then she told him about the afternoon when Elijah came to see her and she turned him away.

"Are you saying now I should have stayed?" Jane said. "That

I should have just told Elijah everything, and risk it?" Just the thought, just saying the words, made her heart race as if in fear.

"I don't know anything for sure, Janie."

"But if he had been unable to get beyond the facts of what I told him, like you said back then, wouldn't my heartbreak have been even worse? And maybe even his, too?"

"I don't know," he said again. "I did think so at the time." He looked at her. "And you thought so, too, didn't you?"

She didn't reply for a moment, felt her heartbeat begin to slow to normal again.

"Yes," she said then. "I did."

"But the truth is, we can never really know."

"Yes," she said. "I suppose that is true."

WHEN THE DRY-CLEANING business finally did fail the next year, in '38, Jane thought she'd go home to the farm, but Grace told her, somewhat mysteriously, to give her a few days, she might not have to leave.

"I don't know, Grace," she said. "I kind of think that's where I ought to be. Anyway, what can you do now? We, I mean?"

"I think I know what I can do. And as for you, we can think about that later, if what I think I can do works out."

"Well, I hope it's legal," Jane joked.

Grace stopped. She was wearing what Jane considered to be a dress just shy of scandalous, was perfumed, in heels, and wore a lot of makeup, and sported a hat made of black cotton with a brim that practically covered one eye, hair down in bangs that practically covered the other.

"As a matter of fact, it's not. You might just say it's conditionally approved."

And then she left. Got into her car, made a U-turn, and headed down the hill into downtown.

When she returned an hour later, she had a bottle of bootleg whiskey with her and told Jane to come sit with her in the kitchen while she had a drink. She poured herself a straight shot of it into a short glass, took a sip, cleared her throat, and removed the hat. Jane was mildly shocked to realize that Grace, with her bright red lipstick, milky pale skin, and yellow-blond hair, was actually a beautiful woman. Sexy, she'd have to say. She'd never realized that ever before. Whenever she'd looked at Grace, she'd only really seen what seemed to be the ugly side of her personality. It had effectively obscured her physical beauty, for Jane.

"What are you staring at?" Grace said.

"Oh. Nothing."

Grace gave her a look, took another shot of the whiskey.

"All right, here's my big secret. I'll be starting tomorrow. Working for Miss Minnie. You know who I'm talking about?"

Jane shook her head.

"You ever heard of a brothel, sister?"

Jane shook her head again. Then nodded. "Well," she said, "kind of."

"It's where men pay women to have sex with them. At Miss Minnie's it pays well."

Jane was just nodding slightly, knowing her eyes were big and no doubt plaintive and stupid-looking. As if to confirm it, Grace laughed, quietly and almost to herself.

"Okay, so I don't want to sling hash or hamburgers, or clean rich people's houses, or work in some filthy factory. Miss Minnie has always liked me. She's been a customer for a long time, didn't you know that?"

"Oh, *that* Miss Minnie. The tall one with the beautiful white hair."

"Right. And the expensive clothes. And the Yankee accent. She's from Michigan. And she is a lady, even if she does manage a house full of ladies of ill repute. And she is in good standing with the police and many well-heeled businessmen in this town."

"And she runs a—what do you call it—a brothel? Grace. If Papa and Mama were to find out—"

"Papa and Mama have never really had any control over me, and you know it."

"Yes," Jane said.

"And there's something else."

"What?"

"She also agreed to do me another favor, and that is to hire you."

"Me! What are you talking about?"

"Not to service the men, for God's sake. Miss Minnie's is a high-class operation. They don't go in for, let's say, the odd experience."

They stared at one another a long moment.

"Anyway, I was teasing you. I'm not going to be a whore there."

"Whore."

"Right. The ones that do it with the men. Miss Minnie has admired my business acumen, my smarts. And she knows I mean business when I do business. I'm going to be what I guess you'd call her manager. Let her take it a bit easier from now on."

"Oh." Jane had been imagining Grace lying in a four-poster bed all day, naked or half naked, fanning herself with a Japanese fan, drinking gin, smoking cigarettes in between rutting with any stranger who walked through the door with his thing in his hand. But now she thought about it, Grace didn't like people, women or men, well enough to have a job like that, with constant intimacy, be it phony and vulgar or not.

"Oh," she said again. "Well, what is it you'd have me doing, then?"

"You might imagine there's a whole lot of sheet-washing going on in a place like that," Grace said. "Sex can be a messy business. They change the bedsheets on every bed several times a day. Now, you know how to run a big washing machine. The pay will not be near as good as what I'll make but it will do its part toward keeping this roof over our heads and food in the pantry. I'll be as skinny as you if all we keep eating is what vegetables you grow in the garden and one hunk of meat every week."

"No. Grace. I don't think I want to do it. I don't think I could."

"No? So, you just expect me to support you? Or Mama and Papa to just support you?"

"I can work a field. Cook and clean. I can earn my keep up there. I can tend cattle, need be. Papa needs help more than ever, nowadays."

"Well," Grace said. She poured herself another shot of the whiskey and lit a cigarette. Apparently going outside to smoke was too much trouble now. "Well, if you want to live on a farm, work a plow, weed a field, pick cotton, stick your arm up the ass of a cow, then I guess that's your business."

"How do you think I would like being in a house where behind every door a caravan of strange men were sticking their stink-horns into the same women all day long? I wonder how long you will like it."

Grace French-inhaled from her cigarette, squinting against the smoke, and blew it out the corner of her red lips.

"I guess I'll find out," she said. "But it'll be them, not me. The only 'stinkhorns,' as you say, that I'll see will be the ones I pluck for myself."

Oblivion

B ut now there was the problem of *how* to go back home. Not the simple act of going home, which could be accomplished by calling and catching a ride with the doctor, or being packed and ready to go home next time her father came into town. The problem was that if she went home she would be questioned about why she was returning, and why now, and what was going on with Grace, and so on. And she had never lied to them, not exactly, and she wasn't good at prevarication, anyway. Lying, or attempting to, or even considering it, embarrassed her, which felt like an oddly humiliating weakness.

And so she lingered, which irritated Grace, although it didn't seem as if Grace's new work disagreed with her. If anything, she came home in a better mood than she'd usually enjoyed coming home from the dry-cleaning and laundry shop. Jane tried to stay on her good side by keeping the house spotless, and the garden in shape, and the yard, and always had supper cooking and dishes washed. Grace grumbled a bit but it was also evident that she was glad she didn't have to do those things. She hadn't done much in the way of those things since Jane had arrived six years earlier.

Then her father came one day—he was not going to the stockyard every week or even every month anymore—and when she went out to his truck, which had no cattle in the empty bed, and spoke to him through the open passenger window, he didn't seem to hear her. She spoke louder, and he turned his head slowly. Then he said, "Why don't you drive us on over, sister?"

He shut the engine off and slowly got out and made his way around the hood, keeping one hand on the truck. He looked shaky and his eyes staked his path but really seemed to see nothing, blind sight. She caught his arm and helped him into the passenger seat. He felt even more bone-thin than he looked. He smelled of liquor already, in late morning, but it didn't feel like that was the governing problem.

"Where are we going, Papa?" she said.

"Stockyard," he said.

"Are you looking to buy something?"

He looked at her as if she'd said something odd or mysterious, then craned his neck around to look into the truck bed through the rear window.

"Well," he said. "I thought I brought along a cow."

"Did you forget to load her up?"

He looked at her again with that look of incomprehension. Then settled back in his seat and looked out the windshield. Raised a hand forward as if to say, *Let's go on now, then.*

So she drove him across town to the stockyard and sat with him through the auction, but he hardly reacted to the business going on. Every now and then he seemed to pay attention to an animal, watch it enter the arena, get shown, and exit. But most of the time he had that same long, unseeing stare he'd had when he arrived at Grace's house. When they were leaving, he asked her to get him something to drink.

"From where, or who?"

He just looked at her.

"Papa, I think the last thing you need right now is liquor. I'm sorry."

He blinked. Looked at her. Then walked unsteadily away and over to a pickup, where he spoke with a man, and came back with a bottle tucked into the front pocket of his overalls.

Jane said nothing but got in behind the wheel. He got in on the other side, pulled out the bottle, took a swig from it after they left the lot. Sipped on the way to Grace's house.

It was late afternoon then, November. The summer's heat finally fully gone, enough to feel a nip in the evening air now and then.

"Are you chilled, Papa?" Jane said. "Want to roll up that window?"

"I'm fine," he said, showing no discomfort aside from his mouth being parted as if to aid his breathing a bit. Cheeks sunken, and weathered skin pulled taut against the thin line of his jawbone.

She parked his truck in front of Grace's house and helped him inside and onto the sofa in the parlor. Grace came home while she was making coffee, took a look around, came into the kitchen.

"What's wrong? He doesn't look right."

"He's not. I don't know what it is. It's not just drink, though I guess it could be, if he's been on a long bender. Mama is not telling us everything, I know that."

She took a cup of black coffee in to him and Grace followed.

He looked at the coffee as if it were a strange thing, then up at Grace and Jane. To Grace, he said, "I know what you've been up to, daughter. Don't think people don't talk."

"I'm making a living."

"As a whore. Bringing shame on your mother."

"I'm not a whore, I'm the *manager* of a *brothel*. I do my work on my feet and behind a desk. Big difference there, you know. And it's my business what kind of business I choose to run, anyway. You and Mama can like it or not. We're surviving, here. Are you?"

"I'm taking Janie home with me, out of this."

"She'll be glad to hear it," Grace said. Then she grabbed her purse off the chair in the foyer where she'd left it and went back out.

Their father was shaking his head. He took off his glasses and wiped his eyes. Jane was shocked. She'd never seen him express much emotion at all, much less break down.

"I'm so sorry, so sorry," he said.

"Papa, for what?"

"For you," he said. "For your life. What you've had to live with."

"Papa," she said, "I'm fine. I am who I am. I know how to live with that."

He shook his head, put his glasses back on, and seemed to pull himself together.

"I'm going home," he said.

"But you can't drive in your condition."

"I'll ask you not to tell me what I can and cannot do, sister," he said. "You can move back in with us in a couple days, after I settle some things and make sure your mama has your room ready. Do you hear?"

"All right."

He looked up at her. "I want to say something to you."

But he couldn't seem to find whatever words he was looking for. He got up, put on his hat, and walked out. In a moment she heard the truck start up. She went to the window and watched it drive slowly away, her father stiff and steady behind the wheel.

HE DIDN'T GO straight home, but drove through downtown and over to the west part of town near the railroad tracks to a street of mostly vacant lots save for a few decrepit old crumbling brick or sagging wooden buildings that had housed various businesses, including a general store, livery, machinist, and such. One older grand home still stood on a large lot surrounded by broad oaks that all but obscured its galleries, where one could see upon driving the lane up to it the unoccupied ladies fanning themselves, smoking cigarettes, some of them sipping what looked like cordials or small measures of liquor. One of them stood, a girl who looked a bit familiar to him, and went inside. Another called out, "Come on up, Popsy." He ignored them and went up to the front door, went in without knocking or taking his hat off, and when a young woman approached him looking a bit apprehensive he ignored her and just stood there as if waiting for something. There was the scent of something like dead roses. He heard his daughter Grace's voice say, "I'll take care of this, Necsa."

He looked at her standing there in the doorway to what looked like an office, wearing the long, coatlike dress and cloche hat she'd had on when she left her house earlier.

"I guess you do look more like business than a whore," he said. "You taken to working evenings now, too?"

"What do you want here, Papa?"

"I want you to leave this place. You don't have to work here."

"I choose to, Papa."

"There's other work, even in these times."

"This work is steady. Besides, here I'm in management, befitting my experience. Would you have me making socks for fifty cents a day? Would a good businessman like you find such slave labor more noble than making good money providing a product that's very much in demand?"

"You could work in a clothing store. You know fashion and such."

"Selling fancy dresses to country club society women. Perfect."

He took his hat off and walked over closer to her and met her hard gaze with a softer one of his own.

"Why have you always hated us?" he said, his voice quieter. "You were never content to be with your own family, cleared out soon as you could. I don't understand it, daughter."

She hesitated so long he thought she might not answer, then said, "Aside from having a good model in my mother, I could look to you."

"I never did you wrong. I gave you a good living and upbringing."

"There's more to that than food on the table, Papa," Grace said. "You know those words you just said to me might be the longest speech I ever got from you, and those words show more care for me than any others you ever spoke. If Mama was mean-spirited, then you seemed made out of stone. The only thing you ever talked to was a jug or bottle. I always knew you weren't talking to yourself. You were talking to some imaginary world full of enemies. Well, I felt like we were among them, Papa. That's what I felt."

"Not enemies, and not my family, in any case. Adversaries, yes. People will take advantage and a man has to be hard, sometimes, if he wants to make it. It's a hard world, as you are finding out."

"Not so hard a body can't have a little fun, enjoy something every now and then. You know what, Papa? I enjoy a drink now and then. You? Did you ever enjoy drinking, or is it only to deal with the demons in your head? Did you ever enjoy sex, like the so-called sinful men who come here do? Or was it just to calm your nerves and make a baby now and then?"

"I'll not have you talking to me like that, right or wrong, girl. And I'll tell you this. If you're still working here when I pass, you shall not inherit anything from me—"

"I hope I haven't."

"Not cash money if there is any. Not land nor home. Not insurance. Not stock. You understand?"

"You in a hurry to go, Papa?"

"No, I'm not." Then he spoke more quietly. "I've had some pains in my chest, but it's not serious. Got some pills for when it hurts me."

She looked at him hard as if to detect a lie, then closed her eyes for a moment.

"I don't need anything from you or Mama," she said. "I do just fine on my own."

"I hope so."

He let himself out and to his truck, his heart indeed on fire, took a largish draft from the bottle he'd left on the seat, and drove home in the receding light of late afternoon. He left his headlights off, as he knew he'd make the home road and quit the highway before dusk. He thought to honk as he passed the doctor's house but wasn't in the mood to hail him or anyone else just then. Off the highway, he drove by memory and what dim light remained like dying firefly glow in the foliage. He descended toward the darker area, where the old bridge his nemesis straddled the little creek. There he stopped, sat a moment looking at the bridge's shadowed outline before him, as he still did not want to violate the sense of this evening with artificial light. Something fragile about it that would break if he did. Real lightning bugs flared down by the water and in the trees. He got out, walked to the bridge, and studied it a minute before going back to the truck and idling over the creaking boards, then gunning on up the hill. He parked beside the shed, saw his wife standing in the open doorway of the house like the backlit figure of a life-sized rag doll. She pushed open the screen door and spoke to him as he approached the porch steps slowly, tired out. His chest ached. He'd lied about the pills, or he would have taken one now for the strain he felt.

"You left that cow you were going to trade standing right there tethered to the post by the shed," she said to him. "Are you going morbus on me now? I can't take care of an old crazy man out here by myself."

"Just hush on me, wife."

"Well, what's wrong with you?"

"Too much on my mind. I'm flustered."

"More woolly-headed, seems to me. Where you going now? You think going down in there and drinking is going to clear your head? Maybe, Mr. Chisolm, you have just simply gone stupid. I've seen men go stupid with drink. My own daddy, for one. At the end there he couldn't even tot a bill—"

"I said to hush," he said, in such a way that she did. She held her mouth in the attitude of her next unspoken words as if someone had frozen or suspended time. He went on around the house and down the shadowy trail to his still, heard the screen door at the house slap to. He moved with such distraction he may as well have been blind, could have walked the trail without sight. In that state he rekindled his fire, hooked a jug off the shelf, sat down before the flickering flames, and woke to himself sitting there on the stump rolling a cigarette, as if he'd sleepwalked from the house to this moment.

He drank headlong into and out the other side of melancholy, laid himself down beside the glowing warmth of the fire's coals to rest and try to empty his mind, the soft glow of firelight on the leaves above.

Copper Pennies

It was nearing noon the next day when Jane came home from a walk to the grocery and saw the doctor's pickup at the curb in front of the house. At first her heart lifted, but then she felt something cold and viscous flood into it.

When she stepped into the parlor, she saw the doctor and Grace sitting in the two chairs by the bay window, partially drunk cups of coffee on saucers on the table between them, seeming to have quietly awaited her arrival into the world from some long, childish dream. The doctor stood, his hat in his hands. She set her sack of groceries down on the floor.

"It's Papa," Grace said. "He passed."

"What happened?"

"Went quietly," the doctor said. "In his sleep."

Dr. Thompson offered to drive them both up home, but Grace said she would drive her own car so she could come into town to check on things if she needed to.

"You know he came to see me yesterday, after leaving here," she said. When neither replied to that she said, "He wanted me to quit my job."

After an awkward silence, Jane said, "Was he still angry, Grace?"

Grace looked at her, an unfamiliar emotion in her face.

"He seemed more sad than angry, I thought," she said. "I hate my last words to him were so harsh."

No one said anything and it was quiet in the room. Death was in the room and they were quiet in its presence. Then Grace gathered her bag and keys and left.

Jane and Dr. Thompson were quiet during the drive up, the doctor taking it slow. At first they drove in the wake of billowing dust and slung gravel from Grace's Plymouth until she pulled well ahead, out of sight. And only then, as if Grace could have heard them before, Jane said, "What happened?"

The doctor, who'd been seeming to chew on something, a habit with his mouth he'd taken up in his age, was quiet a long moment. Then he said, "No mystery. I guess he finally drank himself to death."

"He's been doing that a long time," Jane said.

"Well. That's pretty much how it's done."

They drove a good mile without speaking. The hem of her light fabric dress fluttered against the layered slips she'd taken to wearing and she pressed it down against them, to keep it still. She noticed the doctor glance over discreetly.

"I don't really read it as liver failure," he said. "Most likely his heart. Heavy drink will do that. Plus his heavy smoking."

Jane watched the road ahead.

"I guess it was a worse binge than the usual," the doctor said. "Or one too many."

"How is Mama taking it?" Jane said.

"She's quiet."

After a while, Jane said, "Was he in the house?"

"She found him down at his shed. He'd been down there all

night. She woke up and he wasn't at the house, and she made coffee and breakfast, all but the eggs. When he still hadn't showed she went down and found him there. Lying on the ground next to the little fire pit. It was just smoldering a bit. There was a nearly empty jug. Doesn't mean he drank it all last night, though. He was lying like he'd lain down to go to sleep. Not like he'd fallen. Gets chilly at night, this time of year. Alcohol lowers the body temperature, actually. Could have been exposure involved, too. His little fire seemed long cold, time I got there."

After a while, Jane said, "I wonder what she's going to do now. She always seemed like she just wanted people to leave her alone, but being alone like this, with nobody. I'll be around of course. I was going to move back, anyway. I can't live with Grace. Not anymore."

With that she gave just a glance at the doctor, who seemed to have taken on a momentary rictus himself.

He slowed and turned off the main road onto the dirt road that her father had taken so often on his trips to and from town, crossed the old bridge, and at the top of the rise turned left onto the drive to the home where Jane had grown up.

Grace was in the kitchen with her mother. A single bare bulb burned in its outlet in the ceiling there. They'd had a power line strung to the house the year before. And a phone line, too—the new crank telephone on the wall. Her mother's face was set in some kind of slackened flatness, her hair combed straight back on her head. She looked up at Jane and the doctor, her face set and pale in the glaring light. Jane reached up and pulled the string to turn it off.

Her father was in the bedroom, in his clothes and shoes, on top of the made-up counterpane, arms crossed over one another on his chest. She was surprised, almost alarmed, to see that a bright copper penny rested on top of each of his closed eyes. She almost reached over to remove them but heard something and her mother came in.

"Well," her mother said. "There he is."

She took in a heavy, tired-sounding breath, and let it out.

Dr. Thompson said he would arrange for the grave to be dug, and that the notice would be in the next afternoon's papers for the service and burial on Sunday.

"I'll send telegraphs to your brothers, if you like," he said.

"Thank you," Jane said.

"He'll be fine in there if you keep it cool, closed off from the heated rooms, with the shades down. Mr. Finicker will come by with a casket for when you have him cleaned up and dressed. I doubt you'll need ice beneath him unless we have to wait for burial, but if you think differently, just give me a telephone call and I'll have some delivered."

No one said anything in response and the kitchen was quiet but for the ticking of the stove from the dying noon-meal fire in there.

AFTER DR. THOMPSON left, Grace said she was going back into town to take care of business and arrange time off. Then she left, too.

Later that afternoon, Uncle Virgil came by. He accepted a cup of coffee, apologized for his wife Bea not coming along, but said she would come by tomorrow with the children unless they'd rather them not come along. And then after a few sad pleasantries he cleared his throat and withdrew from his jacket's inside pocket an envelope.

"That's a check from my company, money from the insurance policy your father took out on himself when he took them out on his tenants, if you recall. I had to pull some strings, lord knows they can drag their feet these days." He placed the envelope on the table. Jane's mother sat looking at it a long moment, then got up and left the room. They heard her rocker start up on the porch.

Virgil and Jane sat for a while in silence. Then Virgil got up, thanked Jane for the coffee.

"Do you know who the beneficiary is, Jane?" he said.

She just looked at him.

"The primary beneficiary is you," Virgil said.

"Me."

"Yes."

"Why isn't it my mother? Or Grace or one of my brothers, for that matter?"

"He didn't say," Virgil said, placing his hat on his head. "I don't know. I guess he figured you'd be the one to end up taking care of your mother."

Jane opened the envelope and looked at the figure on the check.

Virgil said, "I guess he didn't think your mother would know what to do with it. She never handled money. I know he thought highly of your good sense, knew you're a smart one. Responsible with things."

"Or maybe he was angry with Grace."

Virgil ducked his head. "Could be."

"He didn't think I was acting very levelheaded when he sent me to live with her."

Virgil looked away, as if knowing this wasn't his territory. Jane studied the check.

"It's more than I thought it would be," she said.

"He did increase it a couple of years ago."

She looked up at Virgil and he was looking back at her.

"How did he afford it?" she said.

"Well," Virgil said, taking his hat off again and straightening the brim. "Must've thought it was better than putting what little he had in some bank to be lost. Increase didn't really cost that much."

Jane looked at the check again.

"I guess he figured his time was short," Virgil said.

When Jane, still looking absently at the check in her hand, did not respond, Virgil let himself out. She was wondering, was this what he thought his life had been worth, or was it simply all he could afford to buy against it? Or had he thought it worth less but, being a businessman, took advantage of the system when he could?

THEY COULD NOT WAIT the days it would take for Sylvester, Jr., and Belmont to travel all the way from Wyoming for the funeral, even had the brothers been able to come. Jane had Dr. Thompson inform them by telegraph that there would be photographs taken, and they could visit when it was most convenient.

They held the funeral service at graveside, there in the plot near their house, instead of the church. Most of the mourners were neighbors and men he'd done business with in cattle. It was an early afternoon. The crops were in, fields turned under. He had apparently at least waited for that. Always a man to finish a job he had already started.

When the words were spoken and the mourners dispersed, she saw a young man at the edge of the little graveyard, standing next to the road. His eyeglasses glinted in the sunlight. She went over.

He took off his hat but not his glasses. He was looking at her. She saw the wedding band on his finger. She looked up to see that he noted she had seen it. He was as handsome a young man as he had been a beautiful boy. Hands squared and strong-looking. A nice, mild creasing of fine lines about his blue eyes and closely shaven cheeks, chin stronger than when he was younger, even though he was still just twenty-six years old. His kind nature still evident in his eyes, his expression. Weathered in a way that suggested farming, and when she asked he said yes, he had a place up north of Scooba. The gray wool suit he wore looked just a bit snug on him, as if he'd put on a little weight since buying it but no doubt would wear it as long as the suit and his frame would allow.

"And family?" she said.

"Yes. Two little boys, I'm afraid," he said with a soft laugh at what that meant to him.

"No more?"

He grinned. "Well, so far. But I kind of think two's enough, these days. Especially boys. They're a handful."

He turned slightly away as if to check the weather. His cheekbones seemed more defined, face matured into a man's, little trace of the boy's softness.

"Well," she said. "It was kind of you to come. Thoughtful."

He nodded.

"I confess I just wanted to lay eyes on you one more time."

Her heart turned over. She swallowed.

"Your father was a good man," he said.

"Yes, he was."

"Did you know that he came to see me, after they sent you to town?"

"No. I had no idea. Why?"

"He told me that he was sorry about it all. That he knew I was a good boy. 'Young *man*,' he said. He said I should go on with my life, that you would be all right, he would make sure of it. He said, 'I take care of my own, son.' I guess I have to say it was something of a comfort to me then."

He took her hand in his strong, callused fingers, leaned down and kissed the back of it, like some Old World gentleman. He took off his glasses and slipped them into his coat pocket, as if to let her see him without them again, then put on his hat and walked away down their drive. She heard a vehicle start up out there, then drive away.

Her hand burning where his lips had touched it. Or more like a tingling of the nerve endings that one can't tell if it's hot or cold, painful or pleasant. It was a lingering feeling, and then after a while, without her noticing its passing, it was gone.

EVERYONE HAD LEFT by midafternoon the next day.

"Leave me alone just tonight," her mother said. And after receiving no answer, she said, "I'll be fine. I would just rather be alone tonight."

"All right," Jane said then. "I'll be back tomorrow."

And so the doctor drove his own way home, and she and Grace drove back to town, quiet, went to their separate rooms in the house. She stood at the window and looked out over the town, the sparse Sunday auto traffic, the trains coming from the east and the west. The steam from stacks at the power plant, the forge, the Nabs plant, the creosote plant, and the hospital's laundry. Puffy white clouds drifting low over the hills to the south and making their way along the valley, moving northeast like a patient fleet of ghost dirigibles carrying the equally weightless, invisible souls of the dead. Quiet.

Grace drove her back up the next day. Surprising Jane, she proposed to their mother that she come to live with them in town.

After a long moment Ida Chisolm said, "I don't want that. I've lived in this house since I was seventeen years old. I can't even hardly remember living anywhere else. It's just"—she waved a hand as if at a fly—"gone."

She had indeed lost something. She slept in, a thing she'd never done. Jane milked their milk cow, gathered the eggs, made coffee and breakfast, although her mother would hardly eat. A few bites of greens or peas at supper. She disdained bread. She had taken up smoking a corncob pipe and would sit on the front porch puffing it.

"I've got half a mind to see if your father left any of his apple brandy down at his shed," she said. And she laughed. It was a single sharp, *Ha*, as if to say, *There, what do you think of that?* But then she frowned and puffed some more on the pipe.

They endured that first winter alone. Her mother would wrap herself in a heavy coat and blankets to sit on the porch in all weather. As if she couldn't stand to be inside except to sleep. Dr. Thompson visited them frequently, and would talk to Jane. When Mrs. Chisolm blurted out that she wanted him to give her laudanum, he hesitated, then said he would. After that, Jane's mother slept in even later, and went to bed immediately after supper, what little she ate.

In the spring Jane went to work in the old garden, planting tomatoes, snap beans, butterbeans, a single row of sweet corn, yellow squash.

Whereas all her life her mother had more often than not been in conflict not only with others but with herself, her own circumstances, angry about one thing or another, mostly dissatisfied and even resentful of her lot in life, now she seemed to have let that go. But in its stead, there appeared to be nothing. As if she had finally fully burned her ability to care about anything in the long-stoked fire of her discontent. And now she was empty.

She did little beyond sit on the front porch, puffing at a corn-cob pipe and rocking. She spoke little. She made no effort to cook and ate almost nothing. It was difficult for Jane to convince her to wash herself, or even brush her hair. She began to look like those people other people called crazy. Those people who would wander the streets of town or even the rural roads, staring at nothing, acknowledging no one, talking to themselves. Her poor father had seemed to be losing his mind, during the hardest times, and here now her mother was losing hers in some different kind of way, not frightening or even bewildering but sad. If her mother talked to herself, it was a silent conversation. She took no interest in her grandchildren when Sylvester, Jr., and Belmont finally visited, and looked at them as if observing a stranger's children, the reason for whose purpose in her presence she could not quite divine.

Jane dealt with what business there was on the farm, totting up the Harrises' crop, selling off to a neighboring cattleman what beef stock her father hadn't already sold. Selling his cattle truck and buying an automobile, a little yellow Ford coupe, for occasional trips to town. By the fall of '39 she was considering whether to take on another tenant or sharecropper to farm or raise cattle on the land her father had always used himself.

Then an oddly hard cold set in one week in early December, and her mother slipped from the house in the middle of the night.

The next morning Jane found her lying in the shorn cornfield, clothed only in her thin nightgown, curled up with her frozen fists to her face, her eyes shut and mouth open as if to take her last breath or mutter some kind of unimaginable prayer.

Jane called Dr. Thompson first, then Mr. Finicker at the funeral home. There was now a more or less permanent preacher at the Methodist church in Damascus and she decided just to let that man come if he heard about it and thought he ought, but made no direct attempt to contact him herself. She figured her mother would have left it at that, if it'd been her decision.

Dr. Thompson and Finicker arrived together, with two young men to help remove her mother from the field.

"Do you want Finicker to take her on to his place?" the doctor asked, to which Jane, after a moment's hesitation, said yes. Funerals in homes were becoming a thing of the past in some quarters and the thought of having her mother's funeral there, in her own home where she had so often been so unhappy, just seemed too dreary. Finicker's men carried her mother on a gurney out to his long funeral car. She stopped them before they closed the door, reached in and pressed a penny onto each of her mother's shrunken, shriveled eyelids. The men looked at her in something like muted astonishment. Then she stepped back and watched them drive her mother away into eternity, vested with her toll to the other side.

Worm

Then she was indeed alone, though Dr. Thompson still visited often. She made her own occasional visits to her tenants, to check in. She put in her garden. One day in July she stood beside the tomato row in a mild state of wonder, watching a doomed tomato worm eat her best plant. The worm's fat, segmented body was studded with the rows of pure white cocoons that had grown from wasp eggs laid under its skin. They looked like embedded teardrop pearls or beautiful tiny onion bulbs growing from its bright green skin. Inside the cocoons, wasp larvae sucked away the worm's soft tissue as casually as a child drawing malt through a straw. The worm seemed entirely unperturbed. No doubt a tomato worm is born expecting this particular method of slow death, a part of the pattern of its making somehow, something its brain or nerve center, whatever it has, is naturally conditioned to recognize and accept. Just as a person hardly registers, until near the end, the long slow decadence of death.

She bent over to dab sweat from her brow with the hem of her skirt. It was July-hot, but a bearable breeze lilted through the clearing where their house and barn and outbuildings had stood since long before her birth, a breeze hinting at something more from the large cumulus that seemed to grow by the minute, a towering mountain of billowing white to the south, its center like tarnished silver.

She heard what sounded like the doctor's pickup coming down the main road, then its wheels bumbling across the bridge over the creek, beyond the trees between there and the house. Its engine churned it up the hill. She knelt and used her thumb and forefinger to pluck the worm from the leaf of the tomato plant—rolled it into her long narrow palm and cupped it there, feeling its weird little stumpy legs work against the tender skin, tickling, an odd stimulation. She snapped off the leaf stem where it had been dining and carried it to the edge of the yard, set it down, let the worm grapple back onto it. It set to eating again right away. For the worm, this stem and leaf were the whole world. Some bird would snatch it up directly. She walked quickly toward the house as the doctor's pickup appeared around the corner of their long drive, a thin drift of red dust rising behind it. In the room she'd slept in growing up, she dabbed a bit of her best perfume onto her wrists, her neck, and dropped her soiled undergarment into a pail she kept covered in the corner, sprinkling in a bit of her cheaper perfume before replacing the lid. Washed herself with water and soap from the basin on the back porch and went back outside.

The blue pickup was parked there in front of the house. The doctor got out then, fanning himself with his hat. He spoke to her and joined her on the front porch, and she fetched them both glasses of sweet tea with chips of ice. A flicker sang its hard staccato song from a high limb in her mother's beloved

apple tree, singing against the softening light of the hot afternoon. The doctor sipped his tea, rocking, that closed-down
expression on his noble but slightly birdlike face, eyes narrowed above his beak.

"You might as well tell me what it is on your mind," she
finally said.

He looked at her as if he'd been interrupted in thought, as
if he'd been alone there on the porch with those thoughts. Not
atypical. He smiled. He was a kindly man. Then he took on a serious look as if the thought in his mind had indeed become about
her. He took a sip of his tea, ice chips tinkling against the glass,
and set it down.

"All right."

And he told her. He'd kept up with things, through his friend
in Baltimore. There'd been a lot of progress since she was a little girl. He thought it was time they asked another specialist to
examine her.

"The very best, so that you can know without doubt whether
or not it's possible to correct your condition. Or to do anything
about it."

"With surgery."

"Yes."

He said the work being done in Baltimore was remarkable.
New developments every year. He didn't think anyone in the
country would be able to examine her with greater certainty than
the men there.

"It may still not be possible yet. It may still be too complicated.
You've been through this before. But they've made great advances
in the last ten years, and I think the emotional risk is worth it.
I think we should be aggressive. And if they cannot correct it

now, they may at least know enough to give you a good idea of when they might."

He spoke his words in a serious manner but still, as always, with the kind of gentle thoughtfulness that was his hallmark as a man and a doctor. His keen eyes in the squint they took on when he was talking seriously. As if he'd got a mote in his eye.

Her father's eyes had seemed so haunted, there near the end. For years had, really.

She peered at the doctor a moment, then looked away, feeling strangely perturbed and not bothering to hide it.

"No doubt expensive," she said.

"Yes," he said. "Of course, now you have the money from your father's insurance policy."

She looked up.

"Did you speak to him about this?"

"I mentioned, years ago, when you were born, that he might put something away toward the possibility."

"Recently, I mean."

"I did tell him, when he asked a couple of years before his death—while you were living in town—that I thought the odds were getting better."

After a moment of looking at him as if he'd said something incomprehensible, she stood up and walked to the edge of the porch.

"What are you saying?"

"Just what I'm saying."

"About my father, I mean, and the insurance policy."

"Just that I believe he would have wanted you to use the money for this, if you wanted."

She turned to face him. He looked down, took out his pocket-knife and a little piece of wood he was carving on. Trying to cut back on the pipe-smoking.

"I believe it's what he had in mind," he said.

"Had in mind," she said.

She looked out over the yard, at the work shed, the now-empty hog pen and its ramshackle fencing, the pasture sloping down to the cattle pond, no cattle there in the midday sun. Hardly seeing it all, really.

"Jane," he said. "You're a hearty person, your condition has no real effect on that. You have no unhealthy habits that I know of. It is likely that you will outlive your sister and brothers, and be alone one day. Without family, if you were able to live a less restricted life—" He stopped there.

Jane said quietly, "This has come to feel pretty normal for me."

It had come over her, some sense of what it would be like to be truly alone. Her mother had become someone who seemed barely there, anyway. The doctor was fading a bit, no denying it now. She felt a heaviness, an almost fluid infusion of a palpable isolation. She would always be the odd one, the one with the secret. Who hurried from company without a word, returned a while later as if nothing were unusual about it. Who had taken to wearing several slips beneath her skirts, and a bit of perfume, in a ridiculously vain attempt to mask the fact of her body, her embarrassment.

But did it matter, really, anymore? She had now lived nearly eight years since moving to town, since giving herself up to the truth of what her life would be. A year out here with her mother, alone, and half a year alone since her death. And she intended to stay. She was not unhappy, she wouldn't put that word to it.

In fact she would not know how, even at her young age of just twenty-four years, to start over. To become someone else entirely. But she took an oblique tack.

"Even if they could make it work, you know I cannot pay. I know my father left that money to me but it seems right that I would manage it, in case others need it in a bad time. For something practical."

The doctor looked away and took a deep breath as if to calm himself. His right hand shook a bit and he placed his left hand there to still it. He closed his pocket knife and put it away in his vest pocket.

"I'll pay," he said.

"No."

"I will," he said. "You understand, Jane. You have always been more than just a patient, to me. Lett and I had no children. I have no one to leave anything to, when I go. I have no one in my life, not here anyway. And no close family left, no one I even really know among them anymore. If you would let me at least do this for you, I would feel as if I have someone in this world who might see me as more than an affable stranger."

"You've never been a stranger."

She looked at him. She thought that indeed he might love her, in some way. The love of one human being for another, which does not demand classification or mode.

"He did it on purpose, didn't he?" she said. "I've thought so, ever since the day."

The doctor looked straight out over the yard, stone-faced.

She said, "You know yourself what can be done and what can't. Don't you? If you just own up to it. You want me to see these people because they're the best experts, but you have been talking to them, corresponding with them, all of my life. You would know if they were able to fix me. Has your doctor friend in Baltimore actually given you some kind of confirmation?"

"What if they were at least able to repair the incontinence?"

"Has your friend actually suggested good odds on that? The man in Memphis said the way I'm made makes that highly unlikely. Has that changed?" Then she said more softly, "What are the odds, Ed? I think you want to believe it, but I think in your heart you either suspect or know that at this point they still cannot. What would be the point, if we're honest?"

He looked startled, emotion in his face. Then looked away.

She thought of her father and her mind felt inflamed with unchecked emotions. She looked out to where she'd left the tomato worm. It was gone, leaf, stem, and all.

"I don't want to make your life more complicated," he said. "I thought, possibly, just the opposite, in the long run."

"Well," she said after a moment, as if to the yard, or to the strangely ravished, vanished worm, the billowing sky, the somewhere-feasting little wild bird—probably the flicker that was gone now from the apple tree, silent.

"Well," she said. "It's not complicated."

They were quiet then in the still of the afternoon. The storm that had threatened seemed to have lost its strength and moved away. And then the doctor got back into his truck and left. She watched him drive off in a late afternoon light that seemed flickering, like the clickety light in a motion picture, color draining as if it, too, were in black-and-white, controlled by a steady hand turning a handle to keep the world in motion, by and by.

What the doctor had said to her, about caring for her. Some

part of her was trying to absorb it, to understand how he had
always helped her to feel less alone in the world. Less strange.

Dear Ellis,

I presented Miss Jane Chisolm w/ new possibility of at least mar-
ginal surgical repair to her condition. She is skeptical, and unwill-
ing to bother without a greater degree of certainty on our parts. No
more exploratory action, I'm afraid. She does have a good measure
of her parents' obstinacy, in addition to her own very independent
nature. I offered to pay for it, myself. I cannot abide the idea of not
at least trying. Finding out what can or cannot be done. Perhaps
it is selfish, but I cannot abide such stubbornness, damned country
stubbornness, when there is absolutely no practical reason not to seek
the medical certainty, and every reason to move ahead should it be
possible to do so.

I did not and never have even brought up the idea of colostomy.
Personally, I wouldn't see it as enough improvement, especially con-
sidering the risks for infection, etc. All things considered, she's been
very lucky in that way.

She believes her father caused his own death, w/ purpose. It
would be impossible to know, of course, given his condition and
habits. Beyond the philosophical sense, of course. How much this
may have to do with her decision, I couldn't say. If I had to guess,
I'd say it's a powerful influence.

Such quiet in this house in the evenings, with my Lett gone
now almost twenty-two years. I have not and I suppose will never
entirely surrender my grief. My peacocks, now so numerous, are a
comfort though they are at least half-wild and sometimes their calls
and cries bring up a feeling of loneliness as much as comfort. A
strange beauty. Sometimes I wonder should I get a dog, maybe, and

wonder why the hell I never did, especially after Lett died. I suppose it makes no sense to avoid it now simply because I'd most likely outlive it. But I probably won't go to the trouble, at this age. Janie Chisolm would take it in, I believe, but I wouldn't want anyone to be beholden.

Ed

Otherworldly Birds

And then there was the long quiet afternoon of autumn, then middle and late winter. Crows angling curious over the fields. Hawks hovering for mice exposed in sparse cover. A light cold breeze. Hard frosted soil. Evergreen pines seen through bare limbs of oaks, sycamores, sweetgums, hickories, maple, poplar, beech. The crooked, crazed, leafless pecans in the neglected grove, the weathered barn, rusted roof tin, rusted barbed wire, implements. Huddled cattle. Weathered grazing horse and mules. Gray scudded sky. She'd made arrangements for Harris, with new help from the return of Mister, to take on another twenty acres. Another eighty came under the hand of a man named Moss and his family, who were friends with the Harrises. The doctor had recommended she take on more colored people instead of whites. "More reliable, more trustworthy," he'd said. "You learned that the hard way." Moss was a big man, with a good sense of his own dignity. She gave him halves, and let him and Harris use of any of her father's equipment they might need, at any time, if they promised to maintain it. She would pay for fuel and major repairs. She told him that if he needed to add on to the cabin the Temples had once occupied, she would supply him with lumber and nails.

All she really had to worry about was preparing her garden and making it good the following summer. She used money from her father's final crop and cattle sales to get through the winter, although, it being only her, there wasn't much cost. She kept her insurance money in a safe-deposit box in town. Days, she could take walks, and talk to Harris or Moss, or Emmalene, or Mister if she caught him out and about. Sometimes she ran into him in the woods, her walking, him hunting with his mutt dog for squirrels. He was still skinny and comical. Even though they'd been childhood friends, he always took his hat off when he spoke to her. He seemed a bit of a rascal, even so, and she didn't doubt what Hattie had told about his rather active nightlife in town. It being still winter, he would disappear down to there when he could, and when he came back Mr. Harris his grandfather would be cloudy for a few days about it.

She discovered, on a dark shelf in the back of the shed beside her father's still, several jars of his apple brandy. Had her mother not even known it was there? Jane would have a little, sometimes, in the evenings on the porch or beside the kitchen stove in winter.

She asked Dr. Thompson if he would recommend a good radio, and the next time he visited he simply brought her one. She set it up in the kitchen, as the only electric outlet was in the bulb socket there. Sometimes she convinced him to come by and stay for dinner, if he had stopped by earlier in the day on his rounds. They would have a little of her father's apple brandy afterward, and listen to a program. Then he would make his way home before too late. If she thought he'd had too much to drink during the day, which was rare enough, she kept on him until he agreed to sleep in her parents' old room across the breezeway. Always, she would hear his car or truck crank up before she could even rise to make coffee, and hear him grinding off down the drive and out onto the road.

Sometimes she would stop in at his house and stay for supper there. Hattie was always glad to see her. She had never married, never had another child. She had grown stout, like her mother Emmalene, but unlike Emmalene she was of a lighter disposition. Jane supposed her life here, as the doctor's housekeeper and helper, was a good bit easier than the life her mother had led growing up and growing old, a midwife and the wife of a sharecropper. Well, of course it was.

She went into town often enough that people began to be friendly (beyond the general sense) to her, speak to her by name, know what she liked to order in the cafés. She would fast beforehand as always, so as not to worry about that. And so they were relatively normal outings. Driving her yellow coupe in her high fog was a kind of dreamy delight. She drove slowly, the world going by like a slow-motion moving picture in color.

Mercury had become populous enough that she was not thought strange for appearing only now and then. Even the somewhat scary-looking woman who ran the ticket booth at the movie theater, pale and skinny with garish makeup, knew her and made small talk. The woman had the voice of a crow. The Phipps couple who owned and ran the Triangle Restaurant were so nice to her—they had known her father—she often had to argue before they would let her pay for a meal. She threatened to stop coming if they didn't stop doing that, and they laughed and complied.

She never ate or drank much, in case she wanted to linger in town a little longer, later.

It was inevitable that men would start to notice her. She wasn't the greatest beauty, not as pretty as she'd been as a girl, but she wasn't plain and certainly not ugly, so she noticed a fair number of men taking notice of her. And they would make eye contact, smile, nod, tip a hat, say, "Morning," or "Afternoon." She learned to give the faintest smile and nod in return, so as not to encourage anyone if she could help it.

But one man started to stand out, and she thought he might be running into her—or passing by, she supposed—on purpose. Then he seemed to show up wherever she had her lunch. Whether the Triangle, or Schoenhof's, Pointer's Grill, the diner in Woolworth's, he seemed to show up soon after she'd taken a seat—generally she sat at the counter, being alone—and sat a few stools from her, and if she glanced over he would catch her eye, smile, and nod. He was a slim gentleman, somewhat older than her but hard to say how much, as he had a young face even though his short-clipped hair was beginning to show some gray. He wore eyeglasses, the small and round wire-rimmed kind. Clean-shaven. Nice suit. His hands, she noticed once, were slim and looked strong without bulk. Hands used to handling things but not workingman's hands.

Finally one day as she left the grill he came out behind her and said, "Excuse me, Miss Chisolm?"

She startled. How did he know her name? Which she asked him.

"I beg your pardon," he said. "I asked Mrs. Phipps." He held out his hand. "My name is Gordon Ray, I work at Citizens Bank. I knew your father, and was sorry to hear of his passing."

"Thank you," Jane said. "Did you do business with my father?"

"Not much. I was just a teller back then. Before everything got so hard. We're lucky to still be in business, I guess."

"Yes. Well, my father wasn't so keen on banks there toward the end, I guess."

"No one was, Miss Chisolm."

They stood there awkwardly for a moment. She emboldened herself and took a good, frank look at him then. He was handsome in a clean, precise, and conservative way. His eyes seemed intelligent and even kind. But she was wary of what seemed his persistent interest in her. She sensed he was a man who would be kind to a woman. But the question was always there: What did he, or would he, expect in the long run?

"Well, it was good to meet you, Mr. Ray."

"Gordon, please."

"Well, you can call me Jane, then. I have noticed you around."

"Yes." He laughed, a bit awkward. "Not a whole lot of options in the lunch department downtown, I guess. And I'm not married so I usually eat out at noon."

"Yes."

"And you? Do you live in town?"

"No, I live on my family's farm, but the sharecroppers are doing all the farming these days, so I'm free to come in every now and then."

"Would you ever like to stay for dinner? I would be honored to treat."

She hesitated. But then her family's tendency to be direct won out.

"Mr. Ray, I must tell you that I have never been on a date with a man in my life, dinner date or whatever kind of date."

He kind of laughed.

"Better late than never." Then added, "Truth is, I haven't had a whole lot of dates myself."

Jane looked at him. Yes, he was the friendly, awkward type.

"Living up in the country as I do, I have to be home early," she said. "Or in any case I don't like to arrive near or after dark."

"I eat early," Gordon Ray said.

All right. She pushed the family bluntness further.

"Mr. Ray, have you not heard anything about me? There must be lots of single young women in this town you could ask out to dinner."

"Not as many as you might think, Miss Chisolm," he said, with a kind of wan smile. "Especially if, like me, you don't put on the he-man act. I come from Tennessee, and believe me I'm all man, but I'm not the kind to go strutting around like some circus wrestler, if you know what I mean. I'm a quiet type. Sometimes Southern women, if you'll forgive me, don't quite know what to make of men like me. Sometimes they get the wrong idea. But I assure you I like women very much."

She stared at him for a second, then laughed, and he joined in.

"Well, I got your dander up, didn't I?" she said. "But you didn't answer my question."

"I'm sorry."

"I said have you not heard anything about me, and since you are sensitive to people making assumptions about you, surely you won't mind the direct question."

"I'll answer you, if you'll let me do it over dinner at Schoenhof's."

"Are you sure you're not a lawyer instead of a banker?" Jane said. But then, for some reason she did not entirely explore in the moment—as close as she would come to a whim—she didn't exactly decline, said she would try to make it but that she had to be home by seven and had a busy afternoon scheduled already. "I hope you won't be offended if I'm not able to come," she said.

"I do hope you can, though. I'll hope to see you there," he said, with a big smile. He shook her hand, touched the brim of his hat, and strode off the one block to his bank with a good bounce in his stride.

Well, she thought, *he's an optimistic fellow, if nothing else.*

She felt like she'd just participated in something like an emotional boxing match, and it felt good, like good exertion. But it had also made her anxious. She was glad of her earlier fasting that day, more than ever.

She occupied herself that afternoon at the new Carnegie library, browsing books and magazines. At around four-thirty she looked up, went outside, and was surprised to realize that the anxiety she'd felt earlier had disappeared. She felt an odd calm in her blood. She felt hungry now and a bit faint, but not dangerously so. She walked slowly back into the center of town. Thinking, if in a cloudy way. She went down to Front Street and into the pharmacy on the corner across and one block down from Schoenhof's. Where she could see out the window from the magazine rack and have little risk of being seen back. In a while, she saw him walk up and stand near the restaurant's door, looking up and down the street. Hands in the pockets of his nice suit. He didn't pull out a cigarette to smoke. Didn't seem like a man of vices, anyway.

She mulled the question, *Just what would come of this?* Surely it could be simple friendship. That was possible between a man and a woman, wasn't it? Yet he had said he was "all man," and just what did that imply? Well, she knew perfectly well what it implied. Especially given the way he had shadowed her, the way he introduced himself to her, the way he had been so politely insistent upon this "date." And, possibly, he was a man with something to prove.

So, what would he tell her he had heard about her? He wasn't a native, with lots of friends. What did anyone outside her family and Dr. Thompson (and Emmalene and Hattie's family, she supposed) really know about her? Her guess was they had some general idea, something in the general vicinity of her condition, her history.

She let her eyes linger on Gordon Ray, standing there waiting on her, now checking his watch. It wasn't yet five-thirty but it was close. He pushed his hands back into his pockets, rocked a bit on his heels. He looked pleased, possibly a little nervous. She felt sorry for him, just then. But she also allowed herself to be pleased that a man would want to ask her to dinner, knowing or having heard God knows what about her. And then she left from the same door she'd come in through, around the corner and out of sight of Schoenhof's and Mr. Gordon Ray, and took the long way around to where she'd parked the little yellow Ford, got in it, and drove up the hill and out of town. Feeling light, in a way, as if she'd escaped a difficult situation. And as far as she knew, she probably had.

She supposed she would have to refrain from taking lunch in town for a while, in order to avoid running into Gordon Ray. She would rather seem to be mysterious than cruel. She felt sorry for him, but of course she was not exactly sentimental about loneliness.

SHE STOPPED AT Dr. Thompson's house on the way home and told him about her encounter. He grew serious, leaning forward and listening as if she were giving a lecture on something. When she finished he sat back, his expression relaxing, as if he were thinking on it.

"I know who that young man is," he said. "I believe he's not from around here, originally. I believe he moved here from Tennessee."

"That's what he said."

"You know people in Mississippi and Alabama can be a little snooty toward people from Tennessee."

"How come is that?"

"I don't know for sure. But my guess would be they think it's not quite Deep South, not quite Appalachian, kind of a state without a clear pedigree."

"What about Louisiana?"

"France, lower part. Northeast part pretty much east Texas."

"Georgia."

"Oh, kind of piedmont in the north, Florida cracker in the south. Middle part's Southern, I guess."

"Well, what about Florida, then?"

"Florida? Florida is nothing. Just what folks slipped and slid down into the swamps, couldn't hold on up here."

She laughed. They'd made a game.

"People sure can get picky about all kinds of silly things," she said.

"You got that right. I expect it would have been all right to go to dinner with that boy. Then again, you're probably right, he's probably been a little lonely and probably would have pressed you to get serious. Probably sooner than one would like, given he must be closer to forty than not. Wants to start a family."

"That's what I figured."

He said, "You know, the Greeks believed that physical love was the lowest form of love. That true love was akin to divine love. Or something like that. That pure love between two people existed on a higher plane."

"What did they mean by that?"

He looked into his glass, shook the ice, and shrugged.

"Well, they were pantheistic, of course. I guess they meant that the highest form of love somehow transcended physical love. Was more powerful. I guess I mean to say that, if you get down to it, you have loved. You've had love. And as I understand it, or it seems to me, anyway, that once you have something like that, you have it forever. So it doesn't matter that you were not allowed to stay with or even marry that Key boy. In fact what you had with him, and still do in your memory, in your mind, is something greater than many people have in the end, when they find themselves trapped in the business of love and marriage. Do you understand?"

"I'm sure I will," she said. "Someday."

"What will you do with the rest of your life, Janie? When you're truly alone."

"I have been studying that."

"How do you mean?"

"I've been studying it all my life."

They were quiet then, looking frankly at one another without discomfort. Interrupted by the call of one of his peacocks over near the edge of the woods.

By this time, as he'd predicted, the doctor had far more peacocks than he could count. The yard was populated with cocks and hens as if it were some kind of strolling park in a big fancy city like New York or Paris, France, birds the leisure class of a Sunday afternoon. No doubt the doctor's reputation as an eccentric had been greatly enhanced by their presence.

"How come the foxes and coyotes don't get them?" she said.

"'Cause they can fly, I guess. Run pretty well, too. Listen, now, are you hungry?"

"As a matter of fact, I am. Thinking about eating at Schoenhof's gave me an appetite."

She stayed for supper.

After eating, between late afternoon and evening, they sat in the back yard while he had another glass of bourbon. She agreed to join him if he made it mostly water and ice.

"Don't tell Hattie I've allowed you to corrupt me," she said.

"Aw," he said. "I know she takes a nip from my supply now and then. At least she doesn't try to hide it by watering it back up to where it was in the bottle."

He went into the house and came out, hobbling just a little, handed her the drink. A cock flew by so close it almost startled her into spilling bourbon onto her blouse.

"Good lord!" she said.

The cock landed on a tree limb at the edge of the yard with a honking sound. Dr. Thompson laughed, sat down.

"You know," he said then, "you being startled like that reminds me. When I was a boy, for a while when I was small, I was afraid of things. I don't know why. But I was afraid of just about everything. I can't even say exactly what, just generally afraid. My parents were worried. I was an only child. I may have been adopted, but if I was they never told me. I don't much favor either one of them, never did. Anyway, we lived on the outskirts of Birmingham, Alabama, in a big house, with woods nearby, like these. My father was a surgeon and I think he wanted me to follow him in that. Anyway, at some point I grew curious about those woods and gathered up the courage to go into them by myself. At first I was afraid of every sound and every little motion from this critter or that. Scared of the swoop of a bird, which would come out of nowhere, it seemed, not like when it happened in our yard. But gradually, as I did overcome my fear, and was able to sit quietly in a little clearing, or in the crook of a small tree, or beside a creek or whatever, I started to study the animals—mostly squirrels and

chipmunks and armadillos, every now and then a fox or raccoon—
and the birds. Study their habits best I could, I mean. And then I
became mostly fascinated with the birds. I became so fascinated
with them that I completely forgot about my fears. I just about
forgot everything else that summer. I must have been eight or
nine, I don't know. Maybe ten years. I'd had some kind of ele-
mentary science at school, I think. And my father gave me a copy
of Audubon's book, and a BB gun, one of the first Daisys, I think,
and some old surgical tools, and helped me in my crude efforts
at dissection. I was fascinated by how these birds' bodies were
put together. How *complex* it was. I would pluck their feathers
before dissection and study how the parts of their bodies fit into
one another, before I removed the skin and then after. I would
carefully skin them. I never did skin them with feathers for stuff-
ing. I wasn't interested in that. I made drawings." He laughed at
himself. "I decided I wanted to become a zoologist, pure science,
much to my father's disappointment. He thought I would grow
out of it, though, and I guess I did.

"In any case, there was a bit of a cooling of my interest, as I got
older. And then I met Lett and medicine seemed like the prag-
matic choice. And she wanted to live down here."

Their glasses were empty and they went quiet, the doctor seeming lost in thought.

"You're kind of talky, Ed," she said. "Have you got into your
medicine again?"

He mocked her expression. "Maybe a bit."

"I should go on," she said. "I don't like to drive in the dark."

One of the peacocks called loudly from the trees, another
called back, and the others made a contest out of trying to join
in, and then after a raucous bit of that all was quiet. Even the
songbirds calmed down.

"The birds are going to sleep for a while," the doctor said. "Roost in the trees down there. Maybe you should give it up and roost in the guest room here tonight."

She thought about it.

"I might."

"Good." Then he said, "There's just enough light left. Let me show you something. Come on."

They walked to the edge of the yard, around Hattie's cabin, then onto a trail into the woods, moving a bit slowly given his stiffness and her town shoes. The woods were pristine, had never been cut. She wished she had walked with him here before and couldn't imagine why she hadn't. The path declined through thick brush and then opened out into an expanse of mostly pine, sweet gum, and birch trees. The trees' high, broad canopy had kept down most of the undergrowth, so that you could see almost the length of this little narrow forest. And there in the relative clearing, standing very still and watching them as if they had interrupted a party, were dozens of peafowl. For a moment it took her breath. Several of the cocks took steps toward them, stopped, and seemed to shudder throughout their bodies, and up went their long tails, fluttering, shimmering even in what little light was left in the day in these shadows.

"My god," she said, "they've gone wild."

"They were never tame," the doctor said. "Not really."

He knelt carefully down and brushed away leaves and pine needles and scooped up a small handful of dusty earth.

"This is what you do with my ashes when I'm gone," he said, and tossed it into the air toward the birds, who seemed to come out of their trance at that. Some took flight toward denser foliage, and mixed in with the blustering of their wings made sounds like the little honk of a horn and a barking sound, almost like a wild turkey. Some squawked like a quieter imitation of a crank being turned to start an old car.

"You know one of the most interesting things about birds, Janie? It's that most of them, all but ducks and geese and a few others—but all songbirds—" then he stopped himself, shook his head. "I may be a little loose-lipped with my bourbon and, uh—it's brought out the awkward scientist in me."

"No, tell me what you were going to say."

He looked at her sideways.

"All right, then. I was going to say they don't have obvious genitalia. It's mostly on the inside. The males and the females have this little puckering down there, called the *cloaca*, and when they're ready to mate the cloaca swell up, and they simply press their little puckerings together and the male's sperm finds the female's eggs and, voilà, baby birds. Do you know what they nicknamed this kind of mating, with birds? They call it a cloacal kiss. Now, don't you think that's just kind of endearing?"

She looked at his long, bushy-browed, kindly face in the fading light.

"I do," she said. "Maybe I'm part bird."

The doctor had a good little quiet laugh at that.

In a moment, she said, "How about the peacocks?"

"They're that way, too."

She could see them, becoming silhouettes as the light became dimmer in her vision, here and there in their roosts, settling in. She looked back toward the trail.

"It's getting dark."

The doctor said, "All you have to do is pretend that you can see in the dark, and then you can."

She made a sound.

"No, really. Just relax your eyes. There. Like that. You see what you can see? You see the trail? You look for what is not the trail. See it?"

"I think I do."

"All right, then," he said. "That's all you need."

"Okay, then."

He hesitated, then said, "You once asked me why I got those first birds."

"I remember. You were lonesome."

"I was. But really I got them simply because they're beautiful, they're strange. People don't know what to make of them. I liked that. I suppose their role in nature is to help control the populations of the things they eat. They're good regulators. And to feed the occasional fox or coyote, no doubt. But I like to think they really exist just because they are oddly beautiful. And are killed out of jealous envy. I like to think they enjoy the fact that we think they're beautiful. I like to think they're vain. I like to think that they think we think they're gods, and that the reason we gaze at them in such wonder is that we are worshipping them. Look at them in there. Like shadows, spirits."

He turned to her, looking unabashedly happy, his face a pale moon in the darkening woods.

"That's what I like to think," he said.

Toward the end she did not fear death, even as it took Dr. Thompson at the age of seventy-four, when she was just thirty-five herself. Somehow he had helped her in that way, too. He left her his house, his woods, money in the bank. He left her to provide a living for his housekeeper, Hattie. If Jane did not want to move in, he wrote, she could just hold on to it until town encroached to drive the price up to premium.

She stayed home, went to town as rarely as possible, grew tomatoes, butter beans, snap beans, yellow squash, onions, sweet corn, and the field corn she fed to the chickens. Greens well into the fall. Her hands, long and thin and strong, worked the good black garden soil. Occasionally one of her plump beefsteak tomatoes would shape itself into some kind of vaguely sexually suggestive conformation, which she would study with interest, standing or kneeling in the garden. Whenever she found one of these on the vine, ripe, she plucked it, studied it in a moment of wonder, and ate it there in the garden heat, her face flushed, the juices from the ripe fruit running down her chin and onto her bony sweating breast.

Her sharecroppers drifted away into time. Fields fallow, meadowed, becoming slowly the brambly woods they'd once been long ago.

Grace, who'd moved to New Orleans after Mercury's brothels were closed during the war, wrote to her once from there, describing her new place of employment (*Fancy*, she wrote, *but Minnie just had the most class*), and then no longer wrote, not even in return to letters from Jane, until one letter came back to Jane with the words *No longer at this address* written on the front of the envelope beneath her return address.

Grace was finally rid of her despised family for good, was what Jane figured, although she was hurt that her sister had not at least made her an exception.

The occasional brief letter or postcard she got from Belmont's or Sylvester's wife in Wyoming was nearly incomprehensible. She had never seen mountains. Never seen endless prairie with no trees.

Cicadas pulsed in the heat of the day, and in the late afternoon, so loud as to overwhelm everything else, the very pressure in the air seeming to swell with their mad song. The all-but-every-day afternoon storms in the summer. Cyclone weather in spring, summer, and fall. Once she stood in the breezeway in such a bile-green darkness and lashing downpour that she was sure the roaring was a cyclone somewhere in the low black sky above, but if so it did not touch down and afterward the skies cleared to moonlight on puddles in the yard like broad, shallow ponds gleaming.

Sometimes there was a feeling of deep sadness, of being alone in a world that seemed all but empty of others. Occasionally she felt a momentary fear that something was going to happen, and she was not allowed to know what it was or understand it. She thought that it might be death, the fear of it. The expectation.

An almost annoying sense of dread. She would have wept in such moments but for some reason the tears would not come, as if the expression of grief itself had abandoned her, the ability to express it too deeply sunk into her mind and heart. She had let it settle in so, in order that it might shrink to a nothing, like some miraculously benign and reticent tumor. But it had not.

She sat on the porch and watched the world around her. The yard, the shed, the garden, the empty pig pen beyond that. Pasture. Pond. Woods. A magnolia she had planted after her father died, along with a row of camellias that flowered every spring. So there were songbirds and squirrels, doves in the yard as well as flocks that flew swiftly over in the early fall, and wild ducks circling in dark, descending swoops to the ponds in winter. Quail bursting up in blustering coveys when she walked the pasture fence lines.

At the age of fifty-eight, simply to give herself a pleasurable vice that brought on memories, she looked for and found her father's old cigarette-rolling machine, bought tobacco, and took up smoking in the afternoons and after her supper in the evenings. Never inside the house—except in winter, by the fire—but on her porch, as her father had so enjoyed doing, along with a little apple brandy from a bottle purchased in town, judging it not as good as what her father had used to make on his own.

The doctor's wild peacocks left the confine of his woods as people and subdivisions indeed began to encroach upon the property, and they rapidly spread their territory out into the country, eventually into the woods around her house. As if they sensed the presence of someone they found familiar. They would leave the woods and strut and peck about the yard.

Sometimes their call in the distance, from down in the woods, was the loud, *AhAHHah*, and sometimes a call she did not like so much, a chilling, *OWWWwww*, that was far too much a cross between a yowling cat and a crying child for her comfort.

But the strange, guttural, jungle call that came late in the evenings, sometimes, a rhythmic, *Oof-a-oof-a-oof-a*, she loved to hear. It would lull her to sleep. She had made her bedroom area in the old living room and mostly kept to that side of the house. Her sleep was early, sound, and she woke early to the dawn and its first, smoky light. Moving about became slower, more effortful. She had lost interest in food and felt weak but not hungry. She would lose her breath in a task. Odd occasional dull pains behind her breast, and into an arm. Tingling hands.

She received a letter one day in 1982, when she was sixty-seven years old, from a doctor at Johns Hopkins. She was confused, wondering what in the world anyone there would be writing to her about at this point in time.

It was from a surgeon named Wilkes, who said he had been a protégé of Dr. Young et al. but especially of Dr. Ellis Adams, who'd been close friends with her own physician, Dr. Thompson. *In brief, Miss Chisolm,* the letter read, *I am writing to tell you that we have just this past month performed the first entirely successful operation on a condition I am fairly certain matches yours, after many years of research and practice. And I am writing to enquire if you would like to take advantage of this, entirely at our expense, of course, in honor of Dr. Thompson and in gratitude for your having contributed to our research in the past. Yours, etc.*

She felt an anger well up in her. She went out for a walk, venturing just to the edge of her woods. Tears welled up but she pushed them down in favor of indignation. She decided she had no anger toward this man or that place. They'd done what they could. But my God, why even bother to let her know, at this point? She went back to the house and composed a brief letter.

Dear Dr. Wilkes,
I thank you kindly for your letter informing me of the new advances and your offer to "fix" me, so to speak. I do appreciate it. But you must understand I am now an old woman, I live alone on my family's farm, and have no interest in going through such an operation as I see no need for it, and there is certainly not the desire.
* Yours truly,*
* Jane Chisolm*

She sealed and put a stamp on the letter, walked to the end of the drive, put the letter into her mailbox, raised the flag, and slammed the mailbox door shut, muttering to herself about what idiots some people could sometimes be.

It seemed that her dreams had become more vivid, and there were more of them. More that she recalled upon waking, anyway. Mushrooms, covering the forest floor. A foreign forest. A fairy-tale forest. Awesome trees towering way, way up, blocking the sky. She sat plucking and eating the fungi, chewing the black dirt at the base of their stems along with their flesh. She'd never known they had eyes.

She woke from another sort of dream and went into the kitchen, and at the table there she wrote a letter, sealed it in an unmarked envelope, and tucked it into her chest of keepsakes at the foot of her bed.

Dear Elijah,
In my dream I walked alone in my meadow in the woods. I
laid myself down in the wild grass there and let you gaze on me
to see what I am. I let the sun beat down on my pale skin so it
became transparent as the skin of an oyster—what is the word—
translucent. And you could see the strange miracle of my body. In
the world of us that gathered in my mind there was no need for
physical perfection in order to enjoy the act of love. This I knew
upon what I will call awakening.
   J

It was late autumn, cooling down. The world had gone again.
She wandered around the house in her slippers and a heavy robe,
the propane space heater she'd had installed hissing its blue flame
in the quiet living room where it sat on the old fireplace hearth.
She was forgetful, leaving her cup of coffee or jelly jar of brandy
in one room and forgetting to bring it with her to the next. Or
setting down her reading glasses and being unable to remember
where she'd set them down when she needed to read a label or an
interesting item in the Sunday newspaper she had delivered each
week.

She had all but forgotten that her life was compromised, had
been compromised, in any way.

From the corner of her eye she saw a blur of bright color like
the moving progress of a rainbow through the air of her yard. The
peacocks, flying from one roosting tree to another.

She heard their calls through the afternoon, and in the dusk
after sunset. Soon it would be winter and they would go quiet for
a while. In the late evening she woke to them again, pulled on her
robe, and shuffled to a window to look down on the overgrown

pasture between the garden and the pond. The moon was almost full after several nights' waxing in the clear cold sky. Its light blue-silver on the grass. At the edge of the yard, a single peacock stood alone, calling to the moon, displaying his magnificent tail as if to woo it, the moon itself.

She settled back into her bed. A cock somewhere deep in the woods gave out the haunting, lulling call that she loved and pulled her down into sleep. She came through her little meadow where the wildflowers trembled, then up the silvery trail and into the yard, where she stopped as if moonstruck. She'd entered a secret avian cathedral, filled with some kind of winged and feathered things she'd never seen. They stood very still, hushed, their gleaming black eyes fixed on her, white beaks open in a strange, alert anticipation.

ACKNOWLEDGMENTS

I'm deeply grateful to the following people and institutions for their kindness and generosity and smarts during the many years I spent trying to figure out how to write this novel (and writing whatever I could when I couldn't actually write this one), and the three years I spent actually writing and rewriting it down: the University of West Florida Department of English; the University of Alabama, Birmingham; the National Endowment for the Arts; the University of Mississippi Department of English and MFA in Creative Writing, and John and Renee Grisham for their endowed chair at Ole Miss; the Lannan Foundation; the University of California, Irvine, Department of English and MFA in Creative Writing; the Taylor family, especially Dr. Marvin Taylor; the Guggenheim Foundation; the Fairhope Writers Colony; the Aspen Writers Foundation and the Aspen Institute; the University of Wyoming Department of English and MFA in Creative Writing. Thank you to all the wonderful colleagues and friends at these places.

Thanks to Dr. Gary Ludwin, for valued information and corroboration and insights concerning important medical facts (any remaining errors would be mine, not Dr. Ludwin's); Angela Beese, for dog talk and encouragement; my Clay family cousins, for memories; Jimmy White, for long friendship and tall tales; my stepmother, Vivian Watson, just for being herself, for saving my father, and for reading a draft of the book and offering insight and advice.

I'd also like to thank the following people: Neltje, for the gift of friendship and a most beautiful place to get away and wrangle with the book at crucial times; also her staff, David and Cindy; Ric Dice, who read the manuscript more times than anyone but the writer should have to and offered great advice and much encouragement; Jason Thompson, for dropping by my office several times in the past couple of years to ask about the book and offer encouragement; Kelly Kornegay, for a last-minute tip that made a big difference; Duncan and Anne Chalk, for long friendship and unmatchable hospitality; Rattawut Lapcharoensap, for letting me sit in his study and whine and moan anytime I wanted; Jon Hershey, who, though I didn't bug him about this book, pulled me out of the basement back when I'd quit writing and so has my eternal gratitude; my amazing agent, Peter Steinberg, for good humor, patience, encouragement, and a keen eye at the perfect time; Dave Cole, for his superb work on the manuscript; the good and (infinitely) patient and supportive people at W. W. Norton & Company, especially Nomi Victor, Dan Christiaens, Marie Pantojan, Erin Sinesky Lovett, Bill Rusin, and of course my incredible editor for all these years, Alane Salierno Mason, whose apparently near-infinite patience I stretched so thin, whose belief in this book often easily surpassed my own, who pressed me with wise advice and encouragement, whose apparently endless support I had no reason to expect to last this long—my gratitude, love, and apologies. My love and gratitude to my wife, Nell Hanley, who not only read many drafts but somehow found a way to live with me while I worked on this book.

Thank you to my beautiful, talented, irrepressible granddaughter Maggie, named after my grandmother, who was such a marvelous source of good stories for me. Maggie, who upon being read a chapter from an early draft of this novel, for some reason said, "Pappy should put a peacock in there." And I did. And it changed everything. Clear-minded, innocent genius. Thanks, Mags.

And thanks to all my old friends on the road who have given me love and support, guest beds, food and drink, good company, and their own unmatchable hospitality, especially Horn, Cawthon, Pettit; McLemore; Denny; Dice; Noble-Horne; Bobo-Brock; Howorth, Franklin-Fennelly, Kornegay, Donelson, Hudson-Formichella; Pritchard; Winthrop; Gessner-de Gramont; Salter; Wier; Peterson-Shacochis; Vaswani-Holter; Esslinger-Sanders; Borofka; Hershey-Blalock; Hathaway-Wickelhaus; Bausch; Carlin; Williams; Huggins; Parrish; Canty; Brown; Harwood; Brewer; Geuder; Chiarella; Butler; Singleton; and Mr. Land; and others I hate to think I may be forgetting at the moment. I'm a little tired.

I'd like to acknowledge the following sources in what was a difficult search for information as I tried to engage in (roughly) educated speculation about rare, complicated, and serious urological issues: *Genital Abnormalities, Hermaphroditism and Related Adrenal Diseases*, Hugh H. Young; *Hugh Young: A Surgeon's Autobiography*; and the website emedicine.medscape.com. Also, for information on Southern daily rural life and country doctors: *The Doctor Stories*, by William Carlos Williams, particularly "Old Doc Rivers" and his cocaine habit; *Up Before Daylight*, ed. James Seay Brown, Jr., particularly the essay "A Plain Country Doctor,"

Lawrence F. Evans (wife conks husband with shovel); *The Country Doctor Handbook*, by the editors of FC&A Medical Publishing; *Never Done: A History of American Housework*, Susan Strasser; *Cotton Tenants*, by James Agee; photographs by Walker Evans.

The lines from the song "Let Me Call You Sweet Heart" come from the popular song published in 1910, with music by Leo Friedman and lyrics by Beth Slater Whitson. The song was first recorded by the Peerless Quartet.

picador.com

blog
videos
interviews
extracts